Narratives of Friendship and Love

(Justin's Story)

Dedication

To my Wife— who believed in my stories long before they ever became pages, thank you for being my steady ground and my greatest encouragement. Your belief has carried me through moments of doubt and reminded me that dreams are worth chasing.

To my Family—thank you for your unwavering support and belief in this project from the very beginning. Your encouragement, patience, and faith carried these pages from idea to reality. This book exists because you believed in me.

Table of Contents

{ 1 }

I want to go

It's 3 a.m. on a subway car loaded with partygoers on their way home from a night of laughs. Of course, there were also some tears. As an observer scanning each of their faces, you can tell just how their night went; you have the loud group standing, laughing, and enjoying time with friends. Just ahead of them is a frowning couple with their arms folded in what can only be described as a raging war of silence. Way in the back, you have another group of friends who embraced the free shots before 11 p.m. promo a little too much and now two of them are trying to keep the delicious but ill-advised street tacos from coming back up. Sadly, the birthday boy (Sleeping Beauty) in the group had already lost his fight and now his friends are trying to keep him from lying in his beef, bean, and cheese burrito. In the window seat at the end of the car there is a young woman trying not to cry. She assumed it was working until an elderly gentleman gave her a napkin from his lunch bag. She politely thanked him before looking out the window again to console herself. Liquid courage was the fuel used by a few men in their early 20s who began a shoving match. Thankfully, the shoving match dissipated when the subway conductor began to speak over the PA system "Sorry for the delay, ladies and gentlemen, we will be on our way shortly." Most of the riders groaned in disbelief while others sat staring at their phones wishing they were home in their beds.

At first glance, a stranded subway seems like a rare occurrence but for Justin it was an all-too-familiar incident. He had been in these situations before; he used to be a die-hard partygoer but now he hates every minute of his time on the train. All Justin wanted to do was get home so he could catch up on the ridiculous sitcom that for some reason he could not stop watching. Justin knew if the train did not get moving soon his wife (Lina) would surely forget or ignore her promise to wait for him before binge watching the remaining episodes on Netflix. Justin checked his phone for bars again with no luck; he knew Lina was waiting for a response text. As Justin sighed in disbelief at his current situation, his best friend Kerry spoke up,

"Stop acting like a bitch and let's party."

Doing pullups on the subway loops, Kerry yelled for Justin to put his phone up and loosen up,

> "Man damn, come on, you're out of the house for the first time in months, relax and get it in with your boy."

You see Kerry was the reason Justin is out so damn late, instead of Netflix and chilling with his wife, as he wanted to be.

***

While Justin looked at Kerry hanging there making an ass of himself, a random long forgotten memory came rushing back to him from nearly 20 years earlier when he first met Kerry. Back then Justin was the new kid on the block after him and his mom moved to the neighborhood following her work transfer. It was summertime and the neighborhood was alive with activity, with much of the action happening at the Earl Joyner Community Park named after the World War II veteran. This was long before smartphones and social media, if you wanted to know about someone or what was happening in the city, the park was the place you would find out. At that time Joyner Park was only about an acre in size but it seemed enormous to them back then. The number of trees at the park could make one forget that you were in the city. The lush green grass was always well maintained by the grounds crew. In the center of the park was a large playground where teenagers would drop off their younger siblings to play; it was a safer time. However, most of the real action found in the park went down near or around the blacktop. The famous blacktop was made up of two full length basketball courts (one hoop with no netting and one hoop with metal netting) covered in asphalt which was hot and sticky during the summer months. As the new guy, Justin learned the all-important unwritten rule of the blacktop. He learned that the court with the metal nets belonged to the teenagers and sketchier crowds, as for the netless courts belonged to everyone else. This valuable lesson was learned the same day he met Kerry. As Justin walked to the park bouncing a basketball along with his little brother, they saw an open court and decided to shoot a few shots, nothing serious just playing around. As they were playing, a rather large man approached them,

"What the hell are you doing here?" assuming Justin and his brother must be lost.

Unaware of the rules Justin was at a loss for words and admittedly somewhat afraid because of what looked to be a giant Samoan yelling at him. Just as it seemed the "Rock's cousin" was about to rip his arm off a soft-spoken voice was heard,

"Chill Tony, he is the new kid."

Justin didn't know if the voice was from a kid or his guardian angel, all he knew was that his life was saved. Tony took a step back,

"This court is not for you; you can walk to the other one or be thrown there!"
Justin grabbed the ball and decided he would take option A and just walk to the approved court.

As Justin made his way to the netless court and safety, he could see a thin short kid running his mouth. Justin watched as the big, mouthed kid talked trash to almost everyone, he was half the size of everyone else, but his mouth and his ego were full grown. The trash talking kid ran around the park flirting with girls regardless of if she was with someone or not. He was using words and phrases that he had no business knowing at his age. To his credit some of the girls were smiling, which only encouraged him more. The girls smiled and laughed saying,

"Kerry, you're a fool!"
Their boyfriends or would-be suitors stood there unamused and not pleased at all. Some of the suitors began to chase the kid now identified as Kerry around the park trying to corner him. Kerry was just too fast for them, and he let them know it with his taunting. He continued to taunt the group while running circles around them, but his luck soon ran out when

he took a wrong turn into a newly roped-off construction area.

Kerry was now cornered with no escape. To the front of him was the group of teens he taunted and behind him was a blockade made of construction equipment. Here like in most places the word of a fight spreads fast. All the kids in the park gathered quickly to see the antagonist get his ass beat. Three of the upset suitors stood in front of Kerry talking shit and threatening him. Even with no escape Kerry refused to back down, instead he upped his game and began talking more trash than all the suitors combined. Kerry called his main adversary Fat Albert (real name Travis), making everyone laugh which only fueled Kerry more. Every time the kids laughed; all Kerry could hear was (get'm!)

> "Your mother is so black she looks like under the bed," Kerry joked, making the crowd laugh (*get'm*).
> "You're so stupid your kids will graduate before you." crowd laughs (*get'm*).

At this point the crowd was in a frenzy. Travis' shit-talking proved to be no match for Kerry. Travis could not keep up with the insults that Kerry was throwing his way. He decided to cut the comedy show short by punching Kerry in the face which knocked him to the ground. Travis stood back admiring his work as the crowd fell silent. He towered above Kerry like he did most of the kids in the park. Kerry got up and gathered his bearings before charging at Travis with reckless abandonment. This action surprised everyone: they assumed Kerry would stay down. Travis was bigger and stronger, but Kerry proved to be faster with his punches coming in bunches. Kerry's punches did not have a lot of power behind them but from the crowd's perspective he appeared to be kicking Travis's ass.

What happened next has been up for debate for nearly two decades now. Kerry believes and reminds everyone who will listen that he dropped Travis with an uppercut to his large stomach, followed by a nasty right cross. Some of the crowd, however, recall seeing Travis trip over a tree branch. Once Travis hit the ground, Kerry started dancing around mocking him. He turned his back to the other teens continuing his celebration when they attacked him. Kerry tried to fight off the two new attackers to no avail, they were all over him. Travis, now back up and even more furious that he fell (knocked down according to Kerry), joined in the beating. They toyed with Kerry, knocking him down and kicking him only to let him get back up to repeat the action over again. The crowd began to express their distain in the attacker's actions, but their complaints were largely ignored. The teens led by Travis intimidated the crowd when they tried to help; one person

(Jalene) joined in the fight to help Kerry but was thrown to the ground by one of the boys. Kerry, to his credit, refused to stay down showing his character and determination.

Just then, Justin emerged from the crowd. Where he was from, a fight was always one on one. The actions of Kerry's attackers upset Justin and even though he did not know him, his upbringing made him join the fight. Justin punched one of the teens, knocking him to the ground. This startled Travis as Justin stepped into his face.

"Who the hell are you?" Travis asked.

Justin responded in his southern drawl calling Travis a coward for jumping the little guy. Kerry, still on the ground bleeding from the mouth overheard this and after spitting out blood responded with,

"Your mother is a little guy!"

Justin ignored the dig while never breaking eye contact with Travis. The fighting stopped, because for the first time Travis was standing eye to eye with the tall southern kid instead of towering over them as he was accustomed to. Travis tried to use his size and words to intimidate Justin, but he learned it did not work on someone that was the same height as him. Justin told Travis,

"Do something or take your scary ass home."

Seeing Travis turn to walk away, Justin went to check on Kerry, but it was all a ruse, Travis turned back quickly and punched Justin in the side of the head. Justin ate the punch, taking a step back to regroup. Surprised that he did not fall, Travis charged Justin, but this ill-fated action did not work, Justin scooped Travis slamming him hard to the ground. The slam was so hard that leaves flew up, the impact knocked all the air out of Travis and left him squirming around trying to find the air that he lost. Justin quickly stood up looking for the other teens, knowing they would take any opportunity to attack him. To his surprise, the other combatants stood there stunned with their mouths wide open. A little afraid and in awe at the fact that Travis was so easily dispatched. In their defense the crowd was also standing there with their mouths gaped open as well.

Kerry, now up, started to go after Travis who was still on the ground looking for his lost air. Justin stopped him saying,

"You don't attack someone on the ground; the fight is over."

Kerry ignored Justin pushing his hand away, still trying to get to Travis. Kerry jumped on Travis removing what little air that he was able to find and raised his fist to begin raining down punches. Justin pulled Kerry off Travis telling him to stop and refused to put him down until Kerry calmed down.

Jalene began to laugh at the sight of Kerry's legs swinging in the air. Kerry understood the humor, but he was not amused, he kicked Justin in the shin causing him to be released. After landing Kerry….

***

"Hey man what the hell are you doing, are you sleeping?" Kerry yelled, bringing Justin back to the train and snapping his flashback.
Justin now laughing,

"No, I'm just remembering your legs dangling as I held you like a baby back in the day."
Kerry dropped from the arm straps, saying,

"Listen I could have kicked your ass, but I was being nice to the new kid."

"Sure, thing bro," said Justin.

"Whatever, what we need to be talking about is getting at these bitches." Kerry said.

"I'm not getting at these women. I'm retired from the game, you know that." Justin said.

"I know, I know you're whipped, I get it, but you can at least be a wingman." Kerry said.
Justin begrudgingly agreed as Kerry started scanning the train for women.

Kerry noticed the young woman he called Lily (doesn't know her) that was sobbing and looking worn out by what seemed to be an emotional night. Kerry winked at Justin saying,

"It's about to go down."

Kerry got his best George Jefferson walk on as he began to stroll over. You can imagine the way he looked trying to be smooth and cool on the crowded subway car. Justin looked on laughing under his breath as Kerry, who was doing his cool strut stepped in the street taco regurgitation left by Sleeping Beauty and almost fell. Justin could not control his laughter anymore; he laughed so loudly he woke the birthday boy but only briefly. Kerry wiped his shoes on the slumbering birthday boy's shirt while trying to remain unfazed. Now smelling of a combination of booze, street taco and vomit, he reached the young woman.

She was still sitting against the window gazing out of it. This gave Kerry the freedom and space he needed to sit down. He sat down as she ignored him sitting with her, which any normal person would take as a sign but not Kerry.

"Hey little mama you're out late, were you waiting for me or something?" Kerry asked as he chuckled.

The young woman unamused looked at him simply and said, "No thanks." as she turned back to the window.

Justin thought Kerry would take the hint but not his boy. Kerry doubled down,

> "I have not offered anything yet (leaning in) sexy."

smiling harder this time.

Now annoyed, she responded,

> "I said no thanks because I don't want anything you're offering, men ain't shit!" Leaning closer and raising her voice slightly.

Kerry, now on the defense, tried to defend the action of whatever dude screwed her over earlier in the night by saying,

> "We all make mistakes and I'm sure it wasn't his fault." with a slight grin on his face.

The woman now in a rage had had enough, she stood up and proceeded to curse Kerry. For the next five minutes all the passengers could hear was the sobbing lady tearing into Kerry asking,

> "Is it my fault that he slept with my cousin, is it my fault that it was in the bed I bought?"

Her rant was broken up only by Justin's laughter. At the end of his dressing down, truly embarrassed and defeated, Kerry stood up and silently walked back to his seat, this time without the George Jefferson strut. He sat down beside Justin who was now looking out the window trying to compose himself. After a few moments of silence, Justin whispered,

"Did you get her number and when is it going down?" referring to Kerry's displayed confidence from earlier.

"Go to hell man you know that was some bullshit," snapped Kerry.

Justin busted up laughing again.

The boyfriend from the silent war couple started laughing saying,

"Bitches be trippin."

For sure referring to his girlfriend and not the sobbing woman. Justin, not a fan of women being called bitch turned and told him to act as if he had some class.

The boyfriend looked at Justin saying,

"Go to hell."

This angered Kerry who was looking for someone to blow up on after being deservingly verbally assaulted by the young lady. He jumped at the chance to get in the face of the rude passenger to relieve his frustrations. Kerry told him that the only bitch on the train was him and if he had a problem then just to say the word. The girlfriend tried to calm the situation, but he had pent up frustration that he needed to get out as well.

Sensing that the subway car was about to erupt in violence the Subway Gods started moving the train as the conductor said,

"Thanks for your patience, let's go home."
The joy from his speech ended what was going to be an unnecessary fight. The warring couple sat back down now with even more to work through, while Kerry also took his seat with a little help from Justin. *A few more stops and tonight would be over, Justin* thought, as Kerry was just happy to have bars on his phone so he could try to set up his Netflix and chill party.

"Mission accomplished," Kerry said, showing his phone.
Justin responded,

"You're going to catch something."
Justin checked his messages from Lina and saw she went to bed and his food was in the microwave.

"This is what you need," Justin said, showing Kerry the text.

"You can keep that shit" said Kerry, continuing on saying "I'm not about that life, I've never been to prison but I'm sure that is what it is like".

"Wow really, that is how it is now", Justin said adding "you know I'm going to tell her."

"I do not care who you tell that is your wife not mine", Kerry said.

"Got it," Justin said picking up his phone pretending to relay the message.

"Quit playing you know Lina is crazy," Kerry said.

"Shut your scary ass up," Justin responded laughing. He had no intention of texting Lina remembering how upset she got in the past with his drunken calls.

Finally, the subway train arrived at the station to the delight of all the passengers onboard. The passengers exiting the delayed train looked disheveled. The silent warring couple exited the train with their arms still folded in discontent, looks like this war is still raging but the boyfriend held the door while carrying her bag. The young lady exited next, stepping around the birthday group as the friends tried to wake the sleeping birthday boy to no avail. Knowing what had happened next; the sober-ish friends began to play Rock-Paper-Scissors to see which two would carry sleeping beauty.

Rock-Paper-Scissors shoot, "Crap," one friend said.

Next up Paper-Rock-Scissors shoot, "Crap," another friend said.

Now that the two carriers (losers) were identified a random thought came out of the winner's mind: what *if he pukes again*.

The winner now realizing that he is now on puke duty let out a lone rumbling,

"FUCK!"

The friends picked up their sleeping friend while trying to avoid the street tacos he left behind. They made their way off the train and struggled up the stairs; it was an interesting sight to see the winner looking and praying his friend did not puke.

Justin and Kerry were next to leave. As they went up the stairs, they had to avoid more street tacos along the way, it seemed the birthday boy did not make it.
Justin set up an Uber once leaving the train,

"3 minutes," he told Kerry who was trying to finalize his late-night rendezvous.
As the Uber arrived, Justin asked again if Kerry wanted to drop him off. Kerry fist pumped Justin like he was Tiger Woods winning the Masters,

"Nah man I'm good I got to go."

"You sure? He can drop you on the way." Justin asked.
Kerry laughed saying,

"Nope, I got this and get out of my business bitch; you're not going to get your jollies off my exploits."

"Whatever man," said Justin laughing.

The two friends parted ways with their patented handshake (slapped hands, upward motion and snapping as they released). Justin's uber left as a woman in a black Honda Civic pulled up, Kerry got in and the two sped off.

{ 2 }

Home Sweet Home

"Would you like water? Would you like to charge your phone? Do you want some gum?" asked the Uber driver (Jamal).

Justin answered, "No thanks to all three."
He began to wonder if Jamal would continue asking questions. Almost on queue Jamal said,

"One last question, would you like to change the music?"
Justin was about to say no thanks for the fourth time until he really started listening.

"You know what Jamal, yes please change the music to literally anything else please."

"No problem man," Jamal said, changing the station to Hot 97.

Both started nodding their heads to the classic rhymes of Warren G and Nate Dogg (regulate). Feeling a kind of kinship with Justin, Jamal proceeded to tell him about his night of ubering in the city. Justin tried to fix his body language in efforts to appear as he was listening and not to appear rude. As Jamal talked, Justin turned on his husband's listening skills (where you nod and add a "really?", occasionally to the conversations with your wife) as he stared out of the back window. Jamal told him a story about picking up a group of sorority sisters at a frat party. He said he pulled up to what he thought was a street fight judging from the amount of college kids on the street. Apparently, these sorority sisters were the life of the party, and two frats were competing for their affection. "Coming around the corner I realized it wasn't a fight, it was an impromptu step off battle between the Q-Dogs and the Alphas."

"Word? That's crazy!" Justin said, proving he was listening.

Jamal continued, "Yea man it was something, shit, I was enjoying the show until my passengers pulled me away."

The uber pulled up to a beautiful Brownstone, Jamal asked,

"Damn yo! This you, this you?" admiring.

"Yeah, it's me," Justin responded.

He dapped Jamal up for the ride. Once Justin exited the vehicle, he stood back and admired his beautiful home after receiving compliments from Jamal. The recently painted Ruby Red shutters bounced off the dark brick wonderfully. After arguing with Lina about the colors Justin would never tell her that even the giant flowerpots blended very well just as she insisted, they would. Justin entered the brownstone quietly trying not to wake Lina and the kids. He went over his nightly checklist to ensure the house was secure before going upstairs. Turn the alarm off, Check. Shoes off to lessen the squeak from the refinished hardwood floors, Check. Alarm reactivated, Check. Water and Advil for the morning headache, Check. Put the food away so Lina doesn't trip, Check. Steal fruit snacks from kids, Check. Hide evidence from kids, Check. Now for the hardest part, making up the stairs. *Half way up, so far so good keep going*, Justin thought. He was feeling good after making it upstairs while avoiding the two creaky steps, big ass Check. Justin was now home free after navigating the treacherous noise makers of the house. The next stop was his bed and finally some much needed sleep, the sleep he had been thinking about since the second round of shots with Kerry.

Moments later Lina was awakened out of a deep sleep by a loud crash.

"Justin is that you?" Lina asked, reaching for her pistol.

A low painful yes came from down the hallway where Justin was struggling to get up.

"You ok babe?" Lina asked while taking deep breaths, still a little startled.

"Yeah, I'm good," Justin said, making his way to the bedroom.

As he limped into the room Lina now sitting up in the bed asked if he needed help.

"No, I'm good," Justin answered slowly taking off his clothes.

After gingerly putting on basketball shorts, Justin leaned over and kissed Lina on the forehead before getting in the bed.

"What happened babe?" Lina asked.

"I tripped over Triston's damn skateboard," Justin responded angrily.

"Oh wow, sorry babe I told him to put it away," Lina said trying to hold in her laugh.

Now having to pee, she made her way to the bathroom trying to avoid eye contact with her hurting husband. Lina turned on the fan and released her held laughter.

"Dammit woman! I can hear you," Justin said angrily which only made her laugh harder.

"Sorry babe," Lina said trying to stop the laughter.

She wiped her eyes as she left the bathroom still apologizing for laughing,

"I told him to put it away before he went to bed."

"Well, he didn't do it. Dammit!" Justin said, feeling the pain in his back.

Lina chuckled as she got back in the bed and rolled over. Justin continued to mutter under his breath as he rolled over a few times trying to get comfortable enough to sleep.

The alarm started blaring after what seemed to be 5 minutes, Justin tried his best to break the alarm as he shut it off.

"Fuck, who set the alarm for 9 a.m.!" Justin yelled,

"You did, fool," Lina yelled from the bathroom.

"Why would I do that?" Justin asked, thinking she was full of it.

"Jasmine has her first soccer practice, and you promised to take her."

"Well damn maybe I did say that. Do you really think it's best for me to take her?" Justin asked, hoping Lina would bail him out.

"Yes, I think it's best, besides, she hasn't stopped talking about how her daddy was going to do this and do that, whatever." (Lina hating a little)

Justin said, "I just got home, come on lovey (trying to be sweet)."

"Well, who told you to shut the club down as if you were young or something," denying his advances. Now a little irritated, Justin sat up to make his request in a firmer voice,

"Lina, I'm tired and still a little drunk, I don't want.—"

"Jasmine, come here, your dad wants to see your uniform." Lina said, cutting him off. Jasmine came running into the room jumping in front of her dad dancing and modeling her uniform. She hugged him,

"Get dressed dad, we have to go," trying to pull him out of bed.

"Ok, ok I'm about to jump in the shower now."

"Great, I will go make some cereal and get my new pink water bottle,"

Justin, now sitting on the side of the bed trying to gather his bearings, began to hope and pray for rain. He opened the blinds filled with so much hope in his heart until he saw the beautiful sunshine reflecting off the deck surface (Justin must be the only person upset at sunshine). Lina adding to his grief walked out of the bathroom in gym clothes with a big, got ya ass grin on her face, Justin simply nodded to acknowledge her victory.

He finally mustered up enough energy to go take a shower and get his life together. After taking the standard drunken piss for nearly eight minutes, Justin stood in front of the mirror wondering how he got himself into this mess and why he took those last two shots (maybe the last six). Now in the shower Justin stood under the hot water which felt great and for a brief moment he fell asleep standing up until his mouth opened and he nearly drowned from the water. After almost choking to death, Justin thought to himself, *well, I'm awake now.* He looked through his closet for a comfortable outfit before deciding on his cool dad sweats complete with his favorite faded baseball cap.

Finally dressed and on his way downstairs Justin felt a twinge in his back which reminded him of the damn skateboard incident from just a few hours before. After looking around for the skateboard trying to avoid another crash, Justin decided to go to Triston's room to give him a stern talking to and maybe even break the board based on his pain level. Walking into Triston's room Justin was confused about why it was so dark. Justin noticed that Triston had put a blanket over the window to block out all forms of light. After removing the blanket Justin could now see Triston in the middle of his bed with the covers pulled over his head. Justin asked,

"Boy what the hell are you doing under there?"

When Triston did not answer Justin walked over and pulled the cover back. What he saw made his grown, I'm not afraid of anything ass run out of the room slamming the door behind him. Justin was now pacing up and down the hallway trying to process what his eyes had just seen. *Was he, no he is too young, but he could have been*, Justin thought? His brain was running at full speed, but it still was not able to keep up.

As he paced the hallway, Justin thought back to his own preteen days and what he was doing at Triston's age. He knew it was a natural pastime for teens but now he had to figure out a way to talk to Triston about it. Justin knew he should practice what he would say before going into his son's room, he did not want a misplaced statement to confuse his son about what was going on with his body. Justin lacked experience in these talks, his dad gave him a horrible talk. Justin refused to do the same, so he came up with the idea of using the only examples he knew. He began to think of what TV dads had told their sitcom sons when situations like this arose. *I could be like the dad from Black-ish (Dre)*, Justin thought but then again his talk didn't work very well with Junior, it led to several shirtless uncomfortable conversations. *Ok what about the (Michael) from My Wife and Kids, he had a good talk with his son but then again maybe not, his son did get a girl pregnant after the talk.* As Justin continued pacing up and down the hallway he began to spiral down the rabbit hole. Certainly, one of the TV dads from his childhood could help him out, *Carl from Family Matters (no), Al from Married with Children (Hell no), Phil from Fresh Prince (no), Steven from Family Ties (no not sure that he ever talked about girls), Rock from Rock (no kids), George from George Lopez (kinda but no),* damn the list got longer and longer than the names Justin could remember. The rabbit hole was deep. Justin had two thoughts: *I have watched a lot of TV and secondly all those dads were no help at all.* As he pumped himself up for the talk, Triston came out of his room startling an already jumpy Justin.

"Hey, dad, are you ok?" Triston asked.

Still jumpy, Justin answered, "yea son, I'm good, I was just about to come talk to you. Let's go have a chat." (Trying not to be weird).

Triston, now looking confused, agreed and followed his dad to his room. Triston jumped on his bed sitting cross-legged waiting for his dad to sit down. Justin almost sat down until he got a visual of what could be on the bed, which made him shoot back up and lean against the dresser instead (really being weird).

Justin started,

"Son you're growing into a fine young man, your body is changing, and I know that can be a little strange or scary"

Nailed the opening, Justin thought.

"I've been there too, you're not alone, every man goes through this; it is nothing to be ashamed of. I know your urges are starting to take over your mind and that it is ok too."

Triston looked on in confusion. *I'm losing him,* Justin thought as he decided to be straight up and not danced around the topic.

"Son, I know what you were doing under the covers, and I want you to know it is ok. I did it when I was your age, but you must lock the door at least. You don't want your mom or sister to walk in."

Triston still confused, "I did it in front of mom yesterday, she thought it was cool."

Justin was now the confused one, "your mom looked at it?"

"Yeah, she gave me ideas on what to look up next." Triston said.

What The Fuck, Justin thought still confused and getting a little angry at the fact that Triston's mother would watch let alone tell him better videos to look up.

Triston continued, "she wants me to be good at it I guess."

Justin stormed down the stairs, "LINA WTF!"

"What?" she responded.

Justin walked into the kitchen where Jasmine was eating cereal and watching cartoons at the table. Seeing that he couldn't blast off the way he wanted to, Justin leaned in close to Lina,

"Why in the hell are you helping Triston find new things to look up?"

"He wants to get better; besides I don't see what's wrong with that."

Everyone has gone fucking crazy, Justin thought.

"Why the fuck are you helping Triston find that kinda stuff?"

Confused, Lina took a step back thinking *WTF is he talking about*. As Justin was still talking all Lina heard was blah blah, as she was too busy trying to remember what she and Triston talked about the night before.

Triston came walking into the kitchen at the wrong time; his parents looked at him how lions look at their prey.

"Get over here," Justin said.

Justin was trying to have a heated conversation in a low tone, so Jasmine did not hear. Justin began to scold Lina and Triston,

"You're his mom, why did you do this and why would you ask your mother for anything like that?"

Lina, now upset,

"What was wrong with Triston looking on YouTube to learn secrets about a game?"

"Because it's wrong and I don't want – wait, what? I'm talking about you helping him find porn." Justin said now a little confused.

"No one showed him porn you fucking idiot." Lina angrily answered.

Oh shit, damn, damn, damn, James, Justin thought standing there perplexed, slightly panicked. Now in full reverse, Justin yelled,

"Triston, why didn't you put your skateboard away last night? How many times have I told you to put the damn skateboard away and why are you watching YouTube under your covers anyway?"

"I just forgot dad, I'm sorry, it will not happen again. I covered my windows and got under the covers to make it feel like the movie theater", Triston answered.

Justin now grinning at Lina, "it's ok we all make mistakes."

She however was still looking at him as if he were the stupid-est fucking person in the world.

"Go clean your room and put all the blankets away when you're done." Justin said.

"Ok dad," Triston responded as he ran off.

"Can you believe these kids?" Justin asked, smiling at Lina who had not really responded since being chas-tised like a child.

"Ok babe, I might have jumped the gun but it's really not my fault." Justin said smiling.
Lina looked up at him with the standard oh hell no face. She moved closer so Jasmine did not see her pick up a butter knife and put it deep into Justin's hip whispering,

"I will cut your fucking balls off if you ever talk to me like that again you fucking idiot."
Justin awkwardly nodded in agreement while telling Jasmine to clean up her cereal bowl and get her soccer bag for prac-tice. After stuffing everything into her gym bag Jasmine hugged her mom goodbye. Justin said,

"Later honey," while moving in for a kiss.
Lina raised the knife indicating what would happen if Justin kept coming forward, he blew her a kiss instead while heading out the door.

{ 3 }

Soccer Dad

Escaping the wrath of his wife Justin jumped in his new Jeep where Jasmine was now waiting.

"We have to go dad; we can't be late."

"Ok Face, we'll be there on time, don't worry."
He started the car and saw the gas light was on which instantly made Justin flash hot (Justin believes Lina thinks "E" stands for extra gas.)

"Damn we need gas," Justin said looking back at Jasmine.

"OH NO, I knew we were going to be late!" Jasmine yelled, starting to freak out.

"Relax, it will be fine, all we have to do is grab a little gas really quick and we'll be on our way." Justin told her.

"Ok dad," Jasmine said looking disappointed.

It is too early for this Justin thought to himself. He sped down the expressway towards practice trying to make up some time. Thankfully, traffic was rather light allowing them to get to the gas station in good time. Justin jumped out and ran into the store to grab Powerade to balance out the alcohol that was still in his system while the gas was pumping. He jumped back in the car,

"Ok let's hit it," pulling out of the gas station. Suddenly Jasmine spoke up,

"Dad, you forgot to get Sam and Dean."

"Who in the world is Sam and Dean?" Justin said looking in the rearview mirror.

"They are my friends from school. Mom talked to their mom and told her that we could take her kids with us today."

Justin called a still steaming Lina who answered the phone aggressively,

"What Fucker?"

"Well first, you're on speakerphone and second who the hell is Sam and Dean?" Justin asked.

"Oh yeah, they're twins who moved into the white duplex down the street. I thought you knew them." Lina said.

Justin cut her off which did not help the steaming issue at all.

"I need their address and please let them know I'm on the way."

Lina agreed to call them but started to tell Justin about cutting her when he cut her off again. He knew it was going to upset her a little more, but he thought it would be funny.

Justin is now speeding back to the subdivision to grab Sam and Dean. He could not help thinking that he knew that naming combination from somewhere. As they arrived at the house Justin remembered where he knew the combo from. He ran up and rang the doorbell while thinking it cannot be. As he was thinking, a pasty male opened the door greeting him,

"I'm Paul," giving a half assed handshake (looking like he was hiding from the sun).

"Morning I'm Justin, Jasmine is in the car, we need to run."

The pale man said,

"Come on guys Jasmine is here."

A blonde freckle faced boy came running out of the house still putting on his shirt followed by a brunette young lady with long pigtails. They grabbed their gear and jumped into the jeep with Jasmine.

"Ok, I will have them back shortly after practice,"

Justin said, informing Paul of the plan for today.

"Oh, I'm going with you," Paul said, putting on crocs and heading out.

Heading back to the Jeep Justin was confused, first what man wears crocs? *Well maybe he is in the medical field* Justin thought. Secondly if Paul was going then why the hell did I have to come get him and lastly, he better not have named his children after a TV show. Justin jumped back in the car and began speeding to practice while trying to ignore the Kidz Bop music that was being sung off-key by the kids in the back. Justin normally has no problem with ignoring the kids bop station but today was a little different. He had only had about 7 minutes of sleep after nearly breaking his damn neck. Not to mention the Triston fiasco, now not only does he have the kids in the back trying to sing despite only knowing about 45% of the words but he now had Paul in the damn front seat trying to sing as well.

"I'm too old for this shit," Justin whispered to himself, quoting his favorite movie line.

Arriving at the park, Justin thanked the lord that the noise had stopped as he exited the Jeep, little did he know that it was the calm before the storm. Jasmine, Sam, and Dean ran towards the practice field, while Justin began to look for a good spot on the sidelines that was far enough away from

Paul but close enough that Jasmine could still see him. Justin saw Coach Gee waving at him as she made a b-line in his direction, Justin began to wonder if Lina signed him up for snack duty or something. Thankfully, Lina did not sign him up for snacks, but she did, however, sign him up to help coach like he did for Triston when he started playing baseball. Damn it man all Justin wanted to do was zone out and maybe catch a power nap.

"Welcome coach Justin," the spunky vertically challenged Coach Gee said.

Her spunk reminded Justin of a cheerleader doing cartwheels. Even though all he wanted to do was sit and chill, it felt good to see the smile on Jasmine's face as he stood in front of them. Justin, a physically intimidating man, a veteran and despite all the training and experience he had; Justin had no idea what was in store for him on this day.

Channeling his inner Coach K, one of the greatest college basketball coaches ever, Justin said

"Circle up dragonflies, let's stretch. *stupid team name* Justin thought: Spread your legs shoulder width apart and bend at the waist."

So far so good Justin thought right before three kids fell trying to spread their legs. It was no problem; they got up and tried again. Two boys fell backwards trying to bend over at the waist, Justin stood there staring in disbelief and said,

"Ok get up and try again."

The rotation of stretching and falling continued to repeat itself for the next 10 to 15 minutes. Justin could already feel his blood starting to boil but he kept reminding himself that this was the first year playing organized sports for the majority of the team.

"Ok grab a ball and let's start kicking!" Coach Gee yelled.

Grab a ball and let's start kicking was a simple set of instructions but Coach Gee might as well have said it in Latin because the kids looked confused as they stood around a bag of soccer balls. Continuing to hold his tongue, Justin simply walked over and dumped the soccer balls out.

"Ok grab one and start kicking," he reiterated thinking surely there should be no more issues.

Nope, Sam and Dean began fighting over the same blue soccer ball, a super cute tiny girl with a cocoa complexion stood there trying not to cry, and his lovely Jasmine grabbed a ball and started kicking in the wrong direction. The sibling fighting, standing around, and Face going in the wrong direction was more than Justin could take. He blew the whistle that Coach Gee lent him as hard as he could, producing a sharp screeching noise that brought all activities to a halt.

After Coach K did not work Justin tried a little Bobby Knight (Great coach, known for being tough),

"Circle it up team, we need to go over the ground rules." Justin said, trying not to curse.
He was unaware if Coach Gee had rules, but she wasn't stopping the behavior, so he decided to take charge and lay out some basic rules for his sanity.

"First no one talks in the circle but the coaches, second no hitting or touching each other, and Third be a good teammate." Justin said.
As he continued, he could tell from the blank stares that he was wasting his breath.

"Ok just remember the first two rules and we will work on the rest."
He broke the huddle and began dividing the team into groups to access their skills. After the groups were set, Jasmine picked which ball the team would use for their scrimmage. As the scrimmage was unfolding there were a few hiccups but overall, the coaches were pleased. It did look more like a rugby scrum than a soccer match but at least the kids were going in the right direction, mostly. The longer the game progressed kids began to drop off, Coach Gee lost a player who

got distracted by butterflies and Justin lost two kids who decided to lay in the grass and contemplate their life choices.
The coaching duo tried to round their players up and get
them back into the game. Justin raised his voice and began to
bark orders which upset some of the parents based on the
looks on their faces. Justin did not give a damn. He thought *if
you sit there while your child eats grass then you can sit there while they
get corrected.*

Finally, after what seemed to be hours, practice was over and
now all that was left was picking up the equipment. A group
of parents approached Justin as he gathered the equipment,
he knew from coaching Triston's teams what was about to
happen next. Some of the parents asked him how they could
make their kids better, others talked about why their kid
should get more playing time, and all of them told Justin why
their kid should start. Justin resisted the urge to tell the parents that most of the kids were bad including his own. Opting
instead to simply nod while saying,

"Practice at home with your kids. We will put out a
lineup after a few more practices."

After biting his tongue with the parents, Justin went over to
the playground where Jasmine and the twins were now playing. Justin sat on the bench giving the kids a little more time

to play while preparing himself for another round of Kidz Bop. As he sat there thinking about how much the park had changed over the years since he was a kid, Paul appeared out of nowhere startling the shit out of him.

"Damn man, I didn't see you. "Justin said, trying to compose himself.

"Sorry I was just walking around being one with nature," Paul said.

"Ok, quick question before you continue being one with nature, where did the twins get their names from?" Justin asked as his curiosity got the better of him.

"It's a funny story, when my wife and I met, we would binge watch a show called *Supernatural*, I proposed after the episode where Dean went to hell. The pregnancy stick turned blue after Jack came back to life, "Justin was nodding at this point.
Paul continued saying,

"Therefore, it was only fitting to name them after a show that was a huge part of our lives."

"Good thing you guys didn't binge watch *Beavis and Butt-head* or *Pinky and the Brain*" Justin said, making a joke about some shows he loved in his younger days.
Paul stood there for a second looking confused, *I guess he didn't get the joke* Justin thought.

"Ok Jasmine, round up your friends and let's go daddy needs a nap."

"Ok dad, I'll drive if you want me to."

"No thanks sweetie, maybe next time." Justin answered, shaking his head.
Heading back home brought more kids bop singing by the kids and of course Paul.

After fighting traffic and trying to ignore the insanity of the group in the Jeep, Justin dropped the Supernatural crew off and headed down the block to his house. Before Justin could pull off,

Paul turned to him and busted up laughing saying, *"Pinky and the Brain."*
Justin nodded, surprised that it took that long to get the joke. The sight of their home-made Justin feel all warm inside.

"Daddy can we go back to Sam and Dean's house after I change?" Jasmine asked.

"No baby, daddy is going to sleep for the next two days, if I can. Ask your mom or Triston, maybe one of them can bring you back." Justin replied.
After parking Jasmine jumped out of the Jeep running to change and ask her mom about going back to play as Justin made his way to the couch.

"How was it babe?" Lina asked.

She could tell how bad it was from the "Fuck Off" expression written all over Justin's face.

"I'm not cut out to coach little children; I'm beat and all I want you to do is let me sleep until Tuesday." Justin got comfortable in his favorite chair. *It's noon, time for a nap* he thought as he put his phone on silent and turned the TV off. Just as he was drifting off to sleep Lina came down and said,

"Babe don't forget his flight comes in at 2pm today."

"FUCK ME!" Justin yelled.

{ 4 }

Kerry's Condo

Thankfully, a massive thunderstorm delayed all incoming flights to the city, which allowed Justin to get a much-needed power nap. After the heavenly delay Justin was now dressed and feeling a little more refreshed. He went downstairs to say his goodbyes to the kids and Lina. He reminded Triston to make sure he cleaned up after himself (not trying to break his neck again).

Lina asked, "please take it easy tonight."

Justin said, "Trust me I'm only having water," agreeing to Lina's request.

Justin had no desire for another morning like the past one. Lina grinned in appeasement but did not believe him at all. She knew Justin was a reformed partier however, she also knew that when the whole gang got together the party would be on and poppin. Justin was aware of this as well, but he truly did not want to go all-out like he and Kerry had done the night before.

The steady rain continued as Justin made his way to the airport. After making his third loop around the arrivals lane Justin decided to wait in the cell phone lot. While waiting, Justin found himself singing along to *Hey Babe* on Kidz Bop, instead of stopping he turned the music up and got his *sang* on. He was singing loud and somewhat off-key in full concert mode when his phone rang.

"I'm at E447 when you come around." his passenger said.

"Ok, I'm on the way," Justin said, bringing his concert to an end.

Pulling up in the pickup lane again, the security guard looked at Justin suspiciously due to this being his 80th loop or whatever. Justin creeped along the lane until he saw his old friend, now a little grayer with more of a Vet bod (like a dad bod just with bad knees). Justin jumped out and embraced his friend before calling him soft for hugging him.

"Let's get out of here man. I hate airports, there are so many people touching and or bumping into me." his passenger said.

The two friends left the airport in a hurry to get the night of partying started (still listening to Kids Bop).

A few minutes later Kerry can be seen laying on his couch in nothing but his boxers. An unknown figure towered over Kerry for a minute or two before yelling,

"Wake up you little bitch!"

There was no movement from Kerry other than him grunting and rolling over. Taking Kerry's rolling over personally the figure moved in closer and yelled louder.

"Wake up you little Smurf looking bitch!" (because of the blue boxers) and this time he added a head slap.

Kerry jumped up looking around for who hit him. Seeing the familiar figure (Travis, yes that Travis), Kerry dove into Travis's arms yelling,

"You fat fuck!"

Seeing this Justin fell on the couch busting up in laughter,

"You two are stupid as hell!"

There might be some confusion at how the three made it from fighting in the park to now laughing and embracing each other in Kerry's condo but we will get back to that a little later. After being slammed on the couch, Kerry stood up yelling,

"Enough, you play too much with your damn fathead self!"

Which prompted Travis to chase him around the room for a few laps.

"Ok, ok chill I'm too old for this shit." Travis said plopping down on the couch.

"Fine only because I'm still a little drunk," Kerry said standing in the middle of the room in his boxers.

"Dude, put on some pants or sit your ass down, no one is trying to see all that," Justin said.

"Shut up bitch, I know plenty of people who like it." Kerry responded, sitting down on the couch. Travis chuckled,

"Right, cool story bro."

Feeling attacked, Kerry stood up taking a defiant stance with his hands on his hips,

"Why do you think I'm in my boxers? I just finished with a beautiful big-breasted hottie."

After looking over the faces of both Travis and Justin who were giving him the look of disbelief Kerry became even more incensed. He began to lay out his bio for them to choke on,

"Hey just because you two are shackled down doesn't mean you have to hate on me damn it. I'm a young, caramel guy that's shredded like Bruce Lee with a great job as a teacher. Plus, my condo is fire."

Kerry now in full rant mode continued,

"Justin, you got married for love years ago which is cool for you, Lina is awesome and much better than you, but marriage is lame. Now Travis with your fat neck self, you want to get married and destroy your player card also. Ok dammit, I will take it, mine is filling up anyway. I'm the player of players, I have a stable of women that satisfy me on the regular. You luckily tricked a good woman to agree to marry you but I'm thriving as a single man. Hell, I just finished up with my cougar a few hours ago. She is the one that picked me up from the subway station; I rocked her and sent her on her way."

Justin started shaking his head in what looked to be judgment, so Kerry continued,

"I got one in finance so I'm always up-to-date with the newest investment trends, one is a manager of Foot Locker, so my gear is always tight, and one is in the Super's office so all my work orders get pushed to the top of the priority list. I have not had an issue in my place for the past six months."

"Dude you're nasty as hell." Travis said, moving from the couch thinking Kerry and his cougar had been there.

"What happens when they run into each other?" Justin asked.

"Nothing, I don't keep secrets from any of them." Kerry admitted.

"Well at least you have that but that sounds awful." Justin said.

Justin began to tell Kerry about the benefits to having one woman as Kerry looked to be listening but in all honesty all he heard was the teacher from *Charlie Brown* saying (womp womp).

"Ok whatever, I'm going to take a shower and get dressed."

Kerry had heard this same conversation from Justin several times, but he could not bring himself to be that open with someone. In the shower, Kerry just let the water run down his face as he tried to understand why the guys wanted him to settle down, after all, years ago they all lived the same life.

Growing up Kerry bounced from pillar to post (house to house) with most of his time spent at his grandmother's house. In his youth, he had several "uncle's" that would hang out with his mom taking advantage of her low self-esteem. His mother had a big heart and just wanted to be loved. She had a knack for finding wounded hood birds that she thought she could save. Needless to say, the relationships never truly worked out for her. This is the main reason Kerry has to be upfront with the women in his life. Her large caring heart often led her to the wrong element of losers most of which were not always the best with children. After a severe beating at the hands of one of his "uncle's", Kerry's grandmother moved him into her house after threatening to kill the suitor. His mother hated it but her love for the wounded birds was too strong.

Kerry's relationship became strained with his mother for years based on how things went down after the beating. He believed she picked the "uncle" over him. An upbringing like that had a dramatic impact on Kerry; he developed humor to mask his real feelings until he was able to bury them all together. In watching his mother be hurt physically and mentally, Kerry recognized that at an early age his heart was just as big as hers, which scared him. Since childhood he had tried to keep most relationships and friendships at surface level to protect himself from being hurt. He allows his heart to be shown to his small circle of friends and even though Justin and Travis reprimand him, he will still give up all for them. To this day, the only girl Kerry ever loved was Jalene. He loved her before she jumped in to help that day when the guy's paths crossed. The fact that she tried to help him only made him love her more. Jalene was able to see the real Kerry through all the smoke and mirrors. This scared him to his core, so he never acted on his feelings for her. He secretly hoped to find that special someone someday (just not today.)

"Dude hurry up! No one wants to see you, so bring your ass!" Justin yelled.
Travis joined,
"If I miss this tuxedo appointment because of you, Red is going to kick our asses. You don't know how much convincing I had to do for her to agree to me getting the tux here instead of back home."
"I'm getting dressed; besides I'm not scared of her, but you had better not tell her I said that." Kerry said as he finished putting his outfit together.
Before heading out the bedroom Kerry took one or three more looks at himself, then went to the front room where an impatient Justin and Travis sat.
"Are you done now?" Justin asked.
Kerry stood looking in the hallway mirror admiring himself again saying,
"I make this look good."
Being a true friend Justin walked by and messed up Kerry's hair just as he finished primping himself.

"You bitch, don't touch my hair. Just because your
shit is gone it doesn't give you the right to touch
mine." Kerry said, now fixing himself once again.

"You look fine, now bring your ass Buckwheat."
Travis said, laughing at his own joke.

Leaving his condo, Kerry sped up to catch up with Justin and
Travis who were on the way to the elevator calling them
bitches along the way, but his timing could not have been
worse. As soon as the letter B came out of his mouth, Miss
Ella (an older small lady with silver hair and a big church hat
on) came out of her condo on her way to choir practice, an
usher board meeting, or some other church-related function.
The four met up at the elevator, Kerry spoke to Miss Ella
who maintained eye contact with Kerry for the entire ride
down the elevator making sure he did not curse again. Justin
and Travis could barely hold in their laughter, but their upbringing made them afraid of Miss Ella. They had grown up
with church women like her, and they still have the scars
from the pinches, those old women loved to pinch the shit
out of unruly children. As Miss Ella exited the elevator and
disappeared, Justin and Travis now free from holding their
tongues burst into laughter at Kerry being caught and them
feeling like 5th graders again in her presence.

After getting in the car and making sure Miss Ella was gone, Justin asked,

"Was she the cougar from last night?"

"Fuck you man, she probably has that fire," Kerry said.

"You will find out first," said Travis.

"Hey man, don't let her church hat fool you, she is about that life. I watched her snap on some of the neighbors for leaving trash everywhere. When the conversation got heated, I went to step in, but Miss Ella told me no thanks, I'm a pistol packing granny. Then she hit them with God Bless You, on the way out." Kerry said.

"Damn, she is my new hero." Justin said.

"Shit, she sounds like my mema." Travis laughed.

"Oh yea, your mema was the best. She could bless you or curse you out with the sweetest smile on her face," Kerry said remembering her.

"Yea that was my mema," Travis smiled.

The group of friends laughed as they jumped on the highway heading to their tuxedo appointment while streaming rap music from their teen years. A debate started about the best song from back in the day. After going back and forth, they decided that each one would pick a song to finally prove their point. Kerry picked *Mind playing tricks on me* by Ghetto Boys and despite them all rapping at the top of their lungs Justin and Travis said

"No."

Next up was Travis with *Straight Outta Compton* by NWA, Kerry damn near blew his speakers out listening to it but just like with the first song the remaining two voters vetoed the pick. Last up was Justin with *No Vaseline* by Ice Cube which the others tried their hardest not to nod their heads, but they failed badly by the second verse of the song. It was close but they each avoided giving in until *Summertime* by Will Smith came on. Kerry let down the windows and the friends went back in time for a short period. The crew was transported back to the early 1990's and began to rap the lyrics perfectly. Just then Travis's cell ringtone played, Major's *this is why I love you* hit song breaking up the party.

"Oh, shit it's Red, I almost forgot about the damn fitting, hey babe sorry I forgot to call you when I got in. Justin did not remind me like I asked him to, you know he ain't shit." Travis said, trying to divert attention from himself.

"Really, is that how we're going to do this shit? Ok got it." Justin said.

"Yeah babe, we are almost at the store, Kerry is driving like my dead grandma, but we are moving, don't worry we will be there." Travis said, ignoring Justin. Kerry started making whipping sounds indicating that Travis is whipped by Red. Justin was cracking up in the passenger seat until she asked to speak to him.

"Hey, what's up girl?" Justin said, flipping off Travis as he chuckled.
She asked,
"If Lina and Jasmine got their dresses for the wedding or if they were still looking?"
He confirmed that they both had them and that they were simply looking for accessories now.
Red said, "tell Travis I will call him back a little later to see how the fitting is going."
As they pulled into the parking lot Justin decided to have a little fun, he started to describe their plans for the night as if Red was still on the phone. Yeah, we plan on hitting the gentlemen's club Peaches for a few drinks to get the night started. He continued saying that he might buy Travis a lap dance or two before getting him a private room. At this point Travis and Kerry were staring at Justin in disbelief.

"What the hell are you doing man!" Travis yelled trying to get his phone back.

Justin jumped out of the car avoiding Travis, Kerry was still in shock and just sat in the driver seat afraid to get out.

"Justin, give me my phone you bitch!" Travis yelled.

"Nope, not until I finish," Justin said as he ran to the opposite side of the car as Travis approached.

"Lastly we will hit up a club so Travis can get one last grind in before marrying you." Justin said, before tossing the phone back to him.

"Hello, hello babe we're not going to a strip club.

Red, did you hear me? Oh, how could you?!" Travis yelled frantically calling Red back.

When she answered Travis began to apologize for Justin's lies.

"What are you talking about? What did he lie about?" She asked.

Travis looked confused until Justin leaned in and told him that Red had gotten off the phone and heard nothing of what he was saying.

"WTF man?" Kerry screamed while laying across the hood of his car laughing.

Now comprehending that Justin was playing Travis said,

"Never mind babe I just hate Justin." Travis said to Red before looking at Justin,

Really dude, why would you do that?"

"Well because it was funny to see you freak out and because you blamed me for not calling." Justin said.

Travis chased Justin to the opposite end of the car again but quit when he could not catch him. Kerry was unaware of the cat and mouse game because he was still laying on his car laughing. To the other shoppers in the parking lot this had to be a sight to see, two grown men running around the car while a third laid across a car laughing. Realizing that they were now being watched, the trio stopped playing and finally made their way into the store to be fitted for their tuxedos.

{ 5 }

R&D's Fashion

They entered the R&D's Fashion which was a high-end establishment that had wall-to-wall mirrors, large windows that allowed tremendous amounts of light in, and a fragrance that welcomed you as soon as you opened the door. The group could not help feeling out of place in the beautifully decorated showroom.

"I'm not sure I have enough money to buy a damn bow tie in this place." Kerry said.

"That's your fault for not asking for the raise that you deserve." Justin said.

"I am waiting for them," Kerry started to explain.

"You're waiting because you're a punk," Travis interrupted Kerry.

"Dude you have been overlooked for way too long." Justin agreed with Travis.

"Ok I'll be all that but look I love teaching and even though I want to murder some of the parents I love helping the kids. I will get my raise, or I might look to work elsewhere." Kerry said.

"Good, you have been waiting for too long." Travis said.

"Hold up, he's not the one ducking promotions," Justin said looking at Travis.

"Look at the pot calling the kettle calling the pot." Kerry added.

"What the hell was that?" a confused Travis asked.

"You know what I meant," Kerry said.

"His words are jacked up but he's right." Justin noted.

"Forget all that, why am I looking for a pink ass tux to wear to your snore fest of a wedding?" Kerry asked, trying to strike back.

"Wow, too far," Travis said, attempting to push Kerry into the clothing rack.

"Ok I'll take most of it back."

"It is a soft ass looking pink," Justin added, laughing at them both.

"Oh, you got jokes now but I remember that mess you had us in at your wedding a few years ago buddy. Shit, I still have nightmares when I think of it." Travis responded.

"You too? I thought I was the only one. Hell, I had to go to counseling because of that damn tux." Kerry said.

"I think Justin and Lina should pay for half of our counseling bill." Travis said high fiving Kerry.

Justin, now sitting on a plush white couch taking verbal fire from both sides decided to end the bullying swiftly by the only way he knew how, violence. He hit an unsuspecting Kerry in the face with a pillow; he then threw a pillow at a laughing Travis but missed as he ran away. Justin got up to get his revenge, but he had to stop as the store manager appeared out of nowhere looking like a retired Mississippi pimp down to the cane. Trying to compose themselves The Three Amigos tried not to laugh as they waited for him to stroll over. With each step towards them it became harder and harder which prompted Kerry to walk away. He felt his will was too weak to contain his laughter, Justin put a couple of throw pillows over his mouth to conceal his facial expressions. Unfortunately, Travis had to stand there, he had nowhere to run or anything to cover his face with. Besides this appointment was for his wedding after all. Surprisingly, Travis was able to pull it off as he began the check-in process with the manager. As the manager and Travis introduced themselves, Justin kicked Travis behind the knee which made him buckle. The manager now identified as Royce was not amused by Justin's actions as he rolled his eyes and continued to lay out the agenda for the day.

"Cut it out bitch you see me talking," Travis whispered.

Kerry, not one to be left out, tossed a bright green bow tie at Travis's head, nearly hitting Royce. Travis could not help but to chuckle as Royce's frustration level increased.

"Ok have a seat and I will bring out the options." Royce said as he stormed off.

With Royce away picking out their options, the three friends began an impromptu accessory fight.

As the war raged on Travis let his guard down looking to make sure that Royce was not coming back. Justin took full advantage of Travis's lapse in judgement and fired a perfect pillow shot to the side of his head.

"You bitch." Travis uttered, but before he could retaliate Kerry threw a bedazzled bow tie that would have decapitated him if he had not dove out of the way at the last minute.

Kerry tried to reload and fire another bow tie, but he got hit by pillows from both sides almost knocking him to the ground.

"You fuckers, it's on," Kerry said as he jumped up and started running at his two adversaries until an elderly man cut him off asking for help.

Kerry quickly shifted gears and helped the man out; he may be a lot of things but being rude to the elderly is not one of them. After helping the man, Kerry returned to the fight blindsiding Justin with a close-range attack as he was ducking from the onslaught from Travis. On the outside looking in the friends had to look like a bunch of big ass kids acting out while their parents were away. The battle started to get bigger as they began to knock things over. Travis yelled for a cease-fire saying,

"We're grown men, cut it out!"

"Ok, ok truce but if you hit me, I will crush you in front of Royce and you know I don't care." Justin said, looking at Travis.

With the fragile peace treaty in place the warring factions retreat to neutral sectors, Travis sat on the couch loaded with multicolored pillows (ammo), Justin sat in an oversized chair near a large bowl of peppermints (ammo), and Kerry leaned against a display table full of cufflinks (ammo). The Cold War raged on for a few more moments until Royce came from the back with the first options. He presented Travis with a retro pink tux with matching ruffles,

"What the hell is this?" Travis asked rather rudely.

"Well sir, this is the tux that the bride Miss Morgan wanted you to try on first."

He handed Travis the tux,

"The dressing room is right behind you sir; let me know if you need anything."

The three men sat in the center as a unified front against Royce and Red's choices.

"Dude, what was Red thinking with this pink ass tux?" Kerry asked.

"Fuck, I don't know."

Justin chimed in being the devil's advocate,

"This has to be a joke, but I think you should try it on just as she asked you to."

"You can kiss my ass. I'm not trying this damn thing on." Travis said.

The humor that Justin and Kerry felt was short-lived however when Royce brought out their groomsmen tuxes that Red picked out. Royce stood in the front of the men trying to hand them off.

"No thank you sir," Justin said.

"Oh, hell no," Kerry added.

Travis smiled,

"We should at least try them on, after all it's what Red wanted."

"Hell No!" both men shouted.

Travis called Red trying to get clarification on how she came to her decision.

"Hey Red, they brought out the selection you picked for us, and I have questions."

"Oh my god great, send me a picture after you guys try them on!"

"Babe, why in the world would you pick a pink tux with ruffles?"

"First off, it's salmon not pink."

"You must be drunk off your ass if you think I'm putting this damn pink tux on and I'm not having my boys do it either." Travis responded defiantly.

"I think you'll look so good, just try it on."

"Nope."

"I said try it on."

"No."

"You heard me."

"Morgan," Travis said, dropping the nickname.

"Travis."

"Dammit."

"Do it for me."

"Fine."

"Love you."

"Whatever."

"What?"

"Love you too," Travis said hanging up the phone and telling the guys to kiss his ass before they even got a chance to start joking him.

"Royce, where was the dressing room?" Travis asked, walking over to him.

"This way sir and I will take pictures for the bride when you're done." Royce said, showing Travis the way.

"Yea, don't forget to take a gang of pictures," Kerry said, pulling out his phone.

"One damn picture maybe," Travis said angrily.

"Wow, you really are a bitch," Justin said in a low tone.

His joke even caught Royce off guard as he laughed before he knew it. Travis looked at Royce thinking, *you too man.* He snatched the tux and followed Royce to the dressing room.

"Oh, hell no I will not be taking a picture in this bullshit! I look like a damn bottle of Pepto-Bismol!" Travis yelled.

Unbeknownst to Travis, Kerry had already made his way back to the dressing room and took a few pictures of Travis in the ruffle filled pink tux. Travis took the tux off and told Royce,

"To either hang it back up or burn it before bringing them more options."
Royce came back with the second outfit, a powder blue tux with butterfly collar and presented to the group but he was cut off before he could explain the design.

"Hey man, stop playing with us and bring out something made in this century," Travis said.

"OK, ok," Royce said as he brought out a wonderful cream tux that Travis loved.
He liked it so much that after he put the tux on, he twirled in the mirror. Ignoring the laughs from Justin and Kerry, he sent a pic to Morgan knowing that he had found his tux. His hopes were dashed when Morgan texted back saying,

"No thanks Colonel Sanders, keep trying."
Defeated Travis slumped his head as he went back to the dressing room. He plopped down on the couch after Morgan rejected his idea to the delight of Royce who also hated the white tux on him.

"Ok guys let's get serious about this dammit, I'm not trying to be in here all night for something you're going to wear once," Kerry said.

Both Travis and Justin agreed, as the three men decided to spread out throughout the store to grab a few selections that the group could vote on. Royce was annoyed by this decision but agreed to help,

"The wedding colors are salmon not pink and black with hints of silver. Now if you need help, I'm here."

Justin declined, "thanks Royce but we got it from here, chief."

"Travis, you look at the tuxedos with tails," Justin said.

"Copy that."

"They are called swallowtails and they are this way," Royce said, showing Travis.

"Kerry, you look for the tuxedos with the priest collars."

"On it."

Kerry walked around lost until Royce helped him out.

"I'll look at the rest," Justin said.

The group split to pick their selections with the help of Royce who was still trying to get on board with the idea.

Minutes later the men turned fashion designers regrouped and laid out their options. Kerry went first laying out his top two choices for the group, first up was a slim white cut design (Marine dress uniform style), and the second option was a black banded mandarin collar with a similar layout. Travis and Justin both said no rather quickly,

"I'm not trying to look like MC hammer on my wedding day."

"Whatever, you fools just don't know how fashion works." Kerry said disappointed.

"Call it what you want but I'm not a bellhop at the Four Seasons," Justin told Kerry as he threw the tux back at him.

Next up was Travis with his designs that were both terribly similar to each other, his first choice had silver stitching in it that would pop with the pink accents.

Kerry said, "you look like a damn butler, take it off and trash it."

Justin disagreed with Kerry and told Travis to "keep it for the final debate."

Lastly Justin laid out two Classic tux's both with sharp lines like a movie villain outfit. Kerry liked the outfit that was until he was swallowed up by the jacket trying to put it on,

"This shit is stupid, I think it is ugly as hell."

"Come on now, you know you like it," Justin said.

Travis joined in, "I'm sure they have one in kid sizes."

"Royce, we need your help!" the men yelled.

He walked back over to the confused and frustrated group after helping another client.

"We don't know which tux to choose." Travis said, explaining the situation to Royce.

"How will we decide?" Justin asked.

"Well, it's my wedding, I should be able to wear what I want."

"Bullshit, we have to stand up there with you." Kerry said.

"Ok damn, we will put them on and vote." Travis said.

"How about each of you put on your favorite tux with the accessories and then you can vote." Royce said.

"Bet, let's do it," Travis said knowing he had a winner as he went to change.
Justin and Kerry fought over the remaining dressing room eager to put on their selections. Justin lost when Kerry crawled under the door while Justin was looking for the key.

"Damnit, hurry up."

"I'll be out when I'm done and you can't rush fine."

Moments later the men were dressed and standing in the mirror admiring themselves. After putting on his choice Kerry did not like the way it felt.

"This tux is some bullshit; I'm not voting for this one." Kerry said going to change.

On the other hand, Travis and Justin both loved their picks.

"Ok we got four people, let's vote now"

Despite trying hard Kerry could not hate on the tux that Justin picked out. Justin and Travis voted for their own choices of course, Kerry voted for Justin's tux, so now it all came down to Royce. He picked Justin's tux, siding with the bride's answer from earlier. With a winner declared, Travis and Kerry changed into Justin's pick to continue the fitting. Royce laid out accessories so the three could match. This proved to be a much easier task now that the tux choice was in. Moving back to the mirrors to continue admiring themselves, they began to have a low-key runway shoot.

"Damn, I look good." Kerry said.

"You're ok but I'm too damn sexy." Justin said.

"Please you two are like the Pips and I'm Gladys Knight or I'm David Ruffin and you're The Temptations." Travis said.

As the fitting was ending Travis found himself standing back watching as Kerry and Justin got their tux's measured and fitted,

"Who would have thought we would be here together; we have come a long way."

"Not me for sure, you two had to grow on me, especially the new kid."

"Whatever, even at a young age real recognized real." They each looked in the mirror and simply nodded. With the fitting wrapped, the friends walked out reminiscing on their lives and how random events can change the course of your life.

{ 6 }

Rob's Steak House

It had started to rain as they were leaving R&D's Fashion.

"Go get the car bitch," Justin told Kerry laughing.

"Fuck you, if you wait for me, you're going to be a left ass." Kerry said.

Travis now on the phone with Red relayed a message to Kerry that if he left them, she would break into his house and watch him sleep for a moment before proceeding to cut his balls off. A shocked Kerry stopped in the middle of the street and turned back with his mouth wide open, Justin stopped laughing as he was shocked and just stared at Travis,

"Damn, dude that was far."

"Shit, she said it. Not me."

"Well, I guess but damn." Kerry said as he began moving towards the car again.

Justin and Travis were both letting their significant others know about the fitting as they watched Kerry come around the corner. Instead of stopping he passed by them with his music turned up and honking the horn. As Kerry kept going Travis flipped him off. He made a loop around the parking lot in an effort to make the guys sweat and wonder if he would come back. Not knowing if Morgan was serious about cutting his balls off, he turned the car around before Travis had the chance to set Red in motion.

Pulling up to the curb, Kerry yelled for Justin and Travis to hurry their slow asses up so they could go grab a drink. They walked slowly to the car to piss Kerry off. The two antagonists began to laugh as they continued their conversation. As the two entered the car,

"Are you guys talking about me?"

"No one is talking about you, fool."

"Keep it that way!"

"Oh, I'm so scared," Justin said laughing.

"Oh, you both want the smoke I see. When we get to Rob's Steakhouse, I'm whipping some ass." Kerry said.

"Are you sure you want to do that before we eat?"

"Hell yes, why not?"

"Well, you might have to eat some soup or drink a smoothie after I break your jaw." Justin said laughing.

Kerry, annoyed, said "you both know I got hands."

"Yeah, little ones," laughed Travis.

Things quieted down as Kerry thought of a comeback which took almost until they pulled up to the steakhouse. Getting out of the car Kerry finally threw out his response,

"I might have little hands, but they were large enough to knock you out," reigniting the great debate between a knock down or slip.

The debate continued as the trio entered the bistro, but all forms of communication suddenly stopped as they observed the layout of the restaurant. They stood there looking around at the rustic cabin style design with marble fixtures. The walls were wrapped with animal skins, carvings, and the floors were adorned with bear skin rugs.

"Excuse me," the trio still looking around.

"Excuse me, Sirs." the hostess said, trying to snap them out of their trance.

"Oh, I'm sorry. We have a reservation under Justin."

"Thank you, your table is ready, please follow me."
As she walked them to their table, Kerry noticed the cute petite Hispanic woman had an amazing figure, so he cut in front of the others to get a closer look at her.

"Will this table work?" she asked.

On cue, Kerry began to shoot his shot. Leaning in,

"It will be just fine Catalina as long as I can still see you from my chair."

"Like a stalker," Justin said looking at Kerry,

"No, not like a stalker."
Catalina just laughed it off as she made her exit.

"Dude WTF, she is bad as hell; she could be the one." Kerry said.

"The one? Is that really what the fuck you just said?" Justin asked.

"Well maybe not the one but maybe the one for to-night."

"She doesn't have time for your shit." Travis added.

"How do you know?" Kerry said, feeling a little offended.

"She looks extremely too smart to fall for someone like you." Travis replied with Justin nodding his head in agreement.

"Fuck you both, I'm getting a number before we leave." Kerry said.

"Good luck with that chief," Justin laughed as he looked at the drink menu.

"Good evening gentlemen, how are you doing this evening?" the waiter asked as he poured water into their glasses.

"We are doing just fine and how are you?" Kerry asked, shifting the conversation.

"Good, sir," the waiter said.

"Come now we're not sir's," Travis said trying to put the waiter at ease.

"Ok, I'm Steve, do you guys want to start off with drinks or appetizers?"

"What is the house special?" Justin asked.

"Yes sir, we have Cognac infused with apples and pear cider. However, a lot of our guests love our bourbon pickleback shot."

"What the hell is that?" Travis asked, looking confused.

"It's a shot of pickle juice chased by a shot of bourbon."

"Oh, hell no," Justin replied, reaching for the drink menu to make a different selection.

"You know what Steve, bring us three of them please." Kerry said.

"I hope you're getting them for yourself." Travis said.

"Oh, you scared now?" Kerry asked just as Steve returned with the shots.

"Bottoms Up." Kerry said as he passed out the shots.

"This shit is stupid," Justin said as he took the shot from Kerry.
Kerry raised the pickle juice and said "cheers," as he waited for the others to respond.
With his shot raised,

"You can't leave me hanging (against the drinking protocol)."

Reluctantly Travis and Justin both raised their glasses, Kerry began the toast,

"Money, Clothes, and Hoes."

"We need a new toast, that shit is 20yrs old." Justin said as their glasses touched.
Justin and Travis tapped their glasses against the table and took the pickle juice shot followed immediately by the bourbon.

"You go to hell Steve." Kerry said.

"Why would anyone buy that?" Justin asked.

"I don't know sir, it's not a favorite of mine but people like to try it."

"Well, they can keep that shit," Travis said, handing the empty glasses back to Steve.

"Please bring me a Blue Moon?" Justin asked.

"I'll take an Iced Tea." Kerry said.

"And for you sir?" Steve asked, looking at Travis.

"You know what, bring another round of pickle-backs," Travis said.

"Really?" Steve asked with a confused look on his face.

"Hell no, dammit, bring me a rum and coke with little ice." Travis said.

"Got it I'll be right back gentlemen."

The guys were overjoyed to see Steve returning with normal drinks. After handing the drinks out he asked,

"Were these better choices?"

"Yes, thanks and don't recommend anymore damn pickleback bullshit to guests." Justin pleading with Steve.

"I will tell the manager sir. Do you gentlemen need more time or are you ready to order?"

"I'm starving," Kerry said as he ordered the bloody T-bone steak.

"That's nasty," Travis said as he ordered his steak well done.

"Is there a house special?" Justin asked.
Before Steve could answer the question Kerry interrupted,

"Fuck No," remembering the pickleback shot.

"True," Justin said, agreeing with Kerry as he ordered the chicken pasta.

Steve went to put in the order, as Kerry and Travis looked at Justin with confused faces.

"What?"

"Who the hell comes to a steak house just to order pasta?" Kerry asked.

"Someone who is buying his own meal."

"You're an idiot, we found a good steak house and you want pasta." Travis said.

Justin tried to explain his decision, but Kerry and Travis kept cutting him.

"You know what? To hell with you both," Justin said signaling for Steve to come over.

"Sir?"

"These people are getting on my nerves. I need something stronger than this Blue Moon. Bring me something with an umbrella to go with my pasta please"

Steve tried not to laugh as he took Justin's order.

"I'll put that in right away and I'll check on your food."

After several minutes, Steve returned with the food and Justin's strawberry daiquiri.

"Well, I know who has the pasta," Steve said, making Kerry and Travis laugh.

"Oh, you got jokes," Justin laughed. Steve topped off the glasses of water after passing out the food,

"If you need anything else just let me know."

"Thanks, we're good for now." Justin said.

"He is working on a tip," Kerry said while cutting into his bloody steak. Travis looked on in disgust as Kerry sliced up his steak,

"It doesn't look like they even tried to cook that damn steak."

"They cooked it just right; you can see the grill marks on it. If you get a steak well-done you might as well save money and just eat an old leather shoe." Kerry said

"Well, I'm about to eat the hell out of this old leather shoe."

"My chicken pasta is amazing, just so you know."

"No one cares," Travis said with Kerry concurring. Steve made his rounds and asked,

"If everything was ok so far?"

"Yes, thanks, just need another round of drinks, please." Justin said.

As Justin was ordering more drinks, Travis began to stare off into space. Noticing Travis was looking above his head Kerry turned around to see what was so important behind him. When he did not see anything, he broke Travis's gaze asking,

"What the hell are you looking at?"
Travis snapped back saying,

"I'm not looking at anything, I'm trying to understand how you could think you of all people could knock me out with those soft pillow punches you were throwing back in the day."

"I can think it because it happened and you both know it," Kerry said, sitting up straight in his chair with his chest poking out.

"It might be your truth, but it's not the real truth."

"What, I laid you out."

"Well, I wouldn't say you laid him out." Justin said, throwing in his two cents.

"Well, if I didn't knock him out then what did I do then?"

Travis answered the question, "you got lucky that's what happened."

"Right, you got lucky Justin was there to save you because it was about to get bad for you."

"Well, that might not be how other people remember it," Justin said, getting back into the conversation.

"From where I was standing, I watched you use your speed to bounce around and get shots in on him."

"Yeah, I was pretty fast back then." Kerry said.

"Whatever, keep going," Travis said.

Justin continued,

"As you were ducking Travis's punches, I honestly believe he stepped on a rock or branch which made him slip as you hit him. Once he hit the ground you began to show off which didn't work out well for your ass at all."

"Bullshit he didn't slip," Kerry said, defending his fighting skills.

"I was dancing around like a young Roy Jones Jr., and he was looking like Butterbean all big and slow. I was so fast that he couldn't see me, when I unleashed this right hand, he was no match for it. When I hit him, I saw a KABOOM pop-up over his head like a comic book"

"Wow, you're full of shit, I'll admit you were faster than I was back then. However, there is no way in hell you could ever knock me down. After slipping, I proceeded to kick your ass to the point this skinny fool had to save you."

"Hold up, I'm not in this dumbass debate."

"You might be right, but you were skinny as hell back then," Kerry said, seemingly switching sides.

"If I was skinny as hell, then you were the height of a damn Chucky doll."

Travis almost spit out his drink laughing at Justin.

"Oh, you can't laugh looking like you ate the Kool-Aid Man."

"You got that one," Travis said as the three laughed. With the debate over the laughter continued as Justin motion for the check

"Thanks gentlemen it was a pleasure having you in here tonight."

"Thank you for putting up with these fools," Kerry said.

On the way-out Kerry decided not to take another run at Catalina,

"We have somewhere to be."

"That's probably for the best," Travis agreed.

A debate about driving vs Ubering started up as they left the restaurant heading towards Kerry's car.

"I'm good to drive, I have only had a shot." Kerry said.

"Dude we are going bar hopping. Do you think drinking and driving is the smartest idea? Travis asked.

After giving the idea some thought they decided that driving was an unnecessary risk.

"OK but you guys know I was the best drunk driver in the group." Kerry said as the guys headed back to the condo to catch an Uber.

"Yeah, that's true you were always the best drunk driver." Justin said.

"We were dumb as hell," Travis said as they all agreed.

Getting back to the condo the guys pass Miss Ella who was staggering like she had a few too many glasses of wine. Travis held the door for her as she switched past him saying,

"Thanks baby."

Travis proceeded to thank her, but she surprised them all when she turned back looking at them saying,

"Now don't be looking at me as I walk by."

It shocked and confused the guys who rode the elevator in a state of awkward silence. The stunned trio walked into the condo and just stood around for a second trying to compre-hend what had just happened.

"Well damn," Justin said, breaking the silence making the guys laugh.

"I need a drink," Kerry said, going towards the kitchen. He yelled "shots shots shots! which is the international call for drinkers.

"Pick your poison, I have tequila, henny, vodka, or some good ol Moonshine."

"I'll take the Henny," Justin said while Kerry and Travis both had vodka.

Kerry toasted the group again, "Money, Clothes, and Hoes".

"We really do need to come up with a different toast." Justin said.

Kerry said, "Winston the Uber driver will be here in 5 minutes."

"Word, just enough time for more shots," Travis said.

"How about another pickleback?" Justin said, making a joke.

"Hell no, pass the vodka," Travis said, pouring another shot for the group.

Travis toasted the group this time,

"Here's to a good night with my brothers and to Kerry for letting us crash here."

"No thanks required, you guys are my family."

"I only ask one thing." Travis said.

"Anything."

"When Miss Ella comes over later just keep it down
or turn the music up," Travis said laughing.

Justin choked on his Hennessy laughing,

"You're dirty for that."

"The Uber is here, let's go," Kerry said.

Thankfully, they did not see Miss Ella on the way out. Now
waiting out they noticed a black Yukon driving up slowly.

"Years ago, that would have made me nervous," Justin said.

"Shit, it still makes me nervous," Travis said, looking
a little uncomfortable.

A soft voice came out of the rolled down window from Yukon,

"Are you Kerry?"

"Yes," Kerry said, walking up to the SUV.

He looked back at Justin and Travis with his eyebrows raised.
Now curious the guys walked even slower to the SUV looking in to see a large African man in the driver's seat. The trio
were confused because the voice did not match the body.
They began to engage Winston in conversation to see if it was
truly his voice or were the shots kicking in already.

"Oh, I see you're going to the Lion's Den," Winston
said to the delight of the ass holes in the car.

"Yep, we're going out to act a fool," Kerry said trying to keep Winston talking.

They had been friends for nearly two decades, so they did not have to coordinate their efforts, they just fell in sync.

"How is your night going?" Travis asked.

"It's going wonderful," Winston, sounding like a Nigerian Michael Jackson.

"I have had a good night of driving," Winston said, continuing to describe his night.

The laughter slowly started rising as the multiple shots started to kick in. Thankfully, they arrived at the Lion's Den before they truly started cutting up. Winston gave Kerry his personal card,

"Give me a call whenever you need a ride."

Kerry exited the vehicle, "word, I will hit you up later after some bar hopping."

{ 7 }

Lion's Den

Leaving Winston's Uber, the triad passed a lengthy line of people taking selfies beside an eight-foot-tall statue of a lion.

"Damn, I want a picture," Justin said.

"Bullshit, you see that line. You will be waiting by yourself." Kerry said.

"True, I'm trying to get a drink, not take a damn picture. Besides, you already have pictures from Munich like that."

"Damn I forgot all about those, I still want one but let's grab a drink and see if the line goes down." Justin responded.

Entering the building, Kerry noted that the bar seemed smaller on the inside compared to how the pictures online suggested. Making his way to the bar,

"I thought this spot was going to be bigger," looking around disappointedly.

"It's all about the camera angles," Justin said.

Travis, however, was amazed by the decoration and commitment to the style of the bar. The staff were all dressed like the cast from the 1970's TV show *Happy Days*. All the waiters were dressed as characters Joanie or Chachi from the spin off show called *Joanie Loves Chachi*. The cooks and bus boys were dressed like preppy kids who were the main antagonists of the show. As they sat at the bar waiting for their first round of beers, a man came walking from what Justin assumed was the back office and introduced himself as Austin the owner. Austin was dressed as the coolest character from the show called The Fonz. His look was complete, he had the boots, the white t-shirt, and a classic leather jacket but what finished the costume was the black comb in his hand. Travis thought Austin was the dad from the show based on his large Italian frame, but he was working the outfit.

"I came to speak to the new faces in the room, I don't think I have seen you guys in here before. Is it your first time?"

"Yes, we have seen ads everywhere but never had the time to come in until tonight," Kerry said.

"Well, I'm glad you found time tonight to come and hang with us, if there is anything I can do for you do not hesitate to ask." Austin said, running the comb through his hair.

Justin spoke up about his love for old sitcoms like *Happy Days*,

> "I grew up watching old reruns on Nick-at-Night like *Green Acres, Happy Days,* and *The Jeffersons* late into the night before the channel went off."

Austin, now grinning from ear to ear remembering that years ago TV Stations did not run 24 hrs., started gushing about the need for more shows like those from years past.

> "It was a simpler time in television, no need for reality shows or shows about people wanting to be a star. Not much grinding needed." he continued.

> "Man, truer words have never been spoken, how in the world did we go from one or two reality shows to dozens about damn near anything and nothing," Justin said jumping on the soap box with Austin.

> "Shit me and my ol-lady watch them all the time. I love the ratchetness of the tattoo shows, all of them and she loves almost all the baller wives ones. You can't tell me you don't like seeing the clips of the unnecessary scripted fights, I know I do." Travis said, knocking them off their soap box.

Kerry joined the conversation, "I like them in small 90 second clips and that's it. I have left girls for watching that mess."

"Whatever man I love them shits, hell I have even tried out for one or two of them," Travis said.

Austin, Justin, and Kerry all looked at Travis waiting for the rest of what had to be a good story. He knew they were looking and waiting with great anticipation, so he took his time drinking his beer, enjoying every second of it. Travis started to explain but Austin interrupted,

"I feel we might need a table for the rest of this story. What are you guys drinking? I am buying." As he walked behind a woman dressed as 60's sex symbol Raquel Welch.

"Well, we have not really picked a drink yet, just having beer at the moment," Justin answered.

"Well gents, I'm having Peruvian Vodka, it has a strong body with a very smooth after taste." Austin said while picking up a blue snake shaped bottle.

With their interest now peeked, the three gathered around Austin, Travis spoke first,

"You know what, we will join you for a round and I'll get the next one."

Austin grinned at Travis, "round no, we're taking the bottle."

He then motioned them to an open table. Walking from behind the bar, he slapped Raquel Welch on the ass while asking her to send over menus when she got a chance. Kerry, amazed by what he saw shook Austin's hand,

"I see how you're running things; I need a place like this."

"Yes, I love this place."

Kerry sensing some confusion,

"Na man I'm not talking about the bar, I'm talking about you being able to tap that fine waitress on the ass."

Now understanding, Austin quickly corrected Kerry,

"Oh No, No, my friend that Bombshell is my wife, she is the brains of the operations. I would have lost my shirt ten times over by now if it were not for her. The only problem is she knows she's the most important piece. That is why she walks around dressed like a Raquel Welch all out of character. She is behind the bar because she likes making drinks and we would lose money if I made them. I'm a heavy pourer. In contrast, I love talking to new customers.

"Well, congrats my guy," Kerry said, sliding his chair up to the table.

"Thanks, she is my life," Austin said pouring the Peruvian Vodka, "Now glasses up, here's to a good night with new friends, and the smart, beautiful

women who keep us together!

"Hell Yea!" Travis and Justin said together thinking

of their much better halves.

Austin stood up,

"I have to make my rounds but here is the bottle, I

will be back after a few laps."

The group took one more shot before Austin got back to

work.

As they sat, Justin noticed that there were bottles of vodka

wrapping around the outside of the bar. He walked over and

began reading the labels of where they were from; Turkey,

Nepal, China, Afghanistan, and even fucking Turkmenistan.

He came back to the table,

"Damn, did you guys notice all these bottles?"

"Yeah, I did but I also noticed the decorum doesn't

match the music at all, even though the layout is fire.

This place is confusing from the sitcom dressed

workers, to the upbeat music, and the wall of liquor

bottles from around the world." Travis said.

"This place is weird but despite the weirdness, I think

we picked a good night to come in here. The music is

hitting and there is some eye candy in here tonight."

Kerry said looking around.

He was right, it was a very relaxed environment with a bunch of chill people. As they poured another drink, a waitress brought over an order of loaded nachos.

"Enjoy gents," Joanie said, walking away.

"Hold up, sorry but we didn't order these," Justin said, catching her before she disappeared into the sea of Joanie and Chachi's.

As she turned around, Justin noticed a fresh cut above her eyelid. Forgetting about the nacho order Justin asked,

"Are you ok?" gesturing towards her eye.

Noticing the change in Justin's demeanor and without a sound Travis swiftly joined Justin followed closely by Kerry. Now bombarded by three men Joanie took a step back. Justin could see the fear on her face and quickly apologized,

"I'm sorry, we meant you no harm."

Trying to reassure her. He asked her to take a seat and tell them what happened; Joanie nervously took a seat and tried to explain,

"It's not what you guys are thinking, I was—."

"Who did this?" Kerry asked, cutting her off.

"Was it the Chachi dude that has been walking around with you?" Travis asked, now scanning the room trying to find him.

"I see him," Justin said as Chachi was walking by the bar.

Justin stood first as Joanie continued to talk unaware of the guy's nonverbal communication.

"What's up man?" Justin asked, distracting Chachi from the approaching Kerry.

Travis, the largest of the three men posted himself in the bartender's line-of-sight ensuring that the work Chachi was about to get would not be seen easily.

"Let me holla at you my man," Justin said towering over Chachi the small, framed man.

"Ah of course sir," the clueless Chachi said, moving away from the crowd with Justin.

Noticing Chachi was being led away Joanie realized what was about to happen and jumped up to save her unassuming and trusting friend. Joanie caught up to them, positioning herself between the trio and the soon to be victim Chachi. Confused by Joanie's actions, Kerry said,

"Let us talk to him really quick."

"It's not what you guys are thinking," Joanie said, trying to diffuse the situation.

"Then please tell us what it's like so we can finish our conversation with Chachi," Travis said, coming up from the rear.

"Ok, ok last week we hosted a Greek reception. Some
guests began to smash plates after a traditional dance.
I got a little too close to the celebration and got hit by
a flying piece of a broken plate." Joanie explained.
As she continued Chachi was still confused about what was
happening around him, but he stayed there and remained silent.

"What? That's bullshit, I don't believe this. Let's talk
to this dude," Kerry said.
He still could remember the wild stories his mom would tell
defending her abusers.
Justin looked at her for more than a few moments trying to
decide whether to finish their conversation with Chachi
or believe her.

"Are you sure? You don't have to be scared," Justin
said, inching closer to Chachi.

"Yes, I'm sure, Oh I have a video." she said, showing
them the video, she took of the party.
With the conflict now diffused, Justin apologized to her and a
still confused Chachi.

"It's ok, you guys are very sweet for trying to protect
me but let's be real I could crush him with little to no
effort."

"Oh damn, Joanie is a G." Travis said, giving her a
high-five in approval.

The group went back to their table while Joanie walked Chachi to safety. After sitting back down Justin poured a drink for his posse and passed them out,

"Damn fellas we still got it," referring to their ability to sense trouble.

They all nodded thinking back to what brought the former enemies together nearly two decades earlier.

***

The three remained locked in conflict, which did not let up. After Justin slammed Travis and punked the other two boys he was quickly welcomed into the neighborhood. The older teens and local bangers respected his hands, and the girls liked his southern drawl and hero mentality. Travis believed that his spot as the next neighborhood tough guy was gone which bothered him for months. Surprisingly, the neighborhood's acceptance of Justin upset Kerry as well, due to the fact people thought he needed to be saved. For the remaining days of summer there was constant tension between the three, however there was not another physical battle between. The summer stalemate lasted into the upcoming school year, but an unexpected event would break said stalemate and bond these friends for life.

Over spring break Justin was cutting through the park when he saw Travis picking up a crying girl off the ground. He was unable to make out who she was, so he moved closer to access what was going on. Reaching Travis and the crying girl Justin realized it was his friend Jalene the young lady who jumped in the fight to help Kerry. He moved in to help her yelling,

"What did you do to her, Bitch!"

"I didn't do anything; I just got here and who are you calling a Bitch?" Travis yelled!

Not believing him, Justin moved to crush him again until Jalene confirmed Travis's story. Putting their conflict on hold the two guys helped Jalene dust herself off while asking what happened. She told them an older boy hit her because she laughed at his lame come-on. She fought back but his friends held her as he hit her a few more times knocking the wind out of her.

Led by Jalene, Justin and Travis silently set out to get revenge on the Ike Turner wannabe. They found the older teen and his friends on the forbidden court and without a second thought, they charged them. Even though both Travis and Justin were tall for their age, they were outmatched and quickly overpowered by the teens. This, however, did not stop them at all, it seemed to fuel them even more. Kerry and a group of kids playing football heard of a fight and came running to watch. Seeing Jalene (his first crush) being held back from helping, Kerry quickly made his way to her. She told him the whole story and now, full of rage Kerry joined in the fight evening the odds slightly. As the fight continued the neighborhood bangers arrived and witnessed the act that would seal their new friendship. Every time one of the young combatants would fall the other two would stand over him until he got up. This impressed the bangers who stopped the fight with their overwhelming force. With the two warring factions now separated, Pookie the local gang leader, and his crew moved in to get answers. What was widely known to everyone except Justin was that Jalene was Pookie's baby cousin. He walked up to Justin,

"Why the hell are you guys fighting on our court?" Justin, now a little nervous, stood up straight holding his ribs,

"No man should hit a woman and she is my friend." Pookie stepped back looking at Justin and his new crew and simply nodded. A nod from Pookie meant that the three were now accepted. Turning his attention to the now retreating teens who were trying to make their escape, Pookie asked,

"Why did all yall hit my cousin?" The teen tried to think of an answer that would save him, but it was too late, Pookie unleashed the worst beating that Justin, Travis, and Kerry had ever seen to this day.

***

Crackling of a loudspeaker broke up their stroll down memory lane,

"15-minute warning, 15-minute warning it's about that time to grab your partner and let's get this sock hop party started."

"What in the hell is a sock hop?" Kerry asked, confused by what he heard.

One of the many Joanie's told him that tonight was the final of a pre-80's old style dance competition. As the couples hit the floor, Justin decided to make it interesting,

"I got $20 on Sonny and Cher in the corner."

"Hell, I got Mork and Mindy," Kerry said.

Not to be outdone, Travis stood up yelling,

"I got Jimmy Hendrix and Grace Mutha Fuckin Jones!"

"Damn, I didn't see them." Justin said.

"Well, I did, and our picks are final."

The guys handed their money to their Joanie to keep everyone honest. As Travis handed the money over, he observed two middle-aged dudes bump into each other and part ways without an issue.

"Did you guys see that?" Travis asked with his mouth wide open.

"Yeah, we saw that shit, I'm shocked it ended so peacefully. Things would have ended differently in most of the places I go," Kerry said.

Seeing Austin making his rounds Justin waved him over to get some answers.

"What's up gents?"

"Bro, why are people so happy in here, are you guys putting something in the drinks?" Travis asked, laughing.

"No, we just treat everyone the same, give them strong drinks and establish a fun environment. It bothers me to see customers with frowns on their faces" Austin explained.

"I like that," Justin said.

"I came over to you for that reason; you learn things as a bar owner, like normally smiling people don't fight."

"Ok one more question before you go. What's up with the style and theme of the bar? It is a cool place, don't get me wrong but it is slightly confusing." Justin said.

"I can respect the question and it's a simple answer, I've had a gang of terrible ideas over the years. I've tried several ideas/themes with most of them failing badly, the brain narrowed down what worked and what failed. She noted people like the relaxed atmosphere, the scene, and the constant mix of music. This is the result of trial and error."

"Cool, what about the bottles?" Kerry asked, picking one up.

"Oh, we love to travel to random countries trying to find the best vodkas so we can bring them back to our customers. Some are empty but we have plenty of others for tasting."

"That's cool as hell," Justin said.

"The trick is finding a better half that is smarter than you," Austin said, shaking Justin's hand before walking away.

Noticing that there was a deck, Justin asked their Joanie if she could grab them some ice and more chasers. Her shift was over, but she had to hook her would-be Heroes up. The deck was a party all to itself, four portable fire pits were placed around the outside of the square with lounge patio chairs in the inner parts.

{ 8 }

Dark Ryder

As the guys sat on the deck enjoying the jazz music and the cool night air Joanie brought them chasers and ice.

"Hey, guys I'm off but I wanted to bring your order and introduce you to (New) Joanie, she will be taking care of you."

"Damn I didn't know you were off when I ordered sorry about that," Justin said.

"Oh no worries, you know I had to take care of my bodyguards. Oh, and by the way Chachi finally realized what was happening and now he's scared of you guys and me for that matter."

"He'll be fine," Travis said, cracking a smile. Joanie continued,

"I gave the money to (New) Joanie and told her about you."

"What did you tell her?" Kerry asked?

"I explained you guys are funny and somewhat over-protective."

"Overprotective is a stretch," Justin said.

"It's nice to meet you new Joanie and it was wonderful to have met old Joanie." Travis said.
Kerry interrupted Justin asking Joanie if she wanted a drink now that she was off. She respectfully declined,

"I would love to, but I have to go grab my son from the sitter."

"Cool, cool, cool," Kerry said, taking one last long look at her as she exited the deck and their lives forever.

"You good my dude? You seemed a little heartbroken," Travis asked.

"Shit of course I'm good, I'm an ol school player," Kerry said, sticking his chest out. "Right, cool story bro, I bet he cries in the bathroom." Justin said laughing.

"Whatever," Kerry said, trying not to let them see him get one last look at Joanie.

When Joanie made her exit, Justin and Travis noticed a man looking a little off, he looked nervous and on edge which was a huge red flag in such a relaxed atmosphere. Their military training made them take note of a possible threat, which in turn made them uneasy. They watched as he was making eye contact and nonverbal signals to a guy on the other side of the deck. Now on the edge of their seats the two old Warriors looked for potential weapons if needed. Thankfully they were both completely off and wrong in every way, the nervous dude knelt in front of a young lady and began to profess his love for her. At that moment, the guy in the corner came in singing *This is why I love you*. Now understanding the situation, the two relaxed and enjoyed the singing. She cried, he cried, most of the people on the deck cried, hell Austin even cried while ordering champagne for the whole deck.

Travis looked at Kerry,

> "You need to stop fucking around and find someone you can trust like that."

> "How do you know without a doubt you can trust Red?" Kerry asked.

Travis replied with a serious look on his face,

> "I love this woman with all my heart; she has helped me in so many ways. I know I can trust her because she has seen my Dark Rider in action and has re-mained by my side."

Not understanding the Dark Rider comment Kerry made a crude joke that Travis largely ignored. Unlike Kerry, Justin knew all too well what the Dark Rider Travis spoke of was all about. Justin calls his, the Darkness.

"Dark rider, man what are you talking about?" Justin tried to change the subject to spare his friend the pain of reliving it.

"No, it is cool, I have a handle on it now thanks to Red and my new outlook on things. The Dark rider is what I call my depression and anxiety. Before I moved for work a few years back I was suicidal, I thought about ending my pain every day. Justin talked me down a number of times but I'm not sure he even knew the true level of my pain."

Looking confused Kerry watched as Travis's body language changed during the conversation. Travis continued,

"Have you ever heard of the military saying, "All Gave Some and Some Gave All?"

"Yes, but only on a t-shirt," Kerry responded.

"It means everyone that deploys to a combat zone leaves a part of themselves over there and what takes that space is emptiness. Well, my emptiness began to grow more during my second and third deployments to the point I had to give it a name, my Dark Rider."

"I call mine the Darkness," Justin added while Travis gathered his thoughts before continuing.

Growing up Travis had one dream and that was to be a Soldier. An old Vet from their neighborhood encouraged them to join if only for a few years. He would tell the kids to be friendly with a supply clerk, medic, or cook, and life would be set. Travis excelled at keeping things in order so being a Supply Soldier fit for him.

"I wanted to do my 20 years and retire, move on, and get a relaxed job. What I didn't know was that supply is much different in a warzone than it is in the rear (home base). Hell, Kerry, you visited me in Germany, I know you remember how chill it was, and I was never at work."

"Oh yea, that was some good times."

"Yea they were, but when we got that call to deploy things got serious fast," Travis said.

Travis was not scared about deploying, he knew it was possible and his leadership trained them well. His first deployment was relatively uneventful, they hit the desert mid-June and it was 120 degrees outside. It was so damn hot his Platoon Sergeant had them cooking eggs on their Humvees in the damn sun. Travis remained inside the wire during the entire deployment which lasted six months. Once the unit returned to Germany, he did sense something a little different going on with friends, but he didn't know what it was at the time.

Travis was all geeked up for his second deployment, he was now a Team Leader with five troops under him. He trained them hard just like he was trained. Travis felt like superman entering the warzone. That was until July 19th when he was assigned to be the gunner on a Humvee tasked with the safety of the other four people inside. Before the convoy left, the commander read a report that both women and children were being sold to terrorists and were being used to start ambushes by walking in front of convoys. They were instructed not to stop for any reason, which meant they were to hit whoever crossed their paths. That is a hell of a thing to tell a 19-year-old kid five minutes before leaving the base.

The woman walked along the road, she kept looking back which was not abnormal, but she started walking slower and slower. Travis got a weird feeling in the pit of his stomach but before he could say a word the woman threw herself in front of the convoy and was run over when the first Humvee did not stop. Travis was the second in the stack and his friend Davey ran up on the curb, he could not bring himself to run over her again. Unfortunately, the woman falling was no accident and before they knew it the world went to shit fast. There were bullets coming at them from both sides, now under fire all their training kicked in. Davey whipped that Humvee off the curb and sped down the street, while Travis began to suppress the enemy gunfire with his M2 heavy machine gun. Travis has taken many lives but the only face he sees when he closes his eyes is the one of a young man no older than a teenager. The teen barely had a beard but what he did have was an AK-47 pointed at Davey. Therefore, Travis did what his training demanded of him and cut the kid down. The convoy lost three people that day. Davey was never the same, he left the military after his contract was up. Travis tried to keep in contact, but he rarely gets online or returns his texts.

Once back in Germany, Travis knew something was different, but it was one of those unspoken things. It was something each person dealt with, hell everyone was dealing with some kind of issue. Drinking, fighting, and other incidences increased drastically. Thankfully, Travis got orders to leave before the unit was deployed again. He thought he was going to be able to ride out his last 18 months in Florida. Big Army had other plans; however, they "Stop Lossed" his unit which meant the Army could freeze all contracts if unit numbers dropped below fighting levels.

"That shit got a bunch of people in my unit," Justin added.

At this point he had a little less than a year left so when the troops at his new command were gearing up for their deployment, he was gearing up to out-process the Army. Just his damn luck Big Army dropped the Stop Loss hammer on his unit. Travis had less than two weeks to get himself ready for his third deployment. Thankfully, since he had deployed before, he got it done without issue. The Platoon Sergeant (Pat) gave him a squad on the eve of their deployment. Normally one needs time to develop a bond with the teams, but it was what it was.

His final deployment to the land of sand started slowly which is the way you want them to go. Troops will take boring over earth rattling firefights any day. The unit had an intense new officer from West Point but thankfully she was different from the other fresh-faced officers. She tried to soak up all the knowledge she could from the lowest enlisted to senior staff. The troops were all impressed with the LT's action under fire; she led the right way. Travis paused his story and took a deep breath; Justin again told him he did not have to finish but Travis insisted he needed to before going back to his story.

Travis's Unit was on a peacekeeping outing to bring food and water to the villagers to win hearts and minds. There was a weird feeling amongst the Soldiers, but they continued their mission. They were in the village for an hour handing out supplies and talking with the tribal leaders. Some of the younger Soldiers were losing badly at soccer with kids in the village. The LT was talking with the women from the village trying to find out if any fighters had been through there when a woman loyal to the terrorist ran over and tried to attack her. The LT quickly subdued her as part of the team went to help. Pat gave Travis a look that he had seen only a few times before, the look meant shit was about to get real. Travis quickly rounded up the platoon and put them on alert. As Pat wrapped up the meeting with the elders, Travis got the troops ready to leave which left Pat alone for no more than five minutes. He rushed back to Pat with his stomach in knots but to his relief Pat came walking out. Leaving operations, Pat would say Load up, Let's roll, in his typical southern drawl. He liked to be the first person out and the last person in the Humvee, that was his way of leading from the front. That, however, proved to be his downfall, Pat covered them as they got loaded up in the Humvees. He didn't see the village elder get within killing distance, but Travis did. Travis yelled for him to turn around as he exited the Humvee but by the time Pat turned, Travis saw his friend take a 9mm round to the face. Coming around the Humvee Travis proceeded to empty his magazine into the village elder, all 30 fucking rounds. He held his friend in his arms until he took his last breath. Travis took a sip of his drink. The normally talkative Kerry sat in silence as Travis looked at the moon.

Travis left the Army shortly after that, but the Dark Rider came with him. He went to all the re-entry classes and training but most of them lied or downplayed their issues afraid of being labeled.

Justin agreed saying, "telling the truth got you labeled back then, and no one wanted that shit."
Travis tried to move on and get a normal job when he got out, but he hated every one of them. He probably had seven jobs within the first year of being out. That transition was hard as hell, the only constant was his Dark Rider who questioned all his actions during his deployment. Most nights he could hear it say things like you could have saved them. When Travis closed his eyes, he either saw his first kill or his dear friend Pat's face. Sleep was not something he got a lot of during that time. On the anniversary of his death, Travis would find himself sitting in the dark with a pistol and a bottle of Guinness which was Pat's favorite drink. Not really something he likes but Travis has committed to drinking one at least once a year until he dies. He was functioning with his PTSD/Dark Rider until it tried a new tactic; it started blaming Travis for Pat's death. It went from he could have saved

him to it was his fault he died. That new tactic pushed him over the edge.

Travis stopped his story and shook Kerry's hand, which confused him.

"What was that for?"

"You saved me without even knowing."

Kerry, now in shock, asked, "how did I do that?"

"One night after not sleeping for a few days my Dark Rider had won, I was tired and all I wanted to do was sleep. I wrote a letter to you both and got in my bathtub to avoid making a large mess. As I took a few deep breaths you called, I sent you to voicemail and continued preparing myself. In your true fashion, you called over and over. I answered the phone annoyed and asked what the fuck you wanted, and you started talking about having some girls that wanted to party, you called them bitches but that's not my style."

"Oh shit, I remember that night, you were stiff as fuck it took you forever to chill. Damn now I know why. You could have told me; I would have made them leave."

"No, I needed you to be you that night, it helped me see what I would be missing. So, thank you my brother." Travis said, raising his glass to Kerry.

Going back to the story: Travis was able to hold his Dark Rider at bay, but he needed a change so when an old Army buddy hit him up about taking a government contracting job back in the desert he jumped at the opportunity. Travis was not good at being a civilian, but he was hella good at being a Soldier.

"Yea, I remember I wanted to beat your ass when you told me you were going back. I was worried that if you went back the darkness would overtake you this time." Justin said.

Travis knew his friends did not approve but he felt like he had to go. Travis was not a super religious person but someone or something had a plan for him. Travis was glad Justin and Kerry showed up to the airport to send him off, it meant the world to him. Once he landed in South Carolina the company had a car waiting on him, hell Travis felt like a star. They took him to their state-of-the-art compound to sign the final paperwork. While there he began to see what kind of person he could possibly become if he went through with the contract. He would be working for good pay but that was not why he had done it before. It was for the brothers and sisters standing next to him. Most of the contractors had seen too much, so death meant nothing to them. He could not help but to question if that could be him one day.

On the last night before the contract signing, Travis and a few of the operators went to a local club called Nelson's Juke Joint to watch a live Blues band. Travis loved small clubs like this but the group he was with were all about drinking as much as they possibly could. He distanced himself from them by walking around the club looking at the pictures on the wall of all the local bands that have played there. While looking at the collection of old photos, a refreshing scent caught his attention, and he felt compelled to follow it. The scent led him to the bar where he saw an angel of a beauty from behind turning down every guy and girl brave enough to shoot their shot at her. Travis knew he had to meet this person but the damn table of Merc's he came with got into a scuffle, so they had to leave. On the way out he looked for her to no avail. Once they made it back to the compound the guys were talking about the fight as Travis went to bed. His Dark Rider came roaring interrupting his sleep, but something was different, the Dark Rider was not as loud as before. It tried to harass him, but the scent of this Mystery Beauty drowned out the noise. In the morning, Travis could not shake the feeling that he needed to find her, hell after all she quieted his Dark Rider with just a scent. So, he turned down the job and set his sights on finding the Mystery Beauty.

"Shit that deserves a shot," Kerry said signaling for Joanie to come over.

"Hey guys, what can I do for you?"

"Could we please get a Guinness and three shot glasses please." Kerry asked.

"Coming right up."

When she returned Kerry split the Guinness into the three chilled glasses and passed them out. He and the others raised their shots to Pat.

{ 9 }

Mystery Beauty

"Damn, Pat was a monster if that was his normal drink," Justin said.

"Fuck," Kerry said slamming his glass down.

"It wasn't that bad," Travis said looking at the shot glass.

"So, do you want another round?"

"Fuck No!" Travis yelled without hesitation.

"Now before we took that death in a glass you were talking about smelling Morgan, which is creepy as fuck." Kerry said.

"Yea, you told me she was hard to find but what's with this smelling shit?" Justin asked.

"Oh damn, I guess I never told you guys the full story of how we met."

"Well shit now you have to tell us," Justin said, taking a seat looking extremely interested in what came next.

"Ok, where was I?" Travis asked, sitting down, and topping off his drink.

"You turned down the job at the contract company," Justin said forcefully.

"Yea I remember you pleading with me not to get on the plane but if I stayed, I would not have met Red."

***

Travis continued his story telling them that as the company's gates closed behind him, he had no idea where he was going to stay or work. All he knew was he had to find his Mystery Woman.

"Ok that's crazy, what did you do? Kerry asked, taking a sip of his drink.

"If you would shut up, I'll tell you."

"Shut up and tell the damn story."

Travis's first stop was the Juke Joint to see if anyone there knew her or had any information. It was slow going at first because of the fight that happened the night before, the owner did not want to tell Travis anything. The bouncer helped him out realizing that Travis had nothing to do with the fight, he helped to get the fools out of there. Travis asked the bartender if he knew anything, but he tried to play dumb claiming to be too busy that night to remember one single woman. It kinda pissed Travis off, but he had to keep cool. Travis told him she smelled like Christmas Day and salvation in a bottle. The bartender laid his head back and closed his eyes. Travis could tell from the smile on his face he remembered her.

"Hold the hell up, she smelled like Salvation and damn Christmas Day?" Kerry asked as Justin laughed.

"Yes, like Mutha Fuckin Christmas Day and Salvation all wrapped into one package."

Justin yelled, "damn," as he was trying to picture that.

"Anyway, as I was saying."

Travis ended up paying 200 dollars for the half assed answers. The bartender told Travis that she came in from time to time but only during the live music weekends with her friends; he thought her name was Mary or something like it. Travis thought it was funny because she didn't look like a Mary to him, but he figured he would ask her. Travis asked if he knew anything else and he said not for 200 bucks and walked off. As Travis was leaving a small spitfire waitress from Philly stopped him wondering why he was asking all these questions. With one hand on her hip and the other pointing at him, this brown skin Fireball thought Travis was some type of stalker or something. Travis tried to reassure her that he was not a creeper, he just wanted to meet his Mystery Girl. He went on to tell her about smelling her scent from afar, but she cut him off saying that sounds like a creeper to me.

"Well, she wasn't wrong," Kerry said.

"Word," said Justin agreeing.

"Whatever."

The problem was she would not take money or favors from him. Travis was hoping he could appeal to her softer side but even that shit failed. Finally, after begging for several minutes, the waitress told Travis she was a teacher at a high school but would not tell him which school. Travis took what little info he could, after all it was more info than he had before walking in the door.

Travis's next step was to find a place to stay. Thankfully, he was able to find a room to rent from a sweet older lady that came up to his waist named Miss Ann. She reminded him of Miss Homes who sold candy and homemade ice cream out of her house when he was a kid. If your neighborhood didn't have a Candy Lady, then your childhood was lacking. Miss Ann mainly wanted someone to talk to, her Vietnam Vet husband had passed a few months before. She liked to hear his military stories.

"I bet she did like your stories," Kerry said.

His burn was short-lived when Justin cut off asking,

"Just like Miss Ella right?"

He now knew what his Mystery Girl did for a living, music she liked, and he found a place to stay with cheap rent. Operations Mystery Woman was now a go. During the week, Miss Ann would talk to Travis about her husband and their lives together and he would tell her the more PG versions of his Army life. He researched the two biggest high schools in the area and visited them, but both were behind gates. So, he tried a little online stalking, but the websites were private also which made for good security but not good for his stalking. Travis went to the bar every live music night so much so that the waitress began to be nicer to him. However, his Mystery Woman had not been back to the bar in weeks, and Travis was starting to get a little discouraged. Around the fourth or fifth week of Operation Mystery Woman, Miss Ann needed to have a knee procedure so Travis dropped her off and swung by the school just to see if he could see signs of his Mystery Woman but no luck. A heavy rainstorm erupted in the city as Travis went to get Miss Ann after the procedure.

On the way back to the Outpatient Clinic, Travis could barely see more than a few feet in front of the car thanks to the rain. He passed a car that appeared to be stuck in the ditch, but he could not tell if anyone was in it or not, so Travis continued to get Miss Ann. After picking her up they headed back to her place when Travis noticed the same car in the ditch but this time, he saw what looked to be a woman walking away from the car. Miss Ann said,

"We should stop."

Travis was more concerned about her getting home but Miss Anne insisted that they stop and help. When Travis pulled the car over and got out, Miss Ann locked the door behind him which made Travis feel like it was either help her or stay in the rain.

"Excuse me, are you ok?" Travis asked, walking up slowly.

The wet woman responded, "I'm fine just trying to make it to a phone."

"I can give you a ride if you would like."
She looked him up and down as if to say no thanks I don't know you.

"Ok how about you get in your car and use my phone to call someone?"
She looked at him with her head slightly turned,

"Why are you trying to help me so badly?"

"Because it's the right thing to do, besides that old lady in the car won't unlock the door until I help you, so we both are kind of stranded out here."
She looked past him at Miss Ann and smiled ever so briefly at her,

"Ok I'll use your phone in my car, but you have to wait here."

Travis said, "cool," and handed her his phone. He waited as she made her way in the rain back to her car. She slipped in the mud and almost slid down the hill. Travis rushed over and helped her up,

"Come on, Miss, let me help you. If I were crazy, I'd have tried something already."

Trying to clean some of the mud off herself,

"Fine I'll get in the car but understand I'm armed so don't try anything."

Travis grinned slightly and said, "yes ma'am."

Miss Ann unlocked the door when she saw the woman walking beside Travis, she tried to get in the backseat but Travis nor the wet woman would let her. Travis said,

"Miss Ann, your knee is busted, get back in the car." The soaking wet woman got in the backseat slowly looking at Travis suspiciously, he told her to relax as she clutched her purse tighter.

"Are you ok baby?" Miss Ann asked as Travis got in the car.

"Yes, ma'am I'm fine, I'm thankful you and your son stopped to help me." the wet woman said.

Miss Ann did not correct her, which was fine with Travis as well,

"It's fine baby, you need help and that's what people do. Call me Ann or Miss Ann, the choice is yours baby."

"Nice to meet you Miss Ann I'm Amber," the wet woman said in response.

Travis was focused on the road in the downpour and did not speak so Miss Ann spoke for him,

"This quiet lug is Travis."

Amber smiled at Miss Ann's description of him.

"Nice to meet you Travis and thank you for stopping."

"No problem Amber, I'm just glad you got in the car. It was cold out there. What happened?"

"I couldn't see the road very well; I didn't notice that the truck in front of me had stopped. By the time I realized what was happening all I could do was swerve out of the way but in doing so I went into the ditch."

"I'm surprised the driver didn't stop to help you."

"Really? You must be new to South Carolina, people don't really do that anymore," Amber said looking out the window.

"Yup, I just got here a few weeks ago, plus we stopped."

"That's true and I'm truly thankful,"
Once he got Miss Ann home Travis told Amber he would be right back, Miss Ann said,

"I got this; you get this young lady home." as she got out of the car.
Travis looked at a soaked Amber and told her he would be right back. He turned the heat up higher and told her the seats in front are heated if she wanted to warm up a little faster. He then ran to catch up with a struggling Miss Ann at the door to help her in the house, she stopped him,

"I'm fine, get that pretty girl home."

"How do you know she is pretty? The rain ruined her hair and makeup."

"I can hear it in her voice, trust me."

"Ok Miss Ann, I will be back."
He headed back to the car to the waiting-soaked Amber thinking to himself *how can she hear her beauty in a voice.*

He got back in the car to see Amber now in the front seat was holding her purse on her lap to remind him she had that fire. Travis smiled,

"Relax little mama, I know you're strapped like an

OG." which made her smile "where to, Miss Lady?"

Sensing the uneasiness and before she could answer he offered to drop her off somewhere other than her house just to be safe. With a sense of relief, Amber agreed and thanked him,

"You can drop me off at a bar, I will have my friends come grab me."

"Ok that works," Travis said, asking for the name of the place.

"Do you know a place called Nelson's Juke Joint?"

"Yeah I've been there a few times."

He did not tell her that he had been there constantly in the last 5 weeks looking for his Mystery Woman. As they made their way to the Juke Joint, Travis started to get a strange feeling of delight. He was unaware where this was coming from, but he soon realized it was Amber's perfume. Travis was sure the look on his face was a bit strange as he debated in his brain about the smell. Noting that Travis's body language had changed, Amber asked,

"Are you ok?"

"Yeah, I'm good just trying to figure out what type of perfume that is."

"Oh, it is called Desire, I really like it," Amber said, making conversation.

"Yeah, it smells refreshing, do you mind if I ask where you got it?" Travis asked as he tried to get a better look at her face.

Pulling up to the Juke Joint, Travis told Amber he would wait with her until her friends got here. She thanked him but Travis was really hanging around to find out if she was his Mystery Woman. Walking into the Juke Joint, Travis saw a live band and his hope started to grow about his chances.

"Do you like live music?"

"Sometimes," Amber responded, looking around for her friends.

Noticing they were not there yet Amber grabbed a table for them.

"I owe you a drink for being so kind to me, what are you drinking?" she asked.

Travis told her if she buys, he flies, meaning she buys, and he goes to the bar to get it. Of course, Travis had no intention of letting her pay but he didn't want to fight about who was buying drinks. On the way back to the table with drinks Travis saw Amber greeting what he assumed were her friends, so he went back to the bar and ordered more drinks. Now with a round for the table Travis handed Amber her money back and passed the drinks to her two friends who were looking at him as if he was a waiter. Amber stood up and introduced Travis to Vanessa, a slender woman with a face full of freckles and Morgan, a beautiful curvy woman with red flowing hair.

"Hello, nice to meet you ladies, I'm Travis."

Morgan said, "oh you must have the 434-area code, I was wondering where she was calling from." Travis looked around for a second before remembering Amber used his phone.

Vanessa told Travis to have a seat as he began to walk away. Vanessa thanked him,

"I can't thank you enough for stopping for my friend."

"No problem, it was the right thing to do."

Morgan looked suspiciously at Travis asking, "The right thing to do?"

"Yes and I see why you're friends," thinking back to Amber looking at him the same way. "I was raised to help people in need so once I saw her in trouble I had to help."

"Did she tell you she was married?" Morgan asked, folding her arms.

"No, she didn't but I didn't ask, I was just helping."

Travis responded, starting to feel a little attacked. Amber told Morgan to relax, she responded,

"I'm relaxed just trying to see what he is looking for."
Now knowing he was under attack Travis sat up straighter in his seat and said in a strong but respectful voice,

"I didn't want shit from her, she needed help, so I stopped to assist not wanting anything from her. I brought her here, waited until you guys got here not wanting shit from her, and now that she is safe, I'll leave."

He stood up, shook Amber's hand, and wished a good night as he went to the bar to close out his tab. As he closed out his tab the waitress said,

"I see you found your girl," but Travis barely heard her due to the music blasting.
Travis took one last look at the table before leaving.

Heading to the car, Travis could not help to think of the scent of Amber's perfume, he wondered if she was the Mystery Woman he had been looking for. He after hearing someone yelling his name. He turned around to see Morgan coming his way. Walking back to meet her, Travis wondered what she wanted to accuse him of now.

"What's up?" Travis asked with his arms folded ready to verbally spar again.

"I owe you an apology, you helped my friend when no one else would and I treated you like shit for it."

Apparently, when Travis left the table Amber lit Morgan's ass on fire for acting like a fool.

"I understand you were just protecting your friend; there's no need to apologize."

"I was trying to protect her; she is young and still a little green, but I shouldn't have acted like that. It shocked me that you would do something like that without expecting anything in return but again I'm sorry." Morgan continued apologizing Travis's hand.

"I totally understand, I may have reacted the same way."

As they sat outside squashing their issues, Travis got another whiff of the perfume and asked if it was Desire. She looked at him wide-eyed, surprised he would know what kind of perfume it was.

"How do you know what it is?"

"Amber is wearing the same one."

"I told her not to wear my stuff."

"It smells great, it must be very popular," Travis said, probing for more information.

"Nope I'm the only one that wears it here, well me and that damn Amber that is. My sister sent it to me." Travis's brain was exploding at that point. *Could this be my Mystery Woman? Play it cool man, relax and don't forget to breathe*, he thought to himself.

"Word, that's awesome you have your own scent, whoever meets you can remember you." Travis said, *nice one* he thought.

Morgan began telling him more about herself, but Travis was lost in thought. He tried to listen, but his brain said *fuck it just ask*. Travis had no choice but to ask if she was in the Juke Joint about a month ago.

Morgan said, "I think we came in for jazz night."
Oh shit, oh shit keep it together, be cool, be cool Travis thought to himself.

"Hey, do you want to go back in and grab a drink?"

"I would like that," Morgan said smiling.
Travis could not feel the ground as he walked back in the Juke Joint, after all he had found his Mystery Woman.

{ 10 }

Morgan not Marry

Travis now trying to keep his cool held the door as Morgan entered,

"My lady," while bowing slightly as she passed by

him, smiling. "Do you want to join your friends?"

Morgan quickly declined that option,

"Let's go to the bar instead."

As they passed by the table where Amber and Vanessa were sitting Travis grinned and tilted his head towards Amber, to thank her for making Morgan come outside.

"Can I help you?" the bartender asked.

"Yes, that Hennessy lemonade looks good. I will try that," Travis said.

"Oh, that does sound good. I will have one as well,"

Morgan said, pulling her out her credit card.

"Oh, no ma'am, I got this."

Morgan insisted,

"I will get the first one and if I want another you can buy it."

Travis was taken back by the forcefulness of Morgan, but he was also secretly turned on as well.

"So, you're telling me I have a one drink audition?"

"Something like that," Morgan said, trying to keep a straight face.

"I can work with that but in most clubs there's a two-drink minimum."

Morgan laughed, as she was unable to keep a straight face any longer,

"Ok we'll see," as the two smiled at each other.

"Here are your drinks," the bartender said, breaking up the moment.

This bitch, Travis thought as the mood was broken. Morgan made him forget all about that by saying "Yes" when the bartender asked if they wanted to start a tab.

"Starting a tab I see, sounds like I'm doing pretty well."

"Relax, you're still auditioning," Morgan said, using Travis's own words against him.

"Yes ma'am, I got you," Travis said as the two continued to flirt back and forth.

Travis noticed a shift in Morgan's demeanor as she started to look annoyed.

"You good?"

"I'm good, excuse me for a second."

She excused herself and headed back to Amber's table. Travis watched as Morgan sat close to Amber and whispered something in her ear. He continued to sip on his Henny lemonade thinking *damn this shit is good, Morgan had better hurry up before he finished hers.* Glancing over to the table Travis noticed two thin men with long dreads who looked a lot like Milli Vanilli sitting at the table, unfazed he continued to enjoy both his lemonade and the live band. The band covered all of Morris Day and The Time's biggest hits. Of course, he was also keeping an eye on his Mystery Woman, but he did not want to do anything to negatively affect his audition. Morgan put his mind at ease as she looked back and gestured to him that she would be back shortly. Travis tipped his drink in acknowledgement. After ordering another round of Henny lemonades for them both, (he drank hers) Travis watched as the two men stormed away from the table just as Morgan made her way back over to him. Morgan grabbed her fresh new Henny lemonade and turned it up, drinking half of it in one gulp.

"Thanks for refreshing it."

"No problem," Travis said, observing Morgan's heightened attitude.

He tried to break the tension,

"Was Milli Vanilli upset about their latest album flop?" which made Morgan choke on her drink.

"You're stupid as shit, no I used to date Vanilli."

"Oh, I see that must have been during your Erykah Badu Neo Soul phase I take it," looking side eyed at Morgan.

"No..... No," Morgan said, defending her choices.

"Did you have braids at the time?"

"Shut up," Morgan said, realizing Travis may be right.

As the conversation continued at the bar, a waitress asked,

"Do you want to grab the open table?"

Travis looked at Morgan to see if his audition was going well. she answered,

"Yes, we'll take the open table."

This delighted Travis who was now trying in vain to hide his smile.

"Shut up, fool," Morgan said, noticing Travis's smile as they made their way to the table.

Now seated, the two continued their conversation, Travis told her about his military service and some of the places he had traveled to. She talked about her uncles who had served as well. Morgan looked at the passion in Travis's eyes as he talked about his desire to travel the world and have unimaginable experiences. Morgan expressed her desire to travel outside the borders of the United States.

"You should travel more; you only live once." Travis told Morgan.

In turn, Travis watched in awe as Morgan described the joy she got from teaching. She told him that her joy comes when the light bulb turns on in the kid's brain as the subject clicks.

"That sounds amazing."

Travis agreed with Morgan's light bulb comment thinking back to his years of training troops.

"Hey, have you seen the crystallized sand cross on the beach?" Morgan asked.

"Sand cross on the beach? No, I haven't."

"A local artist designed a giant rod-shaped cross that was struck by lightning almost five years ago."

"Oh, that sounds like something I need to see."

Travis threw out an offer mentioning they should see it together to see her response.

Morgan upped the ante by,

"We should go tonight."

Travis had to scrabble and gather his thoughts.

"Yes of course we should go tonight," he said, motioning for the check.

Morgan went to tell Amber that she was leaving which left a surprised but happy look on her face.

"Oh, you like him," Amber said, smiling.

"He's just ok," Morgan said, handing her car keys to Amber.

"Oh, you like him... like him."

"Shut up," Morgan responded, putting on her coat and hugging Amber goodbye.

As they left Nelson's Juke Joint the two passed by the still irritated men who tried to intimidate Travis which proved ineffective based on the smile on his face. He watched in the mirror as the two talked and pointed at them, but Travis ignored it because he was walking out with his Mystery Woman. This put him in a great mood. Driving to the beach, each took turns singing songs that came over the radio in their most annoying voices. Travis finished singing *And I am telling you I'm not going* complete with movements while he resisted the urge to tell the smiling Morgan about trying to track her down over the past few weeks. He thought that telling her something like that would make things a little weird since they were on their way to a remote location. When they reached the beach, Travis parked next to a Lifeguard stand which reminded him of the show *Baywatch*. They stood there in silence looking out in the calm ocean as a breeze swept past ever so softly. Morgan removed her shoes and walked down to the water's edge.

"This place is wonderful; I come here when I need to recharge."

She closed her eyes and took a few deep breaths. Travis stood back admiring Morgan's silhouette in the Moonlight,

"It is beautiful if I say so myself."

"Are you even looking at the water?"

"Nope, not at all."

Travis took off his shoes,

"Dance with me beautiful."

"We don't have any music."

Taking her hand,

"We don't need any music."

They began to sway back and forth to the sounds of the water crashing on the rocks. Looking into Morgan's eyes,

"I could do this forever."

Morgan responded, "Don't say things you don't mean."

"Oh, I mean it," Travis said, telling Morgan this was her last first date.

Justin put down his drink and cut Travis's story short,

"Hold up, hold up, did you really tell Red what I told Lina?

"What?" Kerry asked, looking confused.

"You weren't using it anymore and besides it's a fuck-ing great line," Travis said defending his theft.

"Damn man, I'm using that for my next woman!" Kerry screamed.

"You can't use lines like that on the women you date."

Travis begged, "come on man I needed it; she was my Mystery Woman after all and I'm marrying her."

"Ok I understand but if Lina hears that part of the story, she is going to punch you in the throat."

"Hell, Morgan may punch you as well." Kerry said. Travis agreed,

"Red never adds the rest of the story, she doesn't like the fact that she left the bar with me, let alone kissing me on the first night. I got you."

"Ok but remember it's on you." He sat back in his seat remembering when he met Lina.

"Wait, this is bullshit, I need to be able to use that panty dropping line too." Kerry said.

"Nope you can't use it unless you're serious about a woman and you're never serious." Justin said with Travis quickly agreeing.

"Whatever I'm using it, what else do you have that I can use?"

"I got nothing for you."

"Once I see you with the same girl more than twice, I might hook you up but until then kick rocks."

As the three argued over who could use the line, Austin grabbed the microphone and yelled, "IT'S TIME FOR THE FINALS, SO COME ON DOWN PARTY PEOPLE!!" The guys remembering their bet tabled the argument as they made their way to the stage area. Justin looked for Joanie ensuring she did not run off with their money, noticing Justin looking around, she held up the money putting his mind at ease while the others took seats near the stage.

First finalist coming to the stage, the *I Got You Babe* Duo of Sonny and Cher (Justin's team). Sunny grabbed Cher by the hand, and they began their dance melody with the Cha-Cha.

"Oh, no it's the Cha-Cha," the DJ said over the music.

"Yea, Sonny!" yelled Justin.

As the music picked up, so did Cher's dancing speed, she grabbed Sonny's hand as they broke out in a fast-paced salsa number. Cher was moving her hips sliding back and forth across the dance floor when DJ noticed Sonny was not keeping up.

"He is trying, bless his heart," The DJ said, "let's go Sonny pick it up but watch out for that table."

Seeing Sonny's struggle Cher tried to save the couple by slowing down the dance switching to the conga line, but that would prove to be the beginning of the end. Where Cher was accustomed to wearing and dancing in high heel shoes, Sonny was not. Sonny's ankles buckled in the platform shoes during the second turn of the conga line which made him stumble and fall, taking out a couple near the bar in the process.

"Man Down…. Man Down!" the DJ yelled while

blowing a horn symbolizing the end of the dance. After a group of Joanie's helped up the fallen couple, Cher stormed off effectively bringing an end to their partnership. Over the music the DJ could be heard saying,

"And just like that Cher is going solo again," to the laughter of the crowd.

"Shit, there goes my $20."

"Yeah, you're out," Kerry said laughing.

"Ok now that we cleaned Sonny and Cher up off the floor, make some noise for Mork and Mindy coming straight from the planet Ork!" the DJ yelled.

"Ok, here comes the winners!" Kerry said yelling for his team.

"Sit down fool," Justin said, still salty about Sonny's fall.

Mork and Mindy started out hot with a little Mashed Potato that delighted the room.

"Oh, ok I see you, what else you got?" the DJ asked, trying to hype them up.

Mindy did not disappoint, breaking out the twist and dropping it low followed closely by Mork. His twist damn near touched the ground. The crowd cheered and whistled to the joy of Kerry.

"Ok bring it home now," the DJ said, switching up the music.

Mork and Mindy did just that, they broke out with a final dance that the crowd learned later was the St. Louis Shag which is a version of the Charleston shuffle. When the couple finished Kerry stood with his hands raised as if he was dancing in the competition.

"Victory is mine!" Kerry yelled.

"Give it up for Mork and Mindy," the DJ said over the music as the crowd cheered.

"Last but certainly not least, please show some love for two foxy cats coming from that *Purple Haze.* Make some funking noise for Jimmy Hendrix and Grace Motha Fuckin Jones!" the DJ yelled.

Grace wasted little time as she jumped in front of Jimmy and blasted the stage with the jerk.

"Oh, shit I see you Miss Jones," the DJ said.

Not to be outdone Jimmy grabbed Grace by the hand and snapped her to his side which stunned the crowd. He grabbed her by the waist as the twosome began to do the Lambada.

"Oh Shit...Oh Shit it's the forbidden dance!" the DJ yelled.

The pair slid around the floor doing the Lambada and steaming up the room with their sex appeal.

"Shit I need some water or a cigarette," the DJ said alluding to the hotness in the room.

As the room heated up Jimmy and Grace Jones ended their dance melody with the Rumba. The DJ was silent for a second as he just stared at the two of them before asking the crowd if they thought Grace got pregnant during the dance.

"Maybe, you see this sexy man," Grace Jones said, referring to Jimmy.

"Give them a damn hand and maybe a condom," the DJ said as they left the stage.

"Shit, I won this easily," Travis said standing with his chest poked out.

"Bullshit, how do you figure that?" Kerry asked.

"Sex sells and that was sexy, and you know it," Travis said.

"I'm not saying it wasn't sexy but I'm still leaving with the money."

While the ballots were being counted, Austin came over with
a funky looking bottle filled with a blood red liquid.

"How did you guys like the show?"

"It was great, I think Jimmy and Grace won it,"
Travis said.

"Whatever, they were ok, but the show was awesome," Kerry said interrupting.

"Thanks, I was hoping people liked it. While we wait,
I was wondering if you wanted to try a new bottle
that arrived today."
Kerry stood up,

 "I'm no damn vampire and I don't want any, it looks
like blood."

"Of course, it's not blood, it's called Black Mamba.
It's a dry rum from Zimbabwe."

"Really, Zimbabwe?" Justin said now interested.

"Ok we'll try it," Travis said.
Before they could try it, the DJ came on the mic yelling with
an echo effect,

"We have a winner!"
Austin made his way to the dance floor where the eager couples were waiting for the results.

"In third place, the recipient of a $200 tab or gift card
is a Cher-less Sonny." the DJ said.

The crowd cheered well everyone except for Justin who had just lost $20.

"In second place with a $500 gift card or tab is Mork & Mindy," the DJ said.

Again, the crowd cheered but not Kerry who was upset he lost.

"That means your champion and winner of a free vacation is the forbidden lovers Jimmy Hendrix and Grace Motha Fuckin Jones!" the DJ yelled.

The crowd cheered and yelled including Travis who won the bet.

Joanie came over and gave the money to an overjoyed Travis to the chagrin of Justin and Kerry.

"Sorry guys, I wish you all could win."

"It's not your fault, it's that damn Sonny's fault for falling." Justin said, still upset.

Kerry said, "no it's Joanie's fault," jokingly.

The group laughed as Joanie walked away. Austin came back to the table with four chilled shot glasses and said,

"Let's go, gentlemen."

They all stood eagerly to try some of the Black Mamba. They cheered while clinking their shot glasses against each other.

"Fuck me," Travis said, Justin and Austin both just sat down.

Noticing this and leaning against the chair himself Kerry said,

"That was nothing, let's do one more unless you're scared."

Austin said, "it's recommended to have no more than one shot of the Black Mamba at a time."

Kerry played on their egos as he continued to bash them until they stood back up for one more shot. This time however no one said a cheer, instead each man looked at the Black Mamba nervously.

"Down the Hatch, besides what's the worst that could happen?" Kerry said, smiling.

{ 11 }

WTF

Damn it's bright in here Justin thought, he tried opening his eyes, but it hurt too bad, so he closed them back. *Wait is it morning* he thought to himself, he opened one eye at a time very slowly. *Damn it is morning, why the fuck is it morning already.* As he mumbled about how disrespectful the sun was, a thought jumped out, *where the hell am I?* First, he realized he was lying on the floor, so he moved to get up, but his head was splitting so he had to roll over and pull himself up onto the bed. Now sitting on the bed, Justin could see a picture of Kerry with no shirt sitting on the nightstand. *Ok I'm in Kerry's guest room, now I just need to figure out how the hell I got here.* Another thought jumped out *shit what time is it*, he grabbed his phone and saw that it was fucking noon already and he had 10 missed calls from Lina. He missed the Church counseling; he called Lina, but she did not answer so he left a message saying that they got fucked up and he was sorry for missing counseling.

"Damn man, I told her I wasn't getting drunk, I know she is mad as hell."
This was confirmed when Lina called him back and began to lay into him.

"Well, it's good to see that you're alive," Lina said angrily.

"I'm sorry babe," Justin said, starting to explain.
 Lina cut him off,

"Nope, don't call me babe, I asked you not to get drunk. You knew we had counseling this morning and you promised me you would be there."

"Lina, I was not trying to get drunk. I don't even know how it happened."

"Whatever but you did," she responded, cutting him off again.

"You've been ducking counseling for weeks; I told you I needed this, you selfish ass. I'm tired of hearing that men don't go to counseling shit. You go to counseling, or you and Kerry can go back to chasing hoes together."

"Babe chill out, it's not that serious," Justin stupidly said.

"Chill out... Chill Out...., who in the fuck are you talking to about it's not that serious shit!"
Realizing his words were making it worse Justin tried to clarify his statement,

"Babe I didn't mean that it was not important. All I was saying."

Lina cut him off yelling, "Stop calling me babe I said!"

"Damn woman let me finish," Justin said, tired of being cut off.

"Oh, so you're mad now?" Lina asked as she chuckled in anger.

"No, I'm not mad (he had no reason to be), I know I fucked up, but I was just trying to clarify my statement."

"I know what you meant but that doesn't excuse your selfish ass ways and I'm getting really tired of it."

"I know you are, and I will make it up to you."

"I don't need you to make it up to me, I'll make another appointment for this week, and your ass better be there."

"I will be there, I promise"

"Don't promise me shit like that Justin."
This time she sounded more hurt than angry.

"Babe, I will be there."

"Ok, I will make the appointment, the kids and I are out so I'll let you go."

She hung up without saying bye or I love you, which is against the family rules. Justin sat on the edge of the bed upset with himself for blowing off Lina even if it was not on purpose.

"Fuck my head hurts, I need some water."

As he was getting himself together, a noise could be heard coming from the living room.

Travis was that noise in the living room; he woke up shirtless upside down on the couch with his legs hanging over the headrest. *Fuck, why is it so bright* having the same thoughts as Justin about the damn disrespectful sun. After fixing himself on the couch, Travis summed up what strength he had left to close the blinds. As he got up, he felt a sharp pain in his ribs. *What the hell did I do*, he thought to himself as he looked at a large bruise on his right side. With the blinds closed and now holding his ribs he looked for his shirt. Finding it in the kitchen, Travis grabbed some much-needed water along with a bag of frozen peas. He gingerly made his way back to the couch with the peas on his ribs, but he couldn't help to think why does a single guy have such a big ass bag of peas, no one likes peas that much. He tried not to breathe in too deeply because of the pain. Making it back to the couch he contin-ued to wonder how he bruised his ribs so badly. He sat as carefully as he could, just as a bewildered Justin gradually walked from down the hall looking around just as confused as Travis was. Grateful that the blinds were now blocking the disrespectful sun. Justin stopped covering his eyes and walked around slouched overlooking like Gollum from *Lord of the Rings.*

He passed a sitting Travis who was staring at a blank TV screen. After grabbing some water and looking for but not finding any pain pills for his splitting headache, Justin went back and sat on the couch near Travis. As he sat, he started to ask what the hell happened last night, but Travis beat him to the punch,

"Dude, what the fuck?"

"Shit, I was going to ask you the same damn thing."

"Fuck maybe, we should wake Kerry up."

Justin looking a little more confused,

"I thought he was out here with you, I looked in his room and didn't see him."

"Well maybe he's with Miss Ella," Travis said which made them both laugh.

"Shit don't make me laugh, my head is splitting," Jus-tin said with his head in his hands.

"You're right, damn," Travis said, now holding his head as well as his ribs.

"Where could this little fool be? Dude call him, I can't find my phone."
Travis gave up the search just as quickly as he started.

"Lazy ass," Justin replied before grabbing his phone. He put it on speaker, so he did not have to hear the loud ringing in his ear. Kerry answered the phone whispering which was extremely weird.

"Man, what the hell?" Justin asked, commenting on the weirdness of the whispering.

Travis said, "man where are you and why the hell are you whispering?"

Kerry, still whispering, "I have no idea where I am."
Now alarmed they asked him to explain.

"It's very dark in here, I can see a small crack of light, but I can't make out any objects on the other side. I'm starting to freak the fuck out."
Now truly alarmed Travis and Justin's mind switched into go mode, with adrenaline kicking in the pair forgot about their headaches and body injuries.

They began scanning the room looking for clues, they split up and began clearing rooms. Travis looked in the kitchen where he found evidence of more intense drinking. Justin went into the hallway looking for signs of a struggle, he returned once making it to the elevator without finding anything. The whole time the two were looking around, Kerry remained on the phone with Travis.

"Dude, do you remember anything?" Travis asked. Kerry began to answer as the guys listened looking for clues in his story,

"My head is pounding and my fucking shoulder hurts."
As he continued Travis heard a noise coming from the back of the condo. Armed with kitchen knives the two moved to clear the last room, they entered Kerry's bedroom silently looking around and noticed the bed had not been slept in. Justin heard a faint voice; he closed his eyes in an effort to pinpoint where the voice was coming from.

"Take him off speaker," Justin said, with his eyes closed.
Travis did so but in his haste, he forgot to put the phone to his ear, so he didn't hear Kerry freaking out. Summoning up courage for the coming fight,

"Someone is coming. I hear voices outside; I have to fight; I'm not going out like that. If they want me, they will have to earn it."

He told the guys he loved them, thinking this was going to be one of his last moments.

Just then the door swung open, Kerry saw two big knives coming at him, which made all his summoned courage fade quickly. He began screaming louder than a teenage girl in a horror movie.

"Man, WTF?" Justin yelled covering his ears.

"Stop fucking screaming!" Travis yelled.

Kerry opened his eyes, still screaming as he looked around to see the faces of his would-be killers. He recognized the two pissed off faces looking at him,

"Why the hell do you have knives?" he asked, yelling at Travis and Justin.

"We were looking for you, fool," Travis said as he stepped back and sat on the bed.

Justin's adrenaline started returning to normal, he found a chair to sit in. Kerry began to remove a makeshift barricade so he could exit his own closet.

"Why the fuck were you in the closet?" Travis asked, holding his ribs again.

"Shit, I don't know," Kerry said, leaning against the closet door.

Justin looking at the intricately made barricade,

"Did you make it before or after you called us?"

"I guess it was constructed before," Kerry said, realizing he may have been in the closet for hours.

"Why the hell does my shoulder hurt?" Kerry asked, looking at the two of them trying to figure out who to blame.

"Man, that's your shoulder fool, how would we know," Justin said as Travis seconded those words still holding his ribs.

With everyone now accounted for, the bruised group made their way to the living room looking like zombies to try to piece together what happened over the past few hours. Travis and Justin sat on the couch; Kerry put the knives back and grabbed a PowerAde from the fridge. He joined the guys in the living room and stretched out on the love seat.

"Who can stretch out on a damn loveseat?" Travis asked.

"Shut up, you're mad because you can't do it"
Justin looked up,

"Lina is mad as hell at me; we need to figure out what happened."

"Travis what's the last thing you remember?" Justin asked, trying to put a timeline together.

Travis leaned forward, "shit let's see, I remember winning the bet and getting my money from Joanie but after that things get fuzzy."

"Yea I remember that damn Sonny falling, that bitch."

"Yea, yea I remember talking to Austin after that but then it's blank as hell." Kerry said laughing.

"Man, this shit ain't funny," Travis said now looking at Kerry.

"What?"

"Did you slip us something last night? I know how you get down," Travis asked.

"Bitch this ain't no damn movie," Kerry said, defending himself.

"WTF, you better not have done anything, but it would be easier to explain if you did."

"Man, I'm not about that drug life anymore and you both know that, besides I would not waste good shit on you two losers. This is real life, but hell let's follow the movies and check our pockets and phones."

"True you have been cleanish since college but flipping our pockets is a good idea."

Travis said.

After flipping their pockets, Justin spoke up,

"Apparently, I paid the tab."

"Fuck, was it high? We did a lot of drinking," Travis asked.

"Surprisingly no it looks like we got hooked up, all we paid for was the first drinks we ordered. The tip was bigger than the bill."

Travis said, "great and there is nothing in my pockets."

"I got some lint and the card from Winston." Kerry said, now reaching for his phone.

"I didn't make any calls," Justin said.

"Neither did I," Travis said.

Kerry looked at his call list,

"It looks like I called Winston around 3 am."

"At least we know how we got home," Travis said.

Kerry cut him off when he saw that he tipped Winston 100 dollars.

"Looks like we took some pics last night," Justin said as he continued looking through his phone.

"Oh shit, are they bad?" Travis asked nervously.

"No, we are good," Justin said showing him a pic with Grace Mutha Fuckin Jones and Jimmy Hendrix.

"Oh ok, I can work with that."

"Yea, we have a few pics in here but nothing to worry about, cool, cool."

"Wait, what is that?" Kerry asked, looking at Justin pics.

"What's what?"

"What's that bottle?" Kerry asked pointing to the snake shaped bottle on the table.

"Oh, shit I think I remember that," Travis said now sitting on the edge of his seat.

"Looks like I was tagged in a video," Kerry said before loading it.
On the video, Travis could be seen giving a toast,

"I want to thank you guys for a great night with both old and new friends."

"Damn we look fucked up but nothing too bad," Justin said.
As the video continues Kerry was seen saying,

"That was nothing, let's do one more unless you're scared."
Austin could be seen on the video trying to avoid taking another shot by telling them about the recommended one drink minimum of Black Mamba.

Undeterred Kerry said, "down the hatch, besides what's the worst that can happen."

"You bitch, why would you do more than one? Look at my damn face you can tell I didn't need any more." Justin said.

"I hate you so much," Travis said.

"Hey, no one forced you two to drink anything."

"Looks like I shot a few videos last night," Justin said. He pulled up the first video from what looked like the back seat of Winston's Uber. The video started with Travis and Justin in the backseat singing along to *Smooth Criminal* by Michael Jackson. Kerry was in the front seat having what looked to be a deep conversation with Winston.

"Ok first, why the hell are we singing? Second, why is your short ass in the front?" Travis asked.

"Shit I don't know why the hell your big asses were in the back singing in such high-pitched voices."

"Can you remember what you guys were talking about in the front?" Justin asked keying in on the intense look on Kerry's face.

"Man, I have no idea," Kerry said as he racked his brain looking for an answer.

The second video started with everyone in the car singing *If I were a boy* by Beyonce at the top of their lungs while at a red light as other cars looked on. It would seem the beehive approved of their rendition of one of the most popular and inappropriate songs for a group of guys to be singing out loud.

Travis broke the silence, "well at least we were on beat."

"True, true," Justin said, singing the song in his head. In the last video the SUV pulled up to Kerry's condo and the partiers began heading inside. As Travis and Justin stumbled along, Winston and Kerry exchanged a huge hug probably stemming from their heartfelt conversation in the front seat.

"Dude, I really want to know what you guys were talking about." Travis said.

"Well, that was my last video," Justin said disappointingly.

"Damn it didn't explain how I hurt my ribs," Travis said.

Kerry's first video started with him laughing at an argument between Justin and Travis about who was sleeping on the couch vs who was sleeping in the guest room.

"I get the bed, I'm a guest." Travis said.

"Shit, so am I."

Kerry chimed in saying neither of them were guests.

"Well, I flew in, so I deserve it." Travis said changing his tactics.

"Nope, I had a long day coaching youth soccer practice."

"That doesn't seem hard, you get no credit for that shit." Travis said refuting Justin's claims.

"Hey, you guys should race for it."

"Travis doesn't want any of this smoke with his slow ass."

"I got your slow ass," Travis said as he stepped back to get more space.

"Oh, you want it," Justin said while tightening his belt.

Kerry could be heard in the background of the video laughing as the doors of the elevator opened and the race to end all races began. Keep in mind that Kerry only lives a few doors away from the elevator but in their minds, they were running at top speed through the cluttered hallway but in reality, that damn Black Mamba made them look like they were running in sand. Travis raced out to an early lead when Justin started to gain on him. Feeling the pressure Travis kept looking back to see where Justin was, unfortunately his pace checks lasted longer and longer thanks to the Black Mamba. His last pace check lasted a little too long, the video showed Travis running into a large old school vacuum cleaner. He did a massive summersault over the vacuum and landed hard as shit on his ribs. Needless to say, he lost the race, Justin skipped on by him laughing at the hurting Travis. The video ends as Kerry crumbles to the ground laughing at the spectacle in front of him.

{ 12 }

Damn Black Mamba

After reviewing the clips that would win America's Funniest Home Video the guys set back with an uneasy calm on their faces, well everyone but Kerry.

"Who the fuck puts a damn vacuum cleaner in the hallway?" Travis said holding his ribs.

"That shit was funny, and I won."

"Whatever you saw me winning until that damn vacuum got in the way!"

Kerry spoke up, "shit I still don't know how I hurt myself."
Travis gently got up and took his phone off the charger to see if he had any footage of the night also,

"Oh shit, I got a few videos." as he moved to sit back down on the couch.
On the first video Travis could be seen dancing like a fool with Grace Mutha Fuckin Jones celebrating his victory.

"Ok no one wants to see that shit," Justin said, still salty at Sonny for losing him money.

The second video started with Justin walking around the condo talking shit about being the champion, followed by Kerry who was still short of breath from laughing all the way from the elevator. From behind the phone, Travis could be heard saying,

"Whatever man you know I tripped and that is the only reason you won."

Justin and Kerry would not stop laughing, so Travis yelled,

"I am telling Red, and she is going to ride on both you bitches."

Travis took off his shirt to show the camera and Red his rib injury on facetime.

"You see this baby, they hurt me." Travis said looking back into the camera trying to show the pain on his face until the video ended.

Justin and Kerry glanced at each other before asking,

"If he thought he was Facetiming."

At that moment Travis realized what he was recording a video and simply responded with

"That damn black mamba got me."

Both Justin and Kerry leaned back on the couch and nodded their heads in agreement (That damn black mamba got them all).

As the morning continued, the guys seemed to be content with the information that they learned from the phones, well Kerry was still confused as to how he got hurt. However, as the Advil and Powerade began to take effect Travis relaxed knowing the night ended without an issue. Justin's hydration level improved, he tried to relax but he knew that he had a fight coming once this day was over. They dozed off back and forth waiting for the first football game to start. Kerry looked over at Travis and Justin who were now sleeping rather uncomfortably on the couch and decided his bed would be a better place to sleep. He got up and began what seemed to be an awfully long walk down the hall. When he entered the room, Kerry saw the massive pile of clothes spilling out of the closet and remembered his prison escape from hours earlier. He laid across his bed but had to switch positions due to the pain in his shoulder. After re-adjusting, he began to look through his phone again for clues to how he hurt himself. He was screening the previously seen videos to make sure he did not miss anything when he came across a grainy 7 Minute video. The video started in his pocket, once out Travis and Justin could be seen arguing about how the race ended. The conversation shifted when Justin jokingly said,

> "You should just take Kerry's bed; he can sleep his little ass in the dresser drawer."

Travis looked at Kerry and grinned,

"That isn't a bad idea."

Travis grinned so hard it made Kerry freak out and start yelling,

"Oh, Hell No!"

He began running out of the kitchen to beat Travis to his room. The video became hard to view as Kerry ran down the hallway flailing his arms thinking Travis was close behind him. The phone swung back and forth, as glimpses of Travis and Justin could be seen staring at Kerry confused. The video showed Kerry diving into his dark bedroom in a final effort to win the race. What the severely intoxicated Kerry forgot that he had redecorated recently, and that forgotten fact would come back to haunt him. Diving in the darkened room, Kerry slammed into an old-school rocking chair he bought because of a cute salesclerk. On the video, you cannot see anything, but you can hear the painful moaning and groaning of Kerry. After laying on the floor for what seemed to be forever, Kerry could be heard getting up slowly. Being in the room should have ended this remarkably interesting night but not just yet. Kerry could be seen pacing back and forth on his bed paranoid that Travis or Justin would come in and try to steal his bed. Completely gone on that damn Black Mamba Kerry spoke into the camera,

"I'm not leaving my room dammit, I am the King of this fucking castle.

Kerry was continuing his rant until he suddenly stopped and began to stare at the door as if he had heard something. The video ends as Kerry is seen jumping off the bed,

"I got action," stealing a line from his favorite movie *Next Friday.*

Kerry now laying on the bed shook his head thinking about that damn Black Mamba. In what was the last video, Kerry was now in the closet setting up what looked to be a makeshift barricade of clothes and shoe boxes. *I was really really drunk* Kerry thought to himself as he watched the video. The video continued as he sat back against the wall after building his makeshift fort. He seemed to pass out after saying,

"They will never take me alive."

Kerry stopped the video and tossed his phone to the other side of the bed, covered his eyes, and simply said,

"Fuck Black Mamba."

With the mysteries of the night now solved the condo fell silent as the battered and bewildered friends fell to sleep to reset the morning. After a few more hours of much needed sleep the doorbell began to ring. When no one answered it, the unknown party began to bang away.

"Fuck, who is at the door?" Justin asked, sitting up on the couch.

"Kerry answer your door!" Travis yelled.

"I'm going, shut up," Kerry said as he passed the couch. "Who is it?"

The unknown person was starting to annoy them by continuing to ring the bell. He opened the door angrily, but his anger was easily matched and surpassed by the look on Miss Ella's face.
Travis and Justin joined Kerry at the door only to see Miss Ella standing with her hands on her hips and rollers in her hair. Her faded blue robe was held closed by a frayed string that reminded Justin of his mom when she came to school after he had been showing his ass.

"What's up Miss Ella?" Kerry asked, trying to understand the urgency in her presence.

"Do you know which philistine knocked over my dang trash last night?"

Trying to play it off Kerry looked out the door,

"Dang, I am sorry Miss Ella, but I don't know."

Not believing Kerry, Miss Ella asked again, "are you sure?"
She shook her head at Kerry as the frail string hung on for dear life. Justin prayed to himself, *please Lord Do Not let that*

robe open Lord I pray in your most powerful name. Travis stepped in front of Kerry,

"Mam we will help clean it up, but we didn't see anything last night."
Which was somewhat true, Travis did not see the vacuum before running into it.

"Thank you, baby," Miss Ella said, now smiling at Travis.
Needing to stop the awkward moment Justin walked out and began gathering the trash they knocked over unbeknownst to Miss Ella.

"Why do I have to help your clumsy blind ass?" Kerry said, looking at Travis.

"Well, if you don't, I'm telling Miss Ella you did it and she won't give you any special time. You know she will believe me."

"Whatever, this is bullshit."
When Kerry got to the vacuum however he refused,

"You pick that shit up," and walked off.
Justin stood back and said, "Yeah you pick that up, hell you flipped over it."

"Fine I don't care; I'll pick it up." Travis said as he knelt and grabbed the vacuum.

They passed by Miss Ella as they finished, getting back to the condo Justin broke the silence,

"Damn, I thought that string was going to break."

"Shit, I was praying it stayed close," Travis said.

"I didn't notice," Kerry said, which made the others look at him with judgement in their eyes.

"You didn't see it? Really," Justin asked.

"Whatever she can cook," Kerry said, now trying to annoy them.

"I can't even with you right now. I need some food in my life," Travis said, opening the fridge.

"You always need food but I'm hungry too." Justin said laughing,

Justin closed the pantry now looking disappointed,

"Dude you don't have shit in here."

"WTF is this?" Travis said, pulling out some molded shit from the back of the fridge.

"Oh, damn I was looking for that a few weeks ago. Man, my women cook for me."

Justin looked in the fridge,

"Well judging from the mold and the lack of food it must have been a minute since your last meal."

Kerry grabbed a handful of menus and tossed them at Justin,

"Just order something and shut up."

"Ok. wings and pizza?

"Sure, that works for me, but I want a vegan pizza." Travis said.

The statement startled Kerry and Justin who were now staring at him,

"Um what?" Justin asked, looking at Travis with his head tilted.

"Morgan wants me to be healthier."

"Ok I get it, but you really think we're going to order that shit." Kerry said.

As an acne challenged teen walked slowly down the hallway screaming could be heard coming from the condo,

"Run bitch, you better run, what the fuck are you thinking, kill that bitch!"

The voices and threats got louder and louder as he walked down the hallway. The doorbell rang as the guys were watching the game rather loudly and letting the teams know that they were disappointed with their lack of effort. The teen realized that the screaming and threats were coming from the apartment that he was delivering to. He rang the bell nervously; Travis opened the door yelling at the TV only to turn around and see a terrified teen staring up at him.

"PPPizza sir," the teen said.

"Oh, come in, my man," Travis said, backing away from the door.

The still uneasy teen sat the orders down to be checked.

"You good?" Justin asked, seeing the fear in his eyes.

"YYYes I'm ok it is just a little loud," the teen said.

"Oh, you heard us?" Travis asked, realizing what kind of things the teen might have heard.

They gave him a decent size tip and assured him he was ok before plopping back down on the couch to finish watching the game.

"Hey, man what the fuck, that doesn't look like a vegan pizza," Justin said looking at Travis's selections.

"Red has changed my life for the better in many ways and I love it, but I can't eat that shit all the time."

Kerry snapped a picture of Travis eating the meat lover's pizza instead of the Morgan approved vegan pizza while he was distracted.

"Did you take a pic of me?" Travis asked, sensing something was wrong.

"Who me, of course not," Kerry said as he texted the pic to Justin just in case, he needed future ammo.

Justin quickly saved the photo and changed the subject,

"When was the last event you screwed up?"

The distraction worked as Travis began his story saying,

"Oh, shit let me tell you, you guys know that most of Red's family loves me but some of the older ones see me as an uncultured buffoon or something."

"You're cultured," Kerry said, seeming to defend Travis.

"But you're a buffoon," Justin said, taking the back door pass from Kerry and jumping at the opportunity to take a jab at Travis.

"Anyway, shut up fool, they had a function at a large art gallery to unveil her aunt's newest work. No problem there, I know enough about art to have a conversation."

"That's true," Justin said, agreeing with him.

"Ok, so what was the problem?"

"The problem came when we were sitting around having appetizers in front of an open bar."

"Oh," Justin said.

"Yeah, oh, while at the bar tell me why I was the only one with a damn real drink. Everyone else had wine, her Aunt Pam just looked at me with the most disgruntled look on her face. I see someone is trying to turn up, she said sarcastically, and her husband looked at me with what I thought was a gaze of disappointment until I saw him sneaking peeks at Jose. To appease Morgan I switched to wine, cool no problem but they were doing more talking and drinking."

"So, what," Justin said.

"You both know I need a few drinks to be my social butterfly type self, plus the wine had a good body to it."

"I'm sure it did," Kerry said laughing at Travis.

"I told you to text me when things like that happen and we can work on a game plan." Justin said, looking at Travis.

"Well, I forgot dammit."

"Ok, so what did you do?"

"Well, I finished the bottle of course when I heard someone ask Morgan if we planned on Ubering."

"Travis come on now you know better than that," Justin said looking angrily, "Morgan is slumming with you as it is, trust me she doesn't need any more reasons to cut your uncouthed ass off' Justin said.

"Uncouthed? Really that's how it is now?"

"Ok maybe that was too far, how about vulgar or rude demeanor, is that better?" Kerry asked.

"Yes, that is better than the shit that came out of Justin's mouth."

"Whatever, watch the game with your uncouthed ass," Justin said laughing.
As the day turned to night Travis began packing for his return flight.

"Don't take any of my shit. I will be looking through your bag before you leave."

"Trust me I can't fit any of these toddler sized clothes." Travis said.

"Damn toddler size ...really," Justin said laughing at the burned Kerry, "I'm tired as hell right now, Kerry may have to drop you off."

"I'm not getting in his clown car, again."

"You're not welcome in it anyway."

"Ok bring your ass if you're going with me," Justin said, now moving towards the door.

"Ok later, I hate you," Travis said as he and Kerry embraced before exiting on the way to the airport.

"Tell Miss Ella goodbye when you go over there," Justin said while Travis laughed.
Kerry stood in the hallway expressing his hate for them both.
The drive to the airport was largely uneventful which was perfect for both Travis and Justin.

"Hit me up if you go into any more questionable situations. Between the two of us we can make sure you don't look foolish." Justin said, pulling up to the departure drop-off.

"Okay no doubt."

They hugged and Travis made his way inside; Justin laughed as Travis held the door for some flirting Golden Girls reminding him of Miss Ella. He jumped back in his car after one last laugh eager to get home and tell Lina about his crazy night. Somehow, he had completely forgotten about the conversation he had with Lina earlier that morning.

{ 13 }

Dr. Aaron

Justin arrived home and felt the strangest chill in the air; he dismissed it as he continued to the kitchen to see if Lina made his lunch for work or if he had to take from the kids lunches again. *Sweet grilled chicken, I can fuck with that* he thought. After putting his lunch back into the fridge, he made sure everything was locked up tight before setting the alarm and heading upstairs. He made sure he skipped over the two notorious creaky steps on the way up. Justin froze as he had a flashback to what happened the night before, he quickly looked around for Triston's skateboard of death but seeing it against the wall instead of in the middle of the hallway it went a long way to settling his nerves. Heading to the bedroom he noticed one of Face's skates at the top of the stairs which was fine, the problem was that he did not see the second one. Now paranoid again he slowly crept down the hallway to-wards the bedroom, *shit that was close he thought* making it into the bedroom. After changing his clothes Justin climbed into bed and moved in close to kiss Lina goodnight. His attempt for a goodnight kiss was quickly rejected as she felt him come close to her and moved.

"Damn it's like that?" Justin asked, a little surprised that his advances were rejected.

"Yes, it's like that," Lina said as she advised him to go to sleep.

Normally Justin would take the advice, but he was confused by her anger completely forgetting about earlier,

"Who pissed in your frosted flakes?"

Lina sat up and looked at Justin,

"You pissed in my frosted flakes, honey nut cheerios, and my damn raisin bran you inconsiderate ass."

"Inconsiderate ass, wow," Justin said now sitting up trying to understand what he walked in on. I just got home, what could I have done in the 5 mins of being here?"

After Justin had ignored her warnings, Lina turned her head and simply grinned at him. She then began to unleash all her pent-up feelings from not only that day but for every day that she felt taken advantage of,

> "Yes, you just got here 5 min's ago that's true, but you were supposed to be here 12 fucking hours ago so we could go to our counseling appointment."

Oh, damn Justin thought to himself remembering waking up shirtless on the floor.

Lina continued,

> "You then proceeded to ignore all my calls and texts. How do you think that made me feel?"

Justin tried to explain but Lina cut him off,

> "I don't want to hear that I got drunk shit or whatever you were about to say. Before you left, I asked you not to drink too much right…right?"

> "Right."

Lina cut off his attempt at answering,

> "You promised me that you were going to take it easy, and you didn't, so in my book that makes you a liar." looking intensely at Justin.

> "Hold on now, you're taking things a little too far."

Justin said, taking offence to being called a liar.

> "Really, I'm taking it too far?"

She tried not to raise her voice and wake the kids,

> "You selfish bastard, I told you I really needed that damn appointment. You know I've been dealing with a lot between the kids, work, and your often non

emotional ass but I see that was not important enough for you to be here." Lina said feeling hurt.

"It wasn't like that, babe, I really wasn't trying to get drunk, it just snuck up on me." Justin said, now realizing just how bad he had hurt her.

"That was a lame excuse. First don't fucking call me babe and secondly why are you just getting home?"

"Babe I mean, Lina we had a fucking rough morning trying to solve issues that popped up and then I fell back asleep for a few hours. We got up and watched the football games."

Lina tried not to interrupt, "oh, so watching the game was more important than our marriage and trying to solve our issues?"

"That was a low blow."

"Maybe but it's fucking true."

"Ok I should have come back sooner but I was at Kerry's place not like I was out with some other woman."

Lina looked intensely at Justin,

"What in the hell did you just say? Are you justifying not cheating?"

Justin thought those words would comfort her, but he was wrong,

"No woman, that isn't what I'm saying, I'm just saying I was at Kerry's place."

"WTF? That was a stupid ass thing to say Justin," Lina said resisting the urge to hit him.

"You're right that was stupid, but what was so important that we had to go today." Justin asked, trying to shift the conversation.

"I needed to go, that was what was so important. You blew it, and me the fuck off because you don't believe in counseling."

Seeing the hurt in Lina's eyes, Justin finally realized just how bad he had fucked up,

"Listen I didn't blow it off, it's true I don't really want to go to counseling, but I told you that if you needed it then I would go. Today was a colossal fucking mistake and I do whole heartedly apologize for not being there for you. I apologize for worrying you when I didn't answer your calls or text. I really had no intention to miss the appointment."

Pulling her close, he continued, "see if you can get an appointment tomorrow and I will be there."

Moving back to her side of the bed,

"I will call them in the morning to see if they have an appointment, but your ass better be there."

Just like that there was an armistice signed and the fight was put on hold as Lina rolled over. *Damn I hope she gets an appointment* Justin thought as he laid down to get some sleep.

BEEP, BEEP, BEEP, BEEP Justin's alarm blared as he rolled over to check Lina's temperature after a restless night of sleep. As he reached between her hoard of pillows in their king-size bed it felt chilly and instantly knew that the armistice was still in place.

"Morning luv," Justin said trying for a peace offering as Lina looked him up and down before saying morning. Justin began to say damn you cannot add a good to that shit but after many years of marriage he knew just to accept the greeting he got and move on. Lina was already dressed and before she left the bedroom, she told him they had a makeup appointment at 6pm. Justin acknowledged it as she then proceeded to threaten to cut his balls off if he missed this one. Justin assured her that he would be there, Lina told him his food was in his bag and left the room. *Fuck man,* Justin thought it is too early to be threatened with castration, but he also knew that he caused this shit storm, so he just laid back in the bed and hit the snooze button. After hitting the alarm three or four more times he finally got up to get himself ready for work. He yelled out for the kids to hurry them along, but he could tell from the silence that Lina took them to school.

Realizing he was not in a rush Justin began to search through his phone for just the right music to get his day started.

"90's Hip-Hop it is," he said as he began getting ready while listening to the classic hits. Finally making it out of the house he jumped in the jeep and continued to blast the nostalgic music. He pulled into the parking structure at work just in time for Travis to text him with a question. Justin decided to call him instead of replying to the text.

"What's good man?"
 Travis began to ramble about jogging, pancakes, and mimosas.

Confused Justin asked, "dude what are you talking about?"

"Shit my bad, you know Red got me on the health kick."

"Yea I remember."

"So, check this shit out, when I got home from the airport, she woke me up after what felt like 20 mins of sleep just so we could go on a damn run. I wanted to ask her if she was fucking crazy but that's my girl, plus she looked good in those shorts. So, we ran about three miles to her brother's place."

"Ok, I'm not seeing the problem."

"I'm getting there, they were making pancakes and passing out mimosas, so you know I got one of each."

"Ok that messes up your run, but I guess it's not that bad."

"That's not the problem. The problem is that everyone had one plate and maybe a half of a mimosa."

"A half of mimosa, who does that?"

"That's what I'm saying, I want more food and at least six more mimosas," Travis said laughing.

Now understanding why Travis called Justin laughed slightly before telling him to choose either another mimosa or more pancakes but not both.

"That's some bullshit," Travis said angrily at Justin for even suggesting something so damn foolish.

"Ok good luck with that," Justin said as he walked into his accounting office.

Thankfully, he managed to hide out in his office doing budget analysis for his major clients. He was in no mood to deal with office politics today. He only went to the mandatory meetings on his calendar. As he sat in his final meeting, he couldn't get the therapist appointment off his mind. It was coming quickly like an after-school fight.

After fighting traffic, Justin walked into a sibling argument about who had the most homework. Lina gave them what Triston called the mama bear stare and the fight was over.

"Ok, let's just do our homework," Triston said as he took a seat at the table.

He has been around long enough to know what that look meant, and he also knew the consequences of ignoring it.

"Hey dad," Jasmine said before taking her seat.

"Guys, are you good?" Justin asked, waiting to see if the smoke cleared.

"Yea, they're good." Lina said as she leaned in for her forehead kiss.

He quickly took the opportunity to kiss her, just hours earlier she threatened to cut his balls off.

"Are you hungry?"

"No, I'm good."

"We have to go, so you might want to eat something," Lina said as she passed him the fruit bowl.

"OK ok, let me change and I'll grab something."

"Hurry, I don't want to be late."

Justin looked back thinking to himself about all the times that she had made them late. Instead of saying a typical smartass remark he simply said,

"Yes dear," and went to change.

By the time he made it back downstairs, Rosie, the babysitter, was already there and Lina was waiting by the door with his coat and a banana.

"Damn woman I know you don't want to be late but that's a little crazy."

"Let's go," Lina said as she walked out the door with Justin following quickly behind her.

"Do you want me to drive?"

"No, you might try to drive slowly to miss the meeting."

"Wow, really woman?"

"Yes, really man."

When they got on the highway Justin began hoping for a little traffic, not enough to cut their appointment time but just enough to mess with Lina. Unfortunately, fate had other ideas, there was hardly any traffic on the road. In fact, there were so many green lights leading to the parking garage Justin began to think that maybe even God wanted him to go to counseling. Walking into the Psychologists office Justin could not help but notice the drab dull design of the office.

"Where did you find this place?" Justin asked as he looked around with all the judgment in the world.

"Shut up fool," Lina said as she went to check them in.

Sitting down Justin was still finding things to complain about. He went from pointing out how old the magazines were to saying the chairs were uncomfortable.

"Shit, what else do you want to complain about?"

"I'm just saying, I'm not complaining," Justin said, trying to defend himself.

"I like this lady and you will too, why do you think I haven't killed you in your sleep yet?"

Justin looked surprised at Lina as he pictured her sitting in bed watching him sleep with a knife in her hand. As he tried to think of a good comeback a rather stern looking woman came out and greeted Lina. When Justin stood to speak, he could not help but think she looked like one of those nuns that popped kids with rulers.

"Hello, I am Dr. Aaron, but please call me Sofia, rrrright (rolling the r) this way" with a serious Latin accent.

She led them into a colorful room full of family pictures which made the DMV style waiting room look even duller.

While Lina and Dr. Aaron exchanged small talk, Justin looked around as he sat down still feeling very uneasy.

"Relax I'm not here to hurt you or to get all in your business, I am only here to help. Is this your first time or have you seen someone like me before?"

"I saw one before and after my deployments to ensure I was able to process things."

"Yea, Lina told me you served." Dr. Aaron said, leaning back in her chair.

"Yes. I was in the Army for over a decade," Justin said, unsure of why she leaned back.

"Wonderful, my spouse and I met while in Spain."

"Oh, you served?"

"No, my spouse was in the Air Force stationed in Spain, I was a counselor on base specializing in PTSD. I'm sure you told the counselor just enough so they would sign the forms, just as my spouse did." She could see their shared experience made Justin relax ever so slightly. He tried to answer while holding back a smile,

"Well maybe I did something like that."

"You can relax, today you will only be taking a personality test and having a small discussion. Since Lina has already done hers, I will talk to her while you take your assessment."

"Ok I think I can handle that," Justin said as he got up to follow the Dr. to the other room.

"Answer every question and yes I know some of them repeat. Let me know if you need anything. Lina and I will discuss her results until you're done."

Justin began to take the test when a trend became apparent, when given the choice he selected more independent answers over group ones, he also chose more statistical answers over emotional ones. Justin had taken personality tests in the past, but he was impressed by just how in-depth the questions were. As he was testing, Dr. Aaron and Lina decided to wait so they could all discuss their results together. Instead, they discussed the challenges with raising kids in this overexposed world. Justin knocked on the door when he was done.

"Come on in and have a seat beside your wife."
Justin took his seat beside Lina as instructed eager to see their results.

"Ok I'll start with your wife, are you ready Lina?"

"I'm a little nervous but I'm ready."

"My dear you are an ESFP (Extraverted, Sensing, Feeling, and Perceiving) person who loves people, telling stories, and having fun. I don't think you have ever met a stranger."

"Wow, that is me," Lina said, reading over the results. Dr. Aaron went on to explain that Lina's feelings are deep, and they give her life meaning, so when they are brushed aside it hurts deeply.

"Yes, yes I could never explain it to Justin before but that makes so much sense."

"I can see all of that, everyone loves them some Lina. Friends, family, and strangers." Justin said, holding his wife's hand.

Turning her attention to Jusitn,

"How do you think you did?"

"I'm really not sure but I answered them all."

"Ok that's fair, let's see the results."

Justin said, "this feels like an episode of Maury."

Dr. Aaron grinned,

"Justin, you my friend are INTJ (Introverted, Intuitive, Thinking, and Judging). This means you focus more on logic; you're slow to make friends but when you do that bond is unbreakable, you speak in matters of fact, and you have a hard time expressing the inner parts of feelings and love."

"Oh, wow, you can tell that from a few answers on a test?" Lina asked.

"Well yes that and how reserved he was when you came into the office. You both have two completely different profiles and needs but at least now we know where to start."

"People think they need to be with someone that feels and or acts the same way they do but you guys are a good mix and after you learn how to communicate properly, the sky will be the limit. Lina, like we spoke of, you are the entertainer meaning you are very friendly and Justin you are the thinker meaning you are analytical in nature which makes you somewhat less approachable. Both of you are relatively easy going and open to new things which is good for building a strong foundation."

The conversation went on, Dr. Aaron explained how most of the conflicts that were being discussed could be helped by understanding the way they each communicated. Dr. Aaron told Justin he needed to be more sensitive to Lina's feelings while acknowledging it might be difficult, but he needed to work on being more open.

Justin agreed,

"Sometimes I don't always think about her feelings, but I will work on it."

"Good, I like that."

She turned to Lina,

"Mam, you need to give Justin space while you gather thoughts so you aren't overly confrontational which will have a negative result for you both."

"I know there are times where I box him into a corner, and I know I can do better."

"Now understand I'm not saying hide your emotions, I'm saying work with them, so you can express yourself the way you want and to. I'll say after sitting in here with you two for less than an hour I can tell you have built a good foundation and you both seem willing to adapt."

"Thanks."

"So, Justin, was this as gut-wrenching as you thought it would be?" Dr. Aaron asked.

"Why yes…yes it was," Justin said before admitting that he was pleased with how the conversation went. Before leaving and at Justin's request Lina set up biweekly appointments, Lina hugged Dr. Aaron but Justin, still a little standoffish, simply shook her hand.

{ 14 }

New Beginnings

It was an interesting car ride home; they both felt like a weight had been lifted off their shoulders. Over the next few sessions, the conversations with Dr. Aaron got deeper and deeper, Justin told them how inadequate he felt at times. The reveal both surprised and hurt Lina who was visibly shaken. Justin found expressing his feelings normally unsettling and being this vulnerable was extremely unnerving for him. He continued to go, however, for the sake of his kids and his love but mainly for himself. Going to the sessions with Dr. Aaron began to show Justin that he needed a new beginning not only for himself but also for his family. Justin and Lina still had arguments like most couples do but through the sessions with Dr. Aaron they could now see each other's point which made huge differences in the severity of the arguments. Thanks to the guidance of Dr. Aaron their issues started not to boil over as they had done in years past. Justin began solo sessions in efforts to remove the dark passenger from his life. He wanted to prevent passing on the generational curse to his son like his dad did to him. Justin told Dr. Aaron of his childhood torment explaining that his mother was a domestic violence survivor. With her help Justin realized his anger came from PTSD but his need to save people came from not being able to save his mother. His sessions with Dr. Aaron were extremely difficult but the appreciation shown by Lina to his efforts made him continue to push. Lina also took sessions without Justin where they talked about her striving for her goals outside of the household. Their combined efforts helped Lina begin to lower her protective walls, the couple became more affectionate outside of the bedroom which grossed out their kids, but it was bringing them closer.

They reestablished their long-forgotten date nights where at least one night every two weeks was their time. They could do anything or nothing, as long as they were together with no friends or children tagging along. The couple's (old) new tradition of going out started with the much-anticipated Jidenna concert downtown. Lina was an old fan of his genre of music, but Justin was a new lover of the artist and genre. He listened to the songs Lina played as if they were "new" making comments,

"Damn that's the shit, when did that come out?"
Lina laughed them off,

"Some of them have been out longer than we have
been married."

"Oh, damn you should have been playing more of
these." Justin said, turning the music up as the two
got ready for the concert.
"I have been playing some of them for years, you just started
listening."
Justin nodded his agreement,

"You may have a point but better late than never I
guess."
Justin watched as his lovely wife swayed her hips to the music
in her bra and panties.

"Keep moving like that and Jidenna will have to
wait," Justin said, smiling from the bathroom.

"Oh, don't worry I'll be in a swaying mode when we
get back," Lina said as she put some extra sway in her
movements.

"Woman you better stop but I like it," Justin said as
he began to shave.
Lina went into the bathroom trying to hear what Justin said
but she saw her husband swaying to the music as he cut his
hair instead. Seeing her husband enjoying the moment always

did something to her; she went over and slapped a surprised Justin on the ass.

Justin jumped back saying, "keep your hands off my ass woman."
Lina, now walking away, looked back as she swayed her hips out the bathroom.

Justin got dressed in the most neo-soul outfit he could, down to the wooden bracelets and Lina did the same. They came downstairs to the cheering from Rosie and Triston. Jasmine was making kissing sounds as Lina gave Justin a peck on the cheek for helping her with her jacket.

Rosie asked, "what was on the agenda for tonight?"
"First we are going to this swanky new restaurant and then we are going to see that new artist Jidenna."
"New Artist?" Rosie said looking confused.
"You have to excuse him; he just learned about Jidenna."
"Whatever, that's what we have planned."
They each took turns saying their goodbyes to the kids and issuing parental threats/guidance.
Justin held the door of the freshly waxed jeep for his lovely wife. He gave her a little tap on the butt which made her blush. Justin tried to blow the speakers in his Jeep listening to his new favorite artists. Lina attempted to judge him, but she

found herself singing as well. Traffic was light and they made it to the restaurant rather quickly. When they entered the up-scale restaurant, the decor made them feel extremely under-dressed from the hardwood floors to the fine art on the wall. A waiter in a 3-piece suit sat them in a wonderful corner booth. After looking at the menu in French with English sub-titles, Justin wanted to grab Lina's hand and run out, but she looked so happy. So, he looked at the menu to find some-thing edible. Unbeknownst to Justin, Lina was wanting to run out as well, but she didn't want to upset Justin since he chose the restaurant. Looking at the menu they, both fought the urge to upset the other. As the waiter began to introduce the specials Lina could not take it any longer,

"I'm sorry babe but I'm not in the mood for any of this food."

Justin quickly slammed down a tip for the waiter's trouble be-fore grabbing Lina's hand and running out the door.

Laughing as they left the restaurant, Justin and Lina walked to the concert discussing the menu and the elegantly dressed waiter. Making it to the concert venue Justin stood looking on in amazement at how the crowd wrapped around the building. Knowing Justin hated long lines, Lina said come on babe let's get this party started. They began the long walk to the end of the line much to the chagrin of Justin. Now at the end of the line Justin stood there trying not to be annoyed. Lina on the other hand began to talk to the people around her. *She could make friends anywhere,* Justin thought as he looked on. After 5 minutes seemed like forever to Justin, he was unable to wait in line any damn longer.

He turned to Lina, "Babe, I'm going to see what I can do about moving us up."

No other words were needed; Lina knew just what her impatient husband was going to do. He began his long walk to the front thinking to himself that he could not, no, he would not stand in that long ass line. He finally made his way to the front as he noticed a few guys being douchebags to the women checking ids, seeing this he found his way in. The women, clearly annoyed, called for assistance from a bouncer. Justin seized his chance and intervened, shaming the them out of the line. His natural demeanor ensured that they would not question him. When the bouncers arrived, Justin was being thanked for acting. This resulted in him being offered admittance ahead of the line, Justin called Lina who he was sure was talking to her new friends about playdates for the kids and for him and their significant others.

"Babe meet me in the front, I got us in."

Lina said her goodbyes as she started her walk, after all she had no doubt Justin would find a way to get them in.

The venue was a super cute club, but it was sort of empty because it was still early. Lina went to the bar to grab drinks for the couple as Justin did a lap to find the perfect location for their viewing pleasure with limited interference from the crowd. Finding his spot, he went to get Lina before it was taken. Lina handed Justin his Henny and Red bull and asked if he wanted to go upstairs. Justin looked around,

"Yes," surprised that he had missed the upstairs option.

Justin and Lina made their way to the stairs where there was yet another line, thankfully this was much shorter. After paying for the VIP, Justin and Lina sought out to find a perfect new spot. This time it was easier as much of the setting was unclaimed. The crowd started to grow as the first acts began to go on. The music was fantastic, the crowd was lively, and Lina, being true to form, made friends with the muscle-bound couple (Jacky and Brock) next to them. Justin thought the husband looked out of place at the concert, he assumed he would have been more comfortable in the gym listening to death metal instead. That was until he began to sing along with the opening acts, being so new to the genre Justin had no idea who the acts were. Jidenna hit the stage with a bang singing and jumping around hyped by the crowd. His energy excited everyone, even Justin and his new friend Brock. The two began to sing Jidenna's songs as if they were a duet. After his duet and between his third or fourth drink, Justin began to look around the crowd and what he saw annoyed him. He noticed that more than a few people were using their phones to film Jidenna (who was now in the middle of the crowd passing the mic around) instead of being in the moment. Justin decided not to let their foolishness ruin his time which Jidenna himself made easier when he began singing *Chief Don't Run* (Justin's new favorite song).

Brock brought another round of drinks just as Jidenna took a seat on stage to remove his shoes.

He stood up flexing his toes, "That's more like it." Now feeling better, he jumped and kicked in the air before starting to perform his hit song *Bambi* to the joy of everyone. This was one of Lina's favorite songs, so she began to *sang* at the top of her lungs just as Justin had done moments before her. The major difference this time however was that Lina had skills in the singing department. Lina and Justin danced and *sang* at the top of their lungs while Jidenna did his second and third curtain calls. With the night now officially over Lina and Jacky exchanged numbers as they parted ways. On the way back to the parking garage, a delightful smell lofted through the cool night's air.

"Fuck I'm hungry, I forgot we didn't eat," Justin said as he closed his eyes and took a deep breath.

Fortunately, the smell was coming from the pizza place across the street from the garage. Justin looked ahead and saw a large group of partygoers waiting at the lights to cross the street. He looked at Lina,

"We need to cross here, or we will be behind that group."

"Shitting me," Lina said as she grabbed Justin's hand and began to quickly J-walk in the middle of the street.

Her hasty move allowed the famished couple to reach the restaurant just ahead of the partygoers. The combination of fresh bread and hunger urged the couple to order an XL pizza for just the two of them. They sat in a booth near the kitchen, which was perfect for Justin. He could not only continue to experience the pleasant aroma of fresh bread, but he could also see when their pizza was ready. As the couple discussed their enjoyment of the concert and just how wrong Justin was about Brock an enormous pizza was presented to them.

"Damn I'm hungry but not that hungry," Justin said with his eyes wide open.
He closed his eyes after the first bit of the pizza and began humming. Lina looked on in astonishment,

"Babe stop; people are looking at you."

"I don't care; this shit is fire."
Now looking around to see if Lina was right, Justin noticed a
table glaring at him and shaking their heads at his actions.
Unfazed he repeated the act of humming during his next bite
trying to annoy them even more.

"You're a fool," Lina said, noticing him doing it on
purpose.

"You know me, but the pizza is that good."
Lina nodded her head in agreement with a mouth full of
pizza. Now stuffed Lina loaded the remaining slices in the
box while Justin went to pay the bill. Lina noticed a group of
young women blatantly staring at Justin. Being the person she
is, she leaned over as she passed the group,

"Damn, ain't he sexy."
She approached Justin smiling and slapped him on the ass.
He quickly turned as he had done hours before but the smile
on Lina's face relaxed him instantly.

"Let's go home crazy," Justin said as they made their
way back to the garage.
On their way out of the city, Lina opened the sunroof as she
rubbed Justin's leg. In turn he started to run his fingers
through her hair which made Lina lay back and enjoy his
touch. Making it home, Lina waved at Rosie as she ran to the
bathroom. Justin paid Rosie with both money and the remaining slices of pizza. After locking the house and checking

on the kids, Justin came into the room humming *Bambi,* when he noticed his beautiful nude wife walking towards him. She laid him down while humming *The Let Out,* as the two brought a great end to a remarkable date night.

In the morning like the weekends previous, Jasmine came running into their room wearing her soccer uniform ready for action. Lina was awake already and she interrupted Jasmine before she could jump on Justin,

"Morning love, are you ready for the game?"

Jasmine answered her loudly saying, "yes Mom, it's going down (a phrase she heard from her dad)."

"Ok babe don't wake your dad," Lina said as she started to braid Jasmine's hair.

"Too late," Justin said, sitting up slowly.
He started to get out of bed before realizing that his clothes were still on the floor.

"Hey honey, can you get the brush from your bathroom?"
This gave Justin just enough time to run to their bathroom before Jasmine returned with the brush.

"Thanks love," Lina said laughing at the idea of the streaking Justin.

"Mom I'm sad," Jasmine said looking at her mom through the Mirror.

"Why what's wrong, why are you sad? Lina asked,
As Jasmine began to answer, Triston came in looking rather
disgruntled.

"What did you guys want me to do again?" he asked
in an irritated tone.
Lina looked at him and simply smiled. Justin walked out of
the bathroom to Lina saying,

"If you don't fix your attitude and your tone, I'll
throw your little ass out that window. I have told you
way too many times to move that damn skateboard."
Triston quickly fixed his tone while asking the question for a
second time as he tried to stay out of his mother's reach.

"We told you to clean the cars inside and out, rake the
leaves, and cut the grass." Lina said, trying to burn a
hole into his forehead with her eyes.
Justin chimed, "do it correctly or there will be issues."
"Yes Dad," Triston said a little snarky as he walked
out.

"You better get your son," Lina said looking at Justin.
"That's your son," Justin said in response.
"Anyway, sorry babe, why are you sad again?" Lina
asked, turning her attention back to Jasmine.
"I have a game today; I would like for you to go but
dad said you're banned."
Lina looked at Justin as she answered Jasmine,

"Honey I AM NOT banned; I'd go to the practices, but I just think this is a good time for you to spend with your dad."

"Ok mom but you did scare everybody last time." Jasmine said as she rushed off to finish getting ready.

"Fool, why would you tell her I was banned?" Lina asked, throwing a brush at the laughing Justin.

"Babe, you know you are banned," Justin said now on the floor laughing. "You heckled the shit out of DJ!"

"He was making bad calls left and right."

"He's a teenage ref in a beginner soccer league." He continued, "just admit it babe you have a problem, you get extremely too competitive watching the kids play sports."

"I don't think I get that bad," Lina said, shrugging her shoulders.

"Really?.... really?" Justin asked, pausing in mid step looking at her.

"Did you forget about what happened with Triston's softball coach?" Justin asked, looking at Lina with his head tilted.

Lina stood there for a second before she started to answer, Justin cut her off,

"You made a grown man cry with your heckling."

"Why are you bringing up old stuff?" Lina asked, remembering her verbal assault on the coach.

"Besides, he was not coaching to win, so I humbly asked him if his wife got his balls in the divorce," Lina said, not seeing a problem with her question.

"Ok babe, you're banned so just relax and make sure Triston does his chores," Justin said, kissing her on the forehead.

"He better do them right or Jasmine will be an only child, this is my morning to relax," Lina said looking at the sun peeking out of the clouds.

Justin walked downstairs, "let's go Face, get your stuff."

As he passed by Triston, Justin advised him to do everything right reminding him that he was already on thin ice.

{ 15 }

Needed Vacation

Lina relaxed in the backyard laying on her special beach chair enjoying the sun's rays on a beautiful Saturday. The lawn was freshly cut thanks to Triston getting in trouble. She was enjoying the peace and quiet of the Saturday morning while Justin was being soccer dad/coach. The relaxation put Lina in such a good mood she gave Triston a pardon so he could hangout with his friends. To tell the truth they both needed a break from each other, Triston was banned from video games, skateboard, and his phone which meant he was moping around the house, just being a joy to be around. As she was drifting off for her second or third nap Jasmine came running in the backyard covered in mud which startled Lina.

"Wow babe you're a mess," Lina said, stopping Jasmine from jumping on her.

"I know mom it's great," Jasmine responded as they both looked down at the mud drying on her legs.

"What happened babe?"

"Oh! Mom it was a puddle as big as a lake in the middle of the field."

Justin came into the backyard,

"Yes, a damn lake in the middle of the field. Those kids would not stop kicking the ball in the water, which you know is some bull.

Realizing Justin took his new Jeep, Lina asked,

"How is your mistress doing?"

Justin responded proudly,

"She is still beautiful; Face and the twins sat on the rubber mat in the cargo area on."

"In the damn trunk," Lina asked as she tilted her head looking at Justin.

Jasmine yelled, "mom it was great back there!"

She followed that up by asking if she could go to the twin's house, it was just enough to sway the conversation.

"Yes babe, just go take a good shower and put that uniform in the laundry room."

"Ok thanks Mom you're the greatest!" Jasmine screamed as she ran inside followed quickly by Justin as he simply blew a kiss at the smirking Lina.

She shook her head at him and laid back down to get back to finishing her nap, Lina was not about to waste the beautiful rays. Justin and Lina were in a much better place after starting counseling, it was helping to get their thoughts out in a safe space. Justin still felt uneasy about it, but he could see the balance it was bringing to their lives, so he continued to go even after the cold war was over. As Lina slept in the backyard Justin took a shower and got ready to drop Jasmine off at the twin's house. Jasmine came into the room with a brush in her hand.

"What's up Face?" Justin said, looking at her curly hair all over the place.

"I need my hair done and mom's asleep."

"Oh wow," Justin said looking at the task in front of him.

Justin was the guy who took Jasmine's hair out, not the one who did her hair. *Lina and her nap were messing up their system,* Justin knew he had to try something. *Hell, Lina would chew me out for taking her to hang out with wild hair.*

"Ok come here," Justin said as he took the brush and began trying to fake it.

How hard could it be, he had watched Lina do it every morning, *I got this.* After a few minutes it was clear that Justin did not have it, he looked at the massive amounts of products Lina had and grabbed a squirt bottle. Justin squirted Jasmine's hair and began to brush it down. After a few more minutes of struggling by Justin, the war with Jasmine's hair ended in a stalemate.

He tried to encourage her, "It looks good."
Jasmine disagreed but applauded the effort at least,

"It looks ok dad plus I'm just going to see Sam and Dean."
Justin felt the shade coming from his baby girl as she went downstairs. He cut his losses and dropped Jasmine off at the twin's house,

"Be good babe," Justin said as he watched her until she got inside.
He pulled off quickly when Paul looked like he wanted to talk.

When Justin arrived home, he went to see if Lina was still sleeping, she was awake and video chatting with Morgan. As he spoke to Morgan Justin tried to steal a plum from Lina's plate but was caught in the act.

"Stop fool, I washed these, get your own."

"I didn't think you would see me."

"You ass," Morgan said.

"Yes, you're an ass," Lina said in agreement.

"Wow that was a little hurtful."

"Hurtful but true," Morgan said with Lina agreeing again.

"Damn I'm outnumbered!" Justin started yelling for Travis.

"What's good, man?" Travis asked, coming into view.

"Man, your soon to be wife is getting out of pocket right now."

"I know, man she has been on one since their family reunion."

"Oh, you had to go there," Morgan said as she gave Travis a dirty look.

"What? I did nothing wrong."

Which Lina quickly called, "Bullshit."

"Damn, you too Lina?"

"Yes, she knows your ass."

"I got you bro," Justin said, taking up for his friend.

"Shut up fool, what did the other fool do?" Lina asked, looking into the tablet.

"Fool?" Travis asked right before being cut off by both Lina and Morgan.

"Ok, do you remember me telling you of our family reunion coming up?"

"Yes, I remember that you were excited for the re-maining family members to meet Travis."

"Yes, I was but that turned out to be a bad idea," Morgan said.

Tavis intervened, but Lina cut him off,

"Be quiet, you can speak when Morgan says you can."

"Let me tell you about this wonderful man of mine, first of all he showed up fully dressed in all white khaki shorts, a sky-blue polo, and some damn all white Cortez's after I told him we were going to the park early to set up, right."

"I call bullshit, she never told me I was setting up. I don't do manual labor unless I have to."

Justin laughed as Morgan swung at Travis.

"Whatever I told him."

"I know you did."

"He felt some type of way when I asked if he had extra clothes in the car because I know he was not trying to get his Sunday best dirty."

"Ha! Sunday best that shits funny," Justin said.

"Damn, really?"

"My bad you're right."

"Anyway, after waiting for him to change, we finally got to the park and after introducing him to a few cousins, we started moving chairs. Girl, tell me why this big ol' dude was taking one chair at a time."

"Really one chair?! Travis, are those muscles for show?" Lina asked.

"I didn't know I needed to prove anything; besides I'm better at supervising."

Lina and Morgan just looked at Travis as Justin laughed.

"Seeing that he was going to be useless at helping setup, I asked him to go pick up the chicken from the store."

"How did you screw up getting the chicken?" Justin asked.

"No man, I picked that shit up cool smooth."

"Whatever, yes he picked the chicken up but that's about it. He sat it on the table and took a seat with my great uncles like he was tired or something."

"Hell, it was hot I needed a break."

"Then I told him the grill was ready and damn if he didn't look at me like I was crazy. He had forgotten that he told me that he was a beast on the grill, his words."

Justin interrupted, "dude you aren't a grill master, I have never seen you on a damn grill."

"I know man I don't know where she got the idea that I could from."

"She got it from you."

"Exactly but to his credit he tried. Tried."

"Wow Red, I was doing good until your uncles came and tried to take over. They made me screw the ribs up and burn some burgers."

"Dude, I can't imagine you on a grill."

"I know right, I'm the guy that makes the drinks or sets the music."

"Oh, I forgot the worst part, the love of my life ate a piece of chicken before giving me the box."

"What?" Lina said, now sitting up in her chair.

"You heard me."

"I didn't, I told you they shorted us one, besides who counts chicken?"

"That's a good question," Justin said, agreeing with his friend.

"I didn't count the chicken; my aunt ordered 100 pieces. We started putting 2 pieces per plate to make it easier for the family to grab and go."

"Makes sense."

"Thank you, when I got to the last plate all that was left was one chicken leg."

"Well, you must have ordered 99 pieces," Travis said, defending himself.

"Why would anybody order 99 pieces?" Lina asked, smirking at Travis.

"A freak, hell you know them people better than me."

"I'm going to kick your ass. For the rest of the dang reunion this lying ass had people believing that someone at the store shorted us."

"That's what happened, and I stand by it."

"Whatever but other than blackened burgers everything else was good," Morgan said rubbing Travis's leg.

"It's called Cajun besides the chicken leg wasn't that good," Travis said finally admitting to eating the chicken.

"I knew it."

"Ok do you two fools need anything else, we were having a conversation," Lina said trying to get rid of the fellas.

"What don't you want us to hear?" Travis asked while holding his fist up.

"Nobody is worried about your ashy fist; we're going over wedding details."

"I thought we were done with wedding stuff?" Travis said, looking defeated.

"You guys picked the tuxes you wanted, so your part is done but the work continues."

"We can do more than pick out tuxedos," Travis said with Justin cosigning in the background.

"Really? You big kids were acting up in the damn store."

"Whhhaattt? Who told you that?" Travis asked, looking surprised.

"Don't worry about who told me, just know that we know."

"Wait, what?" Lina asked.

"Oh, I guess he forgot to tell you, but our lovely spouses and their jackass friend were fighting with pillows, bowties, and other crap."

"Really Justin?"

"It wasn't that bad," Justin said.

"I don't know where you're getting your info from, but they are truly mistaken." Travis said.

"He was very sure and specific."

"He?"

"He or she," Morgan said, trying to protect her source.

"No, you said he. Damn aw, aw, shit what was his name?" Justin asked trying to remember it.

"It was Royce, trust me woman you can't listen to him. Besides, he was rude." Travis said.

"How was he rude?"

"Well at some point he was and plus he didn't like my tuxedo," Travis said.

"Whatever man, you two are dismissed. Sometimes I don't know what to do with him."

"Well, hell, I have been married longer, and I still have no idea what to do with Travis's counterpart. Justin loves to remind me that I said yes and after so much time together I shouldn't be surprised at anything anymore."

"In their defense what Royce said did sound kinda funny, but I will never tell them that," Morgan said.

"Of course not, girl, they can never know."

"Oh, dude did I tell you I got robbed last weekend?" Travis asked as Justin jumped back into the camera's view.

"What the Fuck?" Justin asked, trying to get more information.

Seeing the look on Justin's face Travis quickly clarified his statement,

"No, not like that dumbass, I was talking about a party Red, and I went to."

"Here we go with this again, can't you call him on your phone."

"Yes, here we go, I was robbed, and the world will know."

"Man, I thought I was going to have to get on the road."

"Come on now, you know I would have told you something like that before now."

"True, my bad."

"Red's brother Joseph is in a motorcycle club, and they hosted their annual formal dress party. I'm like cool, I can clean up pretty well when I need to. First off, Red laid out this banging ass black dress which made me go shopping and you know I hate shopping, but I was not going to stand next to her looking busted."

"Shit I understand Lina does that to me all the time, when we're going somewhere casual and she steps out looking like a whole damn meal instead of a snack."

"So, you get it, I had to rush to the mall and grab an outfit like we used to do back in our clubbing days. I grabbed this bomb ass gray suit with black accessories; shit I was killing the game. I almost bought a kango or a derbie, but I didn't want to go overboard."

"It's good to be humble," Justin said as Travis agreed much to the chagrin of Lina and Morgan.

"The night of the party, Red puts on this fire red lipstick that popped."

"Oh, was that the color you showed me?" Lina asked, cutting Travis off.

"Yes, and it came out great, that was the pic I posted."

"Oh, yea I remember that was a good color on you."

"Ok are you two done?"

"This was our video call before you two butted in."

"Anyway, I grabbed my red tie so we would pop together, and that shit worked. We walked into the party and people didn't know what to do with the amount of sexiness that was in front of them. Come to find out that they were handing out trophies for the best dressed man and woman, best makeup, and a few others. As I looked around, I knew I was a shoe in for best dressed and Red was probably going to win as well."

"Probably win," Morgan said, swinging at Travis.

"It pissed me off that most of the guys were still in jeans, maybe they didn't know what formal meant. Either way I was clean, and the trophy was mine. It was a cool party, the music, the vibe, and even the food was good. Going into it I didn't know what to expect but I was pleasantly surprised. As Red and I were grooving the music stopped as her brother gave a toast and started to call winners for prizes. They handed out a few prizes but nothing that I cared about, then it was best dressed man time. I humbly started making my way to the front when they called some damn old man's name next to me. Needless to say, I was shocked and appalled."

"Damn you lost to an old man," Justin said, cracking up.

"I hate you; he was one of the chapter founders or some bullshit like that. I got robbed."
Lina cut into Travis's complaining asked off and asked if Morgan won anything.

"Yea, I won best makeup and got a giant trophy."

"That's awesome," Lina said while Travis sat back stewing a little.

"Thanks, I was very surprised because I just had a little foundation on."

"It was that fiery red lipstick."

"Thanks, I think it was too."

"Did you try to appeal your loss?" Justin asked as he laughed at Travis.

"I was trying to, but I had to hold Red's trophy while she got multiple free shots from the women's chapter of the motorcycle club."

"So, you held her purse as she got drunk."

"Shut up it was not like that."

"Stop it, Travis looked great in his suit, and he only held the trophy, and I left my purse in the car," Morgan said trying to make it better, but it made them all laugh instead.

"Oh, wow you too Red?" Travis asked as he leaned away from her.

"I wasn't trying to be funny babe; I was just telling them."

"Whatever, I had to carry her drunk tail to the car."

"Come on now, that was funny, and you know it." Justin said.

"That might be true but still," Travis said as he laughed.

After having their fill of the conversation and Lina's food, Justin and Travis made their exit with the help of Lina and Morgan.

"Now that they are gone, are you guys ready for Aunt Gerti and Uncle Pete's vow renewal and more importantly the beach?"

"Oh yes, thank you for inviting us. I can't wait to drop these kids off, I'll miss them, but momma needs a break."

"Of course, we have to stick together, besides with his friends here Travis should leave me alone so I can relax."

"Oh, I know, can you imagine how peaceful a week on the beach would be without them?"

"Yes, I can, and it would be great," Morgan said as she took a sip of her drink.

"Do you guys have anything planned for the girl's day with Aunt Gerti?"

"The other women have not said much but I'm looking at the resort, and they have a wonderful looking spa."

"Oooohhh a spa sounds nice."

"I know right, just think about a whole day at a wellness spa."

"A whole day at the spa sounds simply amazing and I will be the first to sign my name up for all activities."

"Girl I will be right behind you, let the guys ride up and down the island. I will take rest and relaxation any day."

"I totally agree, Justin will not shut up about the excursions and I'm like whatever dude just don't block the sun as I lay out."

"I told Travis the same thing, I'm going to watch a renewal of love but I'm also going to de-stress."

Morgan understands that when they return the stress of their wedding will take over.

"Girl, "I plan on laying on the beach with a large drink that has an umbrella in it."

"Don't worry I'll be there to keep you company, but I plan on having a few empty coconut drinks next me...lol."

"Either way, large drinks or empty coconuts, it all sounds like fun to me."

"Ok let me go, Justin is tearing up the house looking for something with his simple self."

"I understand, I hear Travis banging around in there also. I swear you can't leave them alone for a minute, sometimes I think he is worse than having a kid. Girl, this vacation cannot come soon enough." Morgan said as the two got off the phone to see what their big kids were breaking inside.

{ 16 }

Violation

With baseball season quickly approaching, Justin and Triston played catch in the backyard while Jasmine drew with chalk on the deck. Lina called down for Jasmine to get ready so they could go shopping.

"Yes Mom," she responded, putting up the chalk sticks.

On the way inside she heard Kerry yelling,

"Open up the doe, open up the doe!" as he rang the doorbell.

Jasmine ran to answer the door; she loved her crazy Uncle Kerry. She jumped into his arms,

"Wow, you need to stop growing or we're going to be the same height soon."

Jasmine led him to the backyard before running upstairs to get changed. Kerry threw a fake jab at Triston which made him flinch.

"Got you."

"Barely," Triston rebutted on his way in the house.

"What's up man? You said you needed to talk," Justin said, greeting his friend.

"Yeah, I got something heavy on my mind right now."

"Somebody pregnant?"

"No fool, nothing like that!"

"Oh, then what's up?"

"I'm thinking of applying for an open principal position in Texas."

"Oh wow, that's big."

"Yeah, I know but I'm not feeling the love from my school anymore."

"So, what's making you hesitate about applying?

"Well, I'll lose that one-on-one time with the kids and even worse I'll be stuck with more parents. You know how I feel about some of these parents."

"Oh yeah I didn't think about that, but I think you should at least apply. You could establish the type of change you've been wanting to for years."

"This is true."

As the two talked in the backyard Justin received a phone call from Travis.

"What up Folk? You're on speakerphone, Kerry is here talkin about a possible Big Move."

"What's up?" Travis asked, sounding bothered.

"You good man?"

"Yeah, I'm good. It's just hell, I can't even say it." Travis said.

"Hey man, we're here, what's up?" Justin asked.

"I had my physical today, at this Wellness Center that Red goes to. They had me run for 5 mins, do some push-ups, and hell they even gave me an EKG.

"Ok, what's wrong?" Justin asked.

"Nothing, even though I didn't do as much as I wanted, I did pretty well. Shit, my blood pressure was normal for the first time in years."

"Sounds like Red's routine is working for you," Kerry said.

"Yea, it is but don't tell her."

He began to explain why he called when Morgan came into his man cave,

"Babe, are you still on this?"

"Yes, yes I am."

Now truly confused Justin and Kerry pressed Travis for answers. Before he could speak up Morgan interjected,

"His family has a history of prostate cancer, so he had to have a screening today."

After the big reveal there was silence on the line. Morgan broke the silence,

"I love him, and I truly understand but can you believe he's being so dramatic?"
Her question was quickly answered when both men asked Travis if he was okay.

"What?"

"Yea, I'm good," Travis said.

"I'm sorry bro."
Morgan, believing she still had at least one ally left, asked Kerry what he thought.

"What do I think? What do I think? I want that freaky doctor stripped of his license!"

"You can't be serious; you're some of the quote-unquote manliest men I know. You must be joking, right? You're telling me there isn't one joke between you? Hell, I've seen you three laugh at funerals."

"Nothing is funny," Justin said with both Kerry and Travis agreeing.

"I can't, with you guys right now, tell Lina I'm going to call her later," Morgan said storming out of the man cave.

"Dude how did it happen? I didn't think you were old enough," Justin asked, now worried about his next physical.

"Man, I don't know, I filled out some forms about my family's medical history. My Grandad and Uncle both had prostate cancer like Red said. After the running and the push-ups, I had to meet with a doc to go over the results. No problem there, he came in talkin normal doctor stuff about checking me for a hernia."

"No big deal, turn and cough," Justin said.

"I know I have done a number of those but before he stepped out, he said yeah, when I get back, we will check your prostate and get you out of here." Travis said.

"He said it before walking out?"

"Yeah, I sat there praying I heard it wrong." Travis said.

Travis knew he had a prostate exam coming when he got older, but he was not prepared for it today. The doctor came back into the exam room asking a few more questions but honestly, Travis had no idea what they talked about. He checked for hernia and told Travis to turn around and bend over.

"Shit, just like that?" Justin asked.

"Yes, just like that, I said turn around?! and he said yes, turn around. I felt like his voice got deeper but it might have been the fear. I turned slow as hell like I was about to get a whooping or something. All I could hear was him getting KY type shit."

"Oh hell," Kerry said.

"I think I blacked out for a minute; all I can remember is him saying your prostate looks good. Then he tossed a tissue box on the table and told me to clean myself up. He was gone before I turned around."

"Damn like a $2 hoe," Justin said.

"Wow, I don't know what to say."

"I told Red, and she was sympathetic, but it didn't help."

"She sounded heartless just now," Kerry said.
The phone was silent again before Travis spoke,

"I'll holla at y'all later, I'm about to go have a shot and a long shower."

"I understand," Kerry said.

"Be easy man," Justin said, hanging up the phone.

They each sat in silence hoping that their next physical was nothing like the dread Travis went through. Jasmine broke the horror of their imaginations when she came out to tell them goodbye.

"See you later," Kerry said, thankful for the distraction.

"Have fun Face."

Lina came out,

"I'm going to grab some sundresses and maybe a bathing suit or two if you need anything."

"No, I'm good."

"You don't need any new trunks or sandals," Lina asked, trying to remember the last time she saw him in trunks.

"My trunks are still good, and I still have my old sandals."

"Do you mean those grayish sandals that used to be black?" Lina asked, turning up her nose.

"Yes those, they feel good."

"Oh no, I will be getting you some new ones today."

"Please do," Kerry said making a face.

"Fine, please grab me some sandals."

"Ok, bye babe, we'll be back soon."

Justin kissed her on the forehead and her and Jasmine were off.

"Really man, those sandals sound hideous."

Before Justin could answer, Lina stuck her head out the door,

"I'm getting you trunks and I want to see you in the clothes you plan on packing when I get back."

By the time Justin thought of a good response Lina was already gone.

"Damn, she's gone."

"All right, man I'm out, Lina makes me think I need
to get another outfit or two

After walking his friend out, Justin decided not to return to
the patio. He instead decided to go upstairs and look at his
disputed sandals.

Justin pulled out his grayish used to be black sandals not seeing a problem, *they just need a little TLC.* Triston happened to
be walking by with the trash,

"Dad, do you want me to throw them away?"

"No, there's nothing wrong with these," Justin boldly
responded.

"Ok Dad."

Justin stood looking in the mirror, unable to understand why
his family hated his sandals so much. With his confidence
now shaking, Justin decided to pull out his trunks to see if
they were as bad as Lina said. He tried them on, *not bad at all.*
He decided to call Triston in the room to get his opinion.

"Coming."

Justin stood in the middle of his bedroom with his arms up.
He began to twirl as Triston came into the room.

"Now be honest, what do you think?" Justin asked a
confused looking Triston.

"Truth?" Triston asked.

"Of course."

"Well...well, you kind of look like Grandpa," Triston said looking at the now defeated Justin.

I look like Grandpa; Justin ran to the bathroom mirror.

"Sorry, Dad."

"No need to be sorry, I asked for the truth."

He knew this would be the last time he would be wearing those shorts. It was not that Justin's dad had horrible taste in clothes, it was just he never bought anything. If it were not for the gifts from his grandkids, Justin's dad would not have any clothes from this decade. As a young man Justin promised himself that he would not allow himself to be compared to his father. Justin decided to pull out all the shorts he owned to get Triston's opinion. By the time Lina and Jasmine made it home, Justin was sitting on the ottoman listening to Southern Soul music.

"You ok, Dad?"

"Yea, I'm good." Justin said.

Lina passed Jasmine the bags and asked her to go put them away. Now that they were alone, Lina asked Justin again what was wrong.

"Triston told me I look like my damn dad in those trunks, so I need all new shorts and sandals now."

Justin said, looking away from Lina.

Lina laughed slightly as she kissed him on the forehead before telling him that she already bought him new outfits.

Now feeling a little better, Justin began a new fashion show, this time hoping not to look like his dad. Lina and Justin had different opinions about the styles of clothes he should be wearing but to his surprise, he was pleased with her selections. While Justin was trying on the new outfits and sandals, Lina quickly took the opportunity to trash his grayish sandals and Grandpa shorts.

"Babe, this shirt is fire," Justin said, putting on a white shirt with purple flowers down the side.
Lina handed him some linen pants to complete the outfit.

"Damn, you look sexy," Lina said looking at the now blushing Justin.

"I am pretty damn sexy."
Lina pulled out the remainder of the outfits for Justin to try on.

"Are you sure about this?" Justin asked as he held up a see-through Coral shirt.

"Yes, they go with these black cargo shorts and salmon slides."

"Ok, a see-through pink shirt is one thing, but I draw the line at some damn pink slides."
Lina decided to take the win with the coral shirt instead of pressing her stubborn husband about the salmon slides. Justin was happy to have his confidence back thanks to Lina and

she was happy to get rid of those gray sandals without much of a fight.

With his fashion dilemma now settled, Justin accompanied Lina on an outing to find matching outfits. Neither of the two enjoyed hours of endless shopping but thankfully Lina had a method to her shopping. She knew what stores had what and just when to go there to miss the crowds. Justin did not mind her way of shopping at all. He enjoyed seeing his wife try on the sexy outfits. As they were out Morgan facetimed to get her opinion about an outfit.

"Hey girl, how are you?"

"I'm good, just trying to grab some last-minute things."

"I'm doing the same thing."

"Hey Lina, I'm here too," Travis said moving into the view.

"Oh, hey."

"I need your help; Travis is kinda useless."

"No worries, I got you."

"Wow, I'm right here."

"Babe, I love you but it's true." Morgan said smirking. Lina tried to hold her laugh but she was unable to. Morgan held up two similar onesies',

"Blue or gold?"

"I like the Blue one but the Gold one pops more."

"Thank you, I was thinking that."

"Hold on, I said the same thing," Travis said, standing with his hands on his hips.

"I know you did but you just want to leave."

"Well, maybe..."

Lina walked back over to a waiting Justin who noticed the position Travis was in.

"Dude, are you wearing Red's purse?"

"No, what are you talking about?" Travis said, taking the purse off his shoulder.

Before Justin could think of a joke Lina added,

"He is and so are you."

Both men decided to exit the conversation with the purses slung over their shoulders as Lina and Morgan continued to facetime and pick outfits.

With all the outfits now picked and packed, Lina was on the phone arranging to drop Triston and Jasmine off at gam-gam's house.

"Thank you, guys, so much for keeping them."

"Please, I love them, you're doing us a favor," Gam-Gam said.

As Lina was talking, Justin came in carrying bags followed behind him was Kerry with an empty suitcase. She stared at the

helpless looks on their faces for a moment before putting
them out of their misery,

"What?"

"You scared me, so I brought over my stuff for you
to pick through," Kerry said.

"Ok, bring them in the front room and I will take a
look."

Kerry dropped the suitcase and gave her a huge hug yelling,

"Thank you, thank you, you're so fu... freaking awesome," Kerry said changing his words as Jasmine
walked in the kitchen.

Lina took a seat in the front room as Justin and Kerry walked
behind her. Jasmine followed them wondering what was going on.

"Sit here babe, we have to help Uncle Kerry."
Kerry laid out his top picks in front of Lina. Once he was
done Kerry stepped back and stood silently with his hands
behind his back. Lina walked around the outfits like she was a
judge on a reality show.

"Not a bad start," Lina said to a now smiling Kerry.

"I like the blue shirt," Jasmine said as Lina agreed before passing it to Kerry.

Justin sat and had a beer while Kerry packed everything that
Lina told him to. Once the packing was complete Kerry gave
Lina and Jasmine giant hugs while thanking them.

"Dope, I'm all set," a pleased Kerry said on his way out the door.

"One more day and we're out of here," Justin said as he turned out the lights.

{ 17 }

Paradise

Justin and Lina seemed to run to the car as the children looked on from gam-gam's window. Lina glanced back as the two jumped into the Jeep, with a blown kiss, and a blow of the horn the two were off to Paradise. Justin turned the music up and began singing to it, Lina looked at him surprised he was singing so loudly. Justin noticed the stare and simply turned the music up continuing to sing even louder now. Unable to fight the joy coming from Justin, Lina began to sing along with him. When the traffic picked up, they treated the other traffic goers to an impromptu concert. Most were very receptive to the show but of course there were some unfriendly looks. *Haters gonna hate* thought Justin as he found one of his favorite songs to sing with Lina. She was unsure why he was staring at her so strangely with his head cocked until the melody to *My First Love* started which was one of her favorite duets by Avant and Keke Wyatt. Lina yelled,

"This is my shit."

Justin felt like being petty, so he pulled up to one of the hating cars and began to *sang* Avant's verses loudly in their direction. The couple in the red Honda rolled the windows up and changed lanes, which made Justin and Lina laugh uncontrollably.

"You're such an ass," Lina said looking at the massive grin on Justin's face.

"You laughed so you're an ass as well, but it's a nice ass though."

"And you better not forget it," Lina said as she poked Justin in the ribs as they pulled into long term parking at the airport.

Justin asked Lina to take a picture of the pink turtle on the wall so they could remember where they parked as he struggled to get the suitcase out of the trunk.

"Damn woman, why did you pack so much stuff? We are only going for a week," Justin said, starting the same complaining he was loading the car.

Lina merely gazed over at Justin asking sarcastically,

"Do you want me to take it?"

Justin slapped her on the ass as he sped by her yelling,

"Next stop paradise! Well, a hotel in Florida for a few hours then a short flight to Paradise in the morning,"

Justin and Lina started their Paradise journey at the curbside check-in where Justin slid the baggage handler a $20 tip to jump the line. They got an added benefit when he added TSA Precheck on their ticket which allowed them to skip the massive line at security. The airport was full of travelers going near and far but surprisingly the flight to Florida had maybe fifteen people on it. The flight attendants looked worn out and ready for a break, but their disdain quickly dissipated when they saw the number of people on the last leg of the flight.

The flight attendant announced, "You guys can stretch out wherever you want after we take off."
The passengers settled in after selecting their new open seats. Justin looked at Lina and gave her a grin with an invitation to join the mile-high club. She looked at him for a second,

"No fool, what is wrong with you?"

"I'm just saying."

"I'm not trying to fold myself into a pretzel in that nasty ass bathroom," Lina said as she buckled her seatbelt.

Making it to Florida the two were greeted by a blanket of humidity, instantly Lina's hair started to grow while sweat began to bead up on Justin's forehead,

"Well welcome to Florida."

"And how I hate it," Lina said, speaking of the humidity, not Florida.

They boarded the hotel shuttle just behind a couple that seemed to be having a bad day. As Justin and Lina sat on the shuttle, they overheard a conversation between a short, curvy woman (Andrea) who was pissed her tall lanky man (Darius) sitting across from her trying to avoid eye contact.

"Why don't you just admit that you were checking her out?" Andrea asked, breaking the silence.

"There's nothing to admit, she asked if I could help her with the bags."

"And you jumped into action with your Captain Save-A-Hoe Ass."

Justin chuckled when she called him Captain Save-A-Hoe, Lina looked at Justin and nudged him with her elbow to cut it out. Andrea overheard the chuckle and looked at Justin as to say who the fuck are you laughing at.

"My bad that Captain Save-A-Hoe line was funny,"

which made Darius laugh until Andrea looked at him. Lina apologized for Justin being an idiot as she introduced herself.

"It's not his fault, it's my fault for marrying a jackass," Andrea said looking at Darius.

"Bro listen to this, this woman stopped me as we were walking to the shuttle asking for help with her bags, what was I supposed to do?"

"I guess there's nothing wrong with helping," Justin said, seeming to side with Darius.

"Thank you, brother," Darius said, giving Justin a high-five.

"Oh, hell no, he can help her, yes I have no problem with that, but did he have to hug her after doing so?"

"She hugged me."

"Maybe but you grabbed her ass."

"Wait, what the hell, you grabbed her ass??" Lina asked, jumping into the fray.

"My hand may have grazed her ass, but I did NOT grab it," Darius yelled, defending himself.

"WTF, men ain't shit," Andrea said.

"I hear you," Lina said, now looking side-eyed at Justin.

"Hey, hold up, I got nothing to do with this. This is between them two not us. Besides, I didn't grab anyone's ass."

"Really?" Darius asked.

"Hey, my vacation is just starting, and I don't need any smoke with this woman right now."

"You're right," Lina said.

She gave one last long look at Darius before locking eyes with Andrea and having a nonverbal conversation. Darius just looked at Justin like you dirty bitch you betrayed me and Justin feeling a little bad for not having his back just looked out the window. Andrea and Darius continued to debate whose version of the story was true as Lina and Justin exited the conversation. After what seemed to be forever, the shuttle made it to the hotel to the delight of Darius.

"Be easy," Justin said to Darius who was now trying to avoid eye contact with any women.

He did not want any more fire from Andrea who was just waiting and wishing for him to slip up. Once they checked in Justin and Lina elected to use a separate elevator from Andrea and Darius. They had their fill of the couple's argument.

Entering the room Justin laid across the bed still laughing as he repeated the Captain Save-A-Hoe line.

"You're stupid but understand I'll cut you if you ever graze some woman's ass."

"Why, you always want to cut me?" Justin asked, grabbing her waist.

"You know me, and you like it," Lina said, sliding back into Justin's arms.

"Yeah, I do."

He began kissing the back of her neck. His efforts were quickly blocked when Lina pulled away,   "Eww what are you doing?"

Surprised Justin stood back, "you know what I'm trying to do."

"I know but after being in the airport I need to shower."

"What? I don't care about that."
He took his shirt off and began doing his "Get It" dance. Lina laughed as she resisted his advances on her way to take a shower, not daunted he continued to dance telling her to hurry up. After what seemed like forever, Lina came out of the bathroom wrapped in a towel that was hugging her curves in just the right way with her curly brown hair seemingly blowing in the wind as she walked. *Damn* Justin thought to himself as Lina looked back and gave Justin a smile that sent him into overdrive,

"I'm going to clean up really quick and then it is on."
Justin slapped her ass on the way to the bathroom; he quickly turned around and slapped it again after Lina backed up for another one. In Justin's haste to get back to Lina he turned the water the wrong way which resulted in him being blasted by cold water but in true horny man fashion he pressed by taking the fastest shower that he had taken since his days in basic training.

Justin exited the shower and dried off with one swipe of the towel. He did a few stretches to limber up. Before leaving the bathroom, he did a few wall push-ups to get his blood flowing. Justin walked out of the bathroom to see Lina laying on the bed still in nothing but a towel. He turned out the lights and made his way to Lina's side of the bed thinking *it's about to go down*. Justin dropped his towel and did the sexiest dance he could think of *Magic Mike eat your heart out*. As he danced, he noticed he did not hear a chuckle or any noise for that matter coming from Lina. He turned to see what the problem was and to his surprise Lina was asleep. *WTF*, Justin nudged the bed to see if she was lightly sleeping or if the night was over. Little tap nothing, shit, ok another tap harder this time, still nothing, shit, fuck it hard shake this time, but all Lina did was rollover unfazed by the nudging. Justin, now defeated, went and sat in the chair trying to understand how things went so wrong so fast.

"Fuck," Justin said, as he opened a $4 candy bar, a $6 sprite, and turned on SportsCenter.

After watching ESPN top 10 highlights of the day, he finished drowning his feelings in $10 worth of junk food before going to bed.

After what equated to a long nap, the hotel phone rang waking Lina.

"Good, Great morning this is your wake-up call and heads up the airport shuttle will be downstairs at the top of the hour." the hotel clerk said.

How is she so chipper this early in the damn morning Lina thought. However, all she said was

"Thank you."

Sitting up Lina realized she was still in the towel; *dang I fell asleep.*

"Hey babe it's time to get up," she said, kissing Justin on the neck.

"Oh, now you're awake."

"Ok...Ok… I'm sorry, I must have been more tired than I thought," Lina said, kissing Justin again.

"I get it, at least we are even now."

"Wait what? Even for what?" Lina asked as she paused on her way to the bathroom.

As she stood there naked with her hands on her hips. Justin forgot what he was saying as he looked at her curvaceous body.

"I didn't say anything," Justin said as he dropped his towel.

"Nope you took too long, the shuttle will be here soon."

"How did I take too long, that was the fastest shower ever taken."

"You should've woken me up."

"Dammit woman, I hit the bed and even ended up shaking the shit out of you and all you did was roll over."

"Wow really, are you sure?"

"Oh, I'm sure," Justin said, now standing there in his boxers.

"Sorry babe," rubbing on his manhood.

"Damn you woman why would you do that, now I got a damn chubby."

"Don't worry I might take care of that later if you play your cards right."

Now grinning from ear-to-ear, "ok bet as he rushed to get ready."

On the way to the shuttle, they passed the extra chipper front desk clerk and almost on cue she told them she was sorry to see them leave and begged them to come back. Justin ignored the need to crack a joke and thanked her for the wakeup call.

This time the shuttle ride was peaceful unlike the ride from hours before. Arriving at the airport, they realized just how early their flight was. They breezed through security quickly and walked around the terminal exploring.

"I just want some water," Justin said as he passed by all the closed stores.

"they'll be open soon, let's just sit down."

"True, let's go."

As they sat at the terminal, Justin was still annoyed that he had to wait for water, Lina however was in full vacay mode. She was taking selfies in and around the seat completely in her own world. Her joy became irresistible to Justin who was trying his best to ignore her, but they ended up in a selfie war. The photo-off that erupted was witnessed by airport workers and other early flyers passing by. The joy on their faces brightened up the day of the airline attendant who decided to bless them. Noticing that the waiting crowd was starting to grow, the selfie King decided to take one last combined selfie with a plane to paradise in the background.

"I'm going to review the selfies to see which ones are postable," Lina said.

Justin found himself looking at a young mother playing games with a chubby cheek toddler. His heart almost melted when the Chocolate Shirley Temple looking toddler flashed him the most beautiful smile. She began to glance at him, but when he looked back, she would look away and just like that a game had begun. Lina looked up at Justin as she finished her selfie review,

"What are you doing?"

She was unaware of the game that was being played by Justin and the toddler. Lina tried to speak but the toddler didn't even look her way. Feeling a little slighted, Lina went back to looking at her phone, she did not want any problems with the toddler over her new friend Justin. Lina was motioned over by the woman at the ticket counter, Justin, still engulfed by the game, did not see the act.

"Babe... Babe…," Lina said trying to get his attention, but Justin and the toddler were having too much fun.

Lina decided not to pull Justin away from the game and went to the counter alone to see what the lady needed.

"Excuse me, did you need to see any more information from us?" Lina asked, wondering why she was waved over.

"Oh, no ma'am I wanted to thank you two for brightening up my day. My husband and I have been going through it for a while now and just the sight of you guys blending your different styles gave me hope. My husband is reserved and I'm outgoing and at times it is hard to understand how we fit together," the airline agent said.

Lina just stood there as if she was looking in the mirror,

"Girl I've been there, we're in a good place now but it took and still takes a lot of work," she told the airline attendant who introduced herself as April.

Justin looked around for Lina now that his game was over, his partner had to eat. He found her hugging April and wiping tears from her eyes. Confused, he decided not to interrupt the moment. After Lina and April finished hugging, she told Lina for her spirit and outpouring of love that they were being bumped up to first class for not only their flights today but also for their return flights as well. Lina and April embraced again and exchanged contact information before she returned to Justin.

"What was that all about?"

Lina looked at him and smiled saying, "it was a conversation with my new friend."

"I got that, but what was the crying about?"

"Do you really want to know, or do you just want to enjoy the first-class upgrade?"

Justin wisely decided to simply enjoy the upgrade and not to push the issue further.

Now on the plane Justin moved around in his seat and touched everything he could, like a giant kid; the other first-class passengers could tell it was his first time, but Justin could not have cared less. It was 9 a.m. in the morning but

Justin accepted the champagne offer as a flight attendant passed by. Lina looked at him acting like a kid and simply kissed them on the cheek,

"Next stop paradise," before laying the seat back for a nap.

Sleep was the last thing on Justin's mind as he took everything that was offered to him. The flight was only 90 minutes, but it felt like hours to Lina as she woke up refreshed but for Justin the 90 minutes seemed more like five minutes. Justin started to fill out the customs declaration form, still a little salty about the warp speed flight. He took the mandated selfie to indicate that they had made it. This was solidified as the pilot came across the intercom yelling,

"WELLLCCCOME TTTOOO PAAR-RAADDIISSEE!"

{ 18 }

Beautiful View

Both Justin and Lina had traveled a number of times for work and vacations; however, this was the first time Justin had been in the Caribbean. The closest he had been to white sandy beaches was Afghanistan, he was hoping this trip would be better than those were.

"Damn it's bright," Justin said, shielding his eyes as massive rays of sunshine hit him in the face.

Lina felt the rays as well, but her reaction was much different than Justin. She stepped to the side to let the other travelers go by as she took her hair down from the tight ponytail. She leaned her head back and shook her hair looking like a shampoo commercial. She then turned to see Justin staring at her awkwardly,

"Are you done?"

"Shut up fool let's go," was her response as she closed her eyes one more time to enjoy a few more rays.

Now on the move and after grabbing their bags they caught up with the other travelers at the custom station. *Damn we are going to be here forever* Justin thought as he looked around. Lina, still in total relaxation mode, could care less about the line, all she knew, was that she was in paradise. Justin, unable to relax kept looking around studying his environment; in doing so he saw others conducting the same surveillance. Each time one of the uneasy observers caught the eye of the other they simply nodded as to indicate this side is secure. Lina, well aware of Justin's surveillance demeanor after many years of marriage, began to rub the small of his back. This was a proven tactic she used to calm Justin down and to get his anxiety under control.

Justin now a little more relaxed, kissed Lina on the forehead as to say thank you for snapping him out of his spiral. As they waited in line, Lina saw a tall skinny Islander beginning to round the tourists up, after hearing the name of their resort Justin went to check it out. Lina remained to save their spot in the line. After meeting with the resort liaison Justin waived for Lina to come over.

"Good morning people welcome to the Cccaaarrriiibbbbeeeeaaannnnnn!!! I'm Bob like Marley but not related," he said introducing himself.

Justin thought he looked more like Sanka from *Cool Runnings*.

"Morning," Lina responded, feeling the energy coming from Bob.

"My people, we will get through this line quickly and then we will head up to the reception area to wait for your resort shuttles, your guides have a by name list and let me tell you they are fabulous."

Bob began working his magic by having a few people cut lines at a time. Justin looked as Bob flirted with one immigration inspector to get three or four people into line and got another two tourists in another line while trying to get an immigration inspector a date with one of the beautiful resort liaisons. If his approach failed, he quickly regained his composure and shuffled them to different lines. The large group dwindled quickly as Bob got them all through customs in under an hour. The groups were then broken up into their respective sections and waited for the shuttles as Bob called their names. He stopped once he got to Lina and Justin's names,

"OOOHHH you two are in for a treat."

Justin and Lina both looked at Bob intrigued,

"You two get to wait in the gorgeous suite area for your guide to come get you. Oh, and trust me he is the best I have ever seen, follow me lovers."

Lina and Justin followed Bob into a beautifully laid out suite decorated in rose gold and off white. Justin, now confused, walked in and out a few times just admiring the craftsmanship. He could not understand how they had such a beautiful waiting area in the airport. Bob took the still astonished couple to the front desk of the waiting area to check in,

"Hello, my love, we have guests."
One of the most stunning creatures Justin had ever seen in person came walking from the back,

"Hey babe, oh look at this gorgeous couple. I'm Jade and we are here to serve you, there is food to your left and entertainment to your right."
Justin put on his glasses speaking of the brightness in the suite as Jade walked from behind the counter looking like a large Caribbean Coke Bottle. Lina knew it wasn't that bright, but she decided to let Justin have a look because she even thought *DAMN* as Jade walked out. With Jade gone Justin took off his glasses and asked if Lina wanted something to drink,

"Water please."

Justin came back with her water and a beer for himself, which surprised Lina,

"Do you know what time it is?"

"Yes, I do, and I don't care it's 10am WOMAN, I told you I was drinking from the moment we landed."

"You should have brought me one then."

"Word, I got you," Justin said as he got up to get more drinks just as Bob came in asking for their bags. A baggage handler came walking in looking like Tyson Beckford, which made Lina put her glasses on. When he slung the bags over his shoulder with ease, Lina looked back at Jade like did you see that. Jade smiled the most devilish smile as if to say yes girl I saw that. Justin looked at them and decided to get another drink giving Lina the freedom to have another quick look.

"Let's ride sexy people."
Justin and Lina made their way to the shuttle.

"Hey, babe, do you need your glasses for the brightness?"

Justin quickly responded, "nope, do you need yours." They looked at each other and shared a good laugh. The baggage handler loaded the bags as Lina motioned for Justin to tip him, but the baggage handler stopped him,

"I can't take your money; it was my pleasure."

As the other tourists settled into their seats, Bob got on board introducing the driver and started to introduce the liaison,

"He is the best in the game and not to mention he's easy on the eyes."
Bob exited only to reappear introducing himself as the liaison that was easy on the eyes which made everyone laugh. Bob proceeded to tell the bus how Jamaica produced the best music. Because one of the passengers laughed in disbelief, they were then treated to a Bob Marley, Shaggy, and Sean Paul party mix with a little Shabba Ranks tossed in. He told them that reggae music has always served as a tool for empowerment, and expression of political and social views.

"It was connected to the Rastafari movement, which began in the 1930s in Jamaica. Visitors learn about my home through dance and rhythm."
Bob continued telling them about the island,

"If you look out the right you will see one of our many amazing beaches."
Bob continued to tell them about the island when a refreshingly delicious aroma filled the air.

"What you're smelling is one of our famous Jerk Shacks. If you lovely people have time you have to make it to one of our many shacks to try our world-famous refreshing, crisp, and delicious Red Stripe beer. As I close, please leave Jamaica with little to no regrets."

As the shuttle rounded a large bend in the road, the trees gave way to a stunning resort that was popping with vibrant color and live music.

"Thank you all for listening to my humble words about my beautiful home that I love."

The vacationers filed off the bus, Lina nudged Justin again to give Bob a big tip which he had no problem in doing. Justin stood back and looked in amazement at the beautiful flowers wrapped around the entrance of the resort, he also looked at his wife with an equal amount of amazement as the sun's rays kissed her skin. Lina turned and saw a look in Justin's eyes that she had not seen in a while which made her smile from ear to ear. She moved towards him with her hands stretched out, Justin took her hand, and they made their way into the resort. They were greeted by the resort staff with two coconuts filled with rum punch. One of the resort liaisons called for them to follow her, Justin engulfed by the coconut rum punch forgot to get his wife and luggage for that matter.

"Honey your bag."

"Oh, damn my bad," Justin said, remembering his bag and wife.

"Follow me please," the resort liaison said as they entered a beautiful office to check them in.

Justin sipped on his rum punch as Lina filled out the resort paperwork and heard the sales pitch about being a resort rewards member. Justin nor Lina had no plans on being members, but they were enjoying the punch too much to interrupt her. As she continued Justin caught a glimpse of Travis in some colorful peacock shorts with a boonie cap on. Seeing that sight almost made Justin spit out his rum punch, almost.

"What the hell?" Justin said, startling the liaison who was finishing up the sales pitch.

"Not you, I see somebody I know who is making a fool of themselves."

"No problem, we are done, you can leave your bags here and we will take them to your room."

Justin topped off their rum punches and went to see what the hell Travis was thinking.

"Really dude is this what the hell you put on this morning?"

Travis turned around unfazed by the insult, "hell yea, you know you like them."

Lina told Justin to shut up as she hugged Travis before making her way to where Morgan was sitting.

"Girl this is beautiful," she said, sitting down beside

Morgan who was gazing out over the water.

"Yes, it is, I've been here for a while now," Morgan

said, getting up to hug Lina.

The two threw the peace sign to Justin and Travis as they

moved to the deck overlooking the water to get a better view

and more drinks. Now at the glass-bottom deck Lina com-

mented on the beauty of the water,

"I can see all the way to the ocean floor."

As the two talked, a waiter interrupted,

"Hello ladies, can I help you with anything? Food,

drinks, or water sports?

They both looked at each other instantly declining the water-

sports option but Morgan asked,

"What is that purple drink I keep seeing?"

"Oh, that is our purple paradise."

"Let us both have one please? Oh, and how deep is

the water right here, it's so beautiful?" Lina asked.

"It's about 60 feet deep at this point, I know this view

is amazing," the waiter said as he left to get their

drinks.

While they were looking at the sun bouncing off the crystal-

clear water neither noticed that their purple paradises were

dropped off until Travis asked,

"What in the purple rain are you drinking?"

"Oh wow, I had no idea he brought them," Lina said. Morgan agreed which made Justin a little uneasy saying maybe you should take them back. Unfortunately, before he could finish his thought, Lina and Morgan had already inhaled half of the purple paradises.

"Sorry babe I didn't hear you. It's ok, have a seat and relax," Lina said knowing that would be hard.
Justin took a seat and asked a passing waiter for a rum punch.
"Sure thing, and for you?"
"Let me get one of those purple rains," Travis said, which confused the waiter.
"He wants a purple paradise," Morgan said, pushing Travis's shoulder.
"Yea, yea, purple paradise."
"You're stupid but purple rain is a good name," Justin said now laying back in the chair enjoying the breeze.
As the couples sat relaxing and enjoying the scenery Lina asked,
"How were the flights?"
Travis went to answer but Morgan cut him off,
"This fool asked if he could fly the plane."
Lina looked confused as Travis tried to explain,
"I have seen people fly for years; it doesn't look that hard. They have autopilot. Hell, I can do that."

Morgan asked if Justin could believe what he was saying.

Justin looked up from his drink, "I'm surprised they said no, he can be very convincing when he wants to be."

"Hell, they almost did until this kill joy said something."

Morgan continued, "he wasn't flying me anywhere. I will admit I was worried about getting here because it rained from the moment we landed until this morning actually."

"We brought the sunshine," Lina said.

"Yes, girl and thank you for it, How was it leaving the kids?"

Justin chimed in with his eyes closed, "what kids, we don't have any kids for the next few days."

"Shut up stupid, it was hard, but we needed this vacation. I love my babies, but momma needed these rum punches and purple paradises. The flight to Florida was fine but getting to the hotel was a whole other story, girl. We had a couple fighting about her dude touching some strangers ass."

"What?" Morgan asked.

"Her dumb ass boyfriend helped some thick chick and then felt her ass when she thanked him," Justin said.

"Damn fool," Lina said.

"Yea he was a fool but on the bright side we got up-graded to first class."

"When does the vow renewal party get here?" Justin asked, looking around.

"They arrive tomorrow afternoon," Travis said.

"Ok so we got a few hours of down time, I can deal with that."

"How is your room?" Lina asked.

"Oh, it's wonderful, they have a tub on the balcony."

"Hell yea," Justin said looking at Lina.

"That's nasty, I hope our rooms aren't close," Travis said, interrupting.

"Whatever, it's going down," Justin said with Lina agreeing.

Justin moved to get up as Lina stopped him, "not right now calm down."

"Yea relax dude, your acting like you did on prom night."

"You bitch," Justin said, remembering being impatient as hell that night.

"Oh, that sounds like a story we should hear," Morgan said with Lina quickly agreeing.

"You will never be hearing that or any other stories like that unless we're telling them all."

Travis thought for a second and said, "oh hell no, you wouldn't."

"Oh, I would, well I had been dating this girl." Justin said, sitting up to begin his story.

"Nope, we aren't telling any stories."

"BOO, come on babe that was so long ago let's hear it?"

"Hell, no babe, we came here to relax and enjoy each other."

"Now, I suggest we listen to this live music and chill out"

The women reluctantly agreed and sat back to enjoy the music and the scenery.

"You won today but we will be talking about it soon,"

Morgan said as Lina nodded in agreement.

The group remained quiet enjoying the breeze and music until Justin got a text letting them know their room was ready. They finished up their drinks and bid Travis and Morgan adieu,

"Hit me up later and we will find you guys."

"Cool, will do."

Justin and Lina walked down the passage that was bustling with flowers which Lina loved, however she did not like the tiny frogs that came with it. They made it into the room as Justin had to do a sweep to ensure no creatures made it in the room.

"Oh, babe this is amazing, yes, yes," Lina screamed. She opened the curtain on the balcony to see a screen door meaning she could keep the sliding door open without fear of creatures. Justin kissed her forehead laughing a little,

"What? I was worried about that."

"Nothing love, I understand."

"Whatever, I'm going to freshen up and get my swimsuit on."

"I'll grab my trunks then be in there after you."
Lina made comments about the beauty of the shower. As she exited the bathroom After changing Justin watched his beautiful wife put on lotion as the sunlight danced off the small of her back. He walked over and kissed her from her shoulders to the small of her back. She leaned into him enjoying every kiss, Justin now on his knees kissed and caressed her body, he turned Lina around kissing every inch that the sun hit.

"I could kiss you forever."
He continued kissing the sunspots as he laid her down, now on top, Justin kissed her passionately. They made love and reconnected with each other as only lovers can. After the love-

making session Justin collapsed in Lina's waiting arms as they climaxed together. The two spent lovers laid there for a while,

"Now we have to freshen up again."

"True, but after my nap." Justin said.

{ 19 }

Rum Much

After freshening up again Justin and Lina made their way to the beach. They walked along the shoreline where a normally anxious Justin found himself breathing deeply and enjoying the sun on his face. Lina savored the feeling of the sand under her feet, the coolness of the water on her legs, and the rays on her back. Justin went to grab a few drinks while Lina set out to find seating. She came across two beach chairs that were in the water, and she could not resist taking the opportunity to relax in them. Back with the drinks Justin gave Lina her drink before taking a seat on the sand so the water could run over his legs. The two lovers relaxed as Justin people watched, he could not help but notice the peaceful, almost euphoric look on most of the faces on the beach. He could not understand where it came from, maybe it was the purple rain drinks like Travis thought, or maybe they were smoking on some of that purple kush. Justin continued to scan the beach when he noticed a couple walking the shore towards him and Lina. As they approached Justin sat up almost on instinct, the male looked at his companion,

"Do we cross in front knocking her drink over or do we walk behind her and kick sand on him?"

Justin now looking intently thought to himself *either path ends with a whooped ass.* As the couple got closer, they began to laugh as they moved further into the water avoiding Justin and Lina completely. Feeling husbands energy, Lina told her watchdog husband to stand down, this task was made easier as a separate couple walked by and greeted them warmly.

After some time, Justin reached Lina's level of relaxation so much, he was unaware when Travis and Morgan pulled up chairs beside them. Travis broke the silence startling Justin,

"Damn it's hotter than fish grease out here."

"Dude, you got to be loud everywhere you go?"

"Yes, I do, I want the world to hear me," Travis said, answering them even louder.

"Ok mission accomplished. Anyway, have you guys been to the hammock bar yet?" Morgan asked.

This caught Lina's attention as she turned slinging water on Travis and Justin,

"No, how far is it, I need a refill anyway?"

"Girl it's not far and the hammocks lay out over the water and sexy island men bring you drinks on demand."

"Ok relax with that sexy islander stuff," Travis said as Justin began to laugh.

"Oh yes, that sounds good let's go,"
The women seemed to speed walk down the beach with Travis and Justin far behind like disgruntled children.

"Look at this shit," Travis said pointing to the women.

"You started this mess."

"You're right, my bad but it is a nice hammock."

"When does Kerry get here, I need some comic relief?"

"He is coming in tomorrow with the rest of the vow renewal party. He didn't want to come with us."

"Yea he told me shit like he didn't want to hear our old asses having sex. I hate that guy sometimes," Justin said as they both laughed on the way to the bar.

"Damn, it is nice," Justin said as he looked at the hammocks stretched out over the water. "Shit, I need a picture," Travis said, trying to find a good way to get into the hammock.

After rolling down into the hammock Justin tried to regain his cool as the group laughed at him. He posed as best as he could just long enough for Lina to take the picture, he then put his cool on hold again as he tried to climb out of the cargo net style hammock. Back above-board Justin setback as it was now Travis's turn to check his cool at the door as he took his turn in the hammock.

"I have climbed cargo nets for years, this won't be shit," Travis said looking back at the group.
He almost made it, but he too rolled down into place. Travis tried in vain to act as if he did it on purpose. He had to lay there for a few minutes because Morgan wanted the perfect picture of him,

"Red, take the picture, these nets are hot."

"Come on babe, just a few more. You look too good in the hammock."

"Ok, a few more."

Justin leaned over whispering, "you a bitch," just loud enough for Travis to hear it.
After more pictures he managed to crawl his way out of the hammock and back to the bar,

"Man, the hell with that hammock give me a drink please."

"Of course, sir, what would you like?"

"My man, you saw me struggle to get out of that damn hammock, give me something strong."

After getting their drinks Justin and Travis turned to see Lina and Morgan both relaxing in the hammocks.

"Hold the hell up," Justin said as he stormed over wondering how they got down there without killing themselves.

"You can't be talking to us, we're here and you two are there," Lina said as they both snapped almost in unison.

"Give us our drinks and go sit down until we call you for refills," Morgan said laughing at them.

"Ok, Justin I have tanned enough, come get us up."

"Oh, now you need help," Travis said as he stood over them.

A waiter came by asking if Lina or Morgan needed helped. Justin quickly answered,

"No, they're good we got them."

Now feeling some kind of way, the guys helped the women up as they laughed. Travis asked if they wanted to grab some food at one of the restaurants.

"No thanks, we saw one of those pizza ovens on the beach that looked good."

"Oh, we had one of those earlier that shit is fire," Travis said as the group parted ways.

Justin and Lina went to the pizza joint as Travis and Morgan walked the beach at sunset. At the pizza palace Justin asked if they could get the order to go so they could eat in the room and maybe start round two. After ordering a couple approached them as Justin scanned to see their intentions. A barrel chested, white man came up,

"My friend you have to try the jerk chicken and tater (potato) pizza" in a southern-most drawl.

Justin, now intrigued, turned, and introduced Lina and himself.

"This is my wife Elizabeth and I'm Frank from the Carolinas. When I tried that tater (potato) pizza, I was tickled pink."

"We'll have to try that next time," Justin said.

"Oh, believe me you won't regret it. You guys have a good night now yuher (you hear)," Frank said as the couple continued on.

"You guys have a good night and enjoy this sunset," Lina said as they took their order to go.

"Babe lets go dancing," Morgan said as she twirled in the moonlight.

"Not tonight, Red, we have to meet the family in the morning, and the rum party is tomorrow night."

Morgan danced closer to Travis, he looked into her eyes,

"Ok we can find a party."

They moved to the main lobby of the resort looking for more live music, but they were unable to find anything to the delight of Travis as he quickly made his way to the room.

As the sun rose over the resort, it was already bustling with activity. Staffers were mopping floors, raking the beach, and cleaning the pool all to ensure guests would continue to enjoy their stay. Justin, normally an early riser, left a sleeping Lina to take a walk on the beach. He heard that was something people did on vacation. He ran into the staffers preparing the resort for the day, he tried his best to avoid being in the way too much. Justin was able to relax for the first time in what seemed to be decades. As he stared at the water Travis walked up beside him and just stood there. The two friends did not exchange words; they just looked and relaxed which was a big deal for them both. Far in the distance they heard,

"Look at you two fools, have your wives dumped you for Dexter St Jock already."

They turned and just laughed as Kerry made his way to them.

"Damn, you got here early."

"Shit, I wanted to get here before now, but my boss cut my leave."

"Dude, why are you still there?" Travis asked.

"For real, your ass should have quit by now," Justin said.

"My Boss is just mad because I'm coming here to get me an island wife or two."

"You nasty," Justin said.

"Just remember to keep your dirtiness to yourself when my future in-laws get here."

"Man, I'm looking for island love, they're safe for now."

"Whatever, forget all that, what are you wearing?" Kerry asked, looking at Travis's gator shorts.

"Shit, you know these are hot."

"Right hot as a dirty hoe in Vegas," Justin said as the three laughed while making their way off the beach. They went to get some breakfast, while they ate and had bottomless mimosas causing the volume of their voices to increase.

"Jesus, can you guys be quiet? I don't want to hear your bullshit conversation," a guest said. Startled, the three got up to address the disrespect coming from the other table. They made their way around the corner, they met up with a tall older black gentleman standing there with a Hawaiian shirt on. Before Justin or Kerry could say something, Travis said,

"I hate you, we thought it was about to go down." The stranger started laughing uncontrollably, still confused Justin and Kerry looked at Travis who was also laughing.

"Oh, my bad this is Joseph, Morgan's older brother, a retired Air Force man with a sense of humor almost as jacked up as ours," Travis said introducing his future brother-in-law.

"Oh damn, that was a good one," Justin said, now sitting back down.

"Is everyone else here or are they arriving later?"

"No, we're all here, I came to find you and Morgan."

"Ok, let's roll."

Joseph led the way and introduced his wife Shawn, Morgan's other brother Norman, and his wife Sarita.

"Nice to meet you all, even you Joseph," Justin said, adding that Lina was asleep and would be down later. Morgan came running out and hugged each one of them before asking about the bride and groom. Norman answered,

"Uncle Pete and Aunt Gerti will be joining us tomorrow; they'll be separated so they wanted to spend tonight together."

"Oh, that's nasty," Joseph said, making the guys laugh way too hard.

"Shut up you fools, it's sweet right," Morgan said looking at Travis who was trying desperately to avoid eye contact with her.

"Ok I got you," Morgan said as she and the ladies went to breakfast.

Lina hugged the group of Morgan and the others but declined to join them for breakfast instead she ran up and kissed Justin, hugged Travis, and slapped Kerry in the back of the head.

"Babe we have to go, we are going paddle boarding."

"I'm sorry what?"

"You heard me, let's go."

"Yea go paddle boarding you bitch," Travis whispered getting his revenge for the hammock comments.

 Kerry laughed as Justin accepted his fate and went to try paddle boarding.

After some instructions from a staffer the two were making some headway on the boards, well Lina was getting the hang of it. Justin, however, was only able to stand for about 2.3 seconds before falling into the refreshing cool island waters (how the instructor described it). With paddleboarding now complete, Justin and Lina met up with Kerry who was trying to mix purple paradise and rum punch together,

"Dude one drink isn't enough, you need two?"

"Hell, yea I do, I'm going to get my money's worth." Morgan waved as she jogged by, minutes later, an exhausted Travis came running up and almost fell trying to slow down and catch his breath.

"Dude what the hell, you good?" Justin asked.

"Yea I'm good, Morgan wants us to get in better shape for our damn wedding," Travis said, still trying to catch his breath.

"You're a shape, you're a circle," Kerry said laughing.

"Shut up fool, she's serious about this shit."

"Maybe, I should tell her about the meat lovers pizza." Morgan came running back down the beach before Travis had a chance to get up.

"Oh, are we taking a break?"

"Babe, Justin called me, so I had to stop," Travis said, trying to shift the blame.

"Come on babe, we got 2 more miles, let's go." As the defeated Travis got up and began to jog,

"Don't forget the Rum Party tonight guys."

After getting ready, Justin people watched, and Lina watched for little creatures as Morgan and Travis walked up. Now together the two couples set around listening to live music when Kerry walked up with two drinks in his hands.

"Damn double fisting already?" Travis asked.

"Dude we're literally on the way to a Rum Party," Justin said.

"Hey man this might be some bull; I need to be prepared."

Arriving at the gazebo, the group met up with Joseph and the others who were already there. The already beautiful gazebo had been transformed into a spectacular casino environment complete with a DJ booth. A tall slender staffer with a kango introduced himself saying I am Linford, and I will be your DJ for tonight. He went on to introduce Clive the dice man who was a retired sprinter who looked to still have wheels and Pops the dealer who was the oldest of the three. He told stories that reminded them of one of their great uncles. Linford continued,

"We'll teach you all how to play some of our games and of course let you try some of our world-famous Rum, so if you're ready to party let's get this journey started."

Clive said, "Come round let me tell you about our game called Ludo."

"Ludo?" Justin repeated.

"Yes, Ludo is a strategy board game where you race to get four tokens across the finish line with one dice."

"I'm good at dice, this will be my game," Kerry said, taking the dice.

"Oh, ok, we got a player." Clive said.

"That was luck," Travis said, passing by the table to get more Rum.

As the game continued it turned into a mashup of luck and frustration as Kerry and Justin began losing badly to Sarita. Lina sat at the table with Mrs. Carolyn, Gerti's best friend, Morgan, Joseph, and Shawn. Pops began to explain the card game Kalooki,

"Kalooki is a card game kind of like your American rummy, we call it Jamaican Rummy."

"Oh ok," Mrs. Carolyn said as she danced in her chair.

Linford played the music as the group played pool and other board games enjoying the time with each other. As time passed Clive, Pops, and Linford relaxed and started enjoying themselves as well. Noticing this, Travis and Justin tried to convince Clive it was ok to have a drink, after all he was still on the clock. The reluctant Clive relaxed in time, and he even mixed the group local drinks not on the resort's menu. Linford played a great mixed set of Jamaican and American dance hall music which took the party to the next level. The vibe was so infectious that other guests and staffers came to dance or have a drink. Linford ignored the three-hour time limit set by the resort and continued DJing off the clock.

As the drinks flowed and Mrs. Carolyn finished kicking ass at Jamaican Rummy the group began dancing to old school hip hop, Sarita had a flashback to when she was younger and began to break dance to a Queen Latifah beat. Linford began feeling her flow unleashing his rendition of the Stanky-leg which Justin joined in. Next was the running man which a drunk Kerry tried but could not catch the beat. The Dougie in which Joseph tried and failed badly. Linford began to twerk with Mrs. Carolyn, fresh off her third or fourth purple paradise before she remembered she was a woman of God. Norman seeing what he thought was the regression of his wife went to sit her down, but his efforts were made in vain, every time he sat her down, she bounced back up hitting the dance floor with a different dance. He got a drink and she hit the Chicken noodle soup, he ordered food, she hit the Robot, and he got a napkin she broke out with the Pop and Lock. Shawn was feeling the music as she two stepped in front of

Joseph who was still nursing his Dougie fail. Justin and Lina were shoulder leaning in the moonlight, while Travis and Morgan started the cupid shuffle which made everyone get up, even Norman. Everyone in the gazebo was dancing and having a good time including a number of hotel guests. Justin glanced over the crowd when he noticed Kerry had stopped dancing and was just looking up at the stars. He went to check on him but before he got there Lina and Morgan reached him first and began to talk to him. Justin continued over when Lina waved him off which confused him, but he listened and went to get a refill of Rum instead. Eventually management came back for the third time and shut the party down assuming the guests had kept the staffers from clocking out, but little did management know Linford and the others had clocked out hours ago.

With the party now over the group moved to the waterfront, sitting in beach chairs, and enjoying the view. Morgan asked Sarita if she really popped and locked out there?

"Yes, I did, and I would do it again. You know how it is when you have kids, I almost forgot how much fun it was to cut loose."

"True, I can understand and attest to that," Lina said, giving her a high five.

Over time the group started to dwindle and with Kerry leaving to find more punch all that was left was Morgan, Travis,
Justin, and Lina.

"Babe are you ready?" Lina asked.
He asked for a few more peaceful moments which she was
more than happy to give him.
Morgan rubbed Travis's hand,

"We need to get some sleep; you guys have your excursion with my Uncle Pete, and we have our wom-
en's day with Aunt Gerti."

The couples said their goodnights and turned in for the night,
Kerry came back and noticed everyone was gone. He stood
there for a second thinking; *well damn must be bedtime* before
going back to his room.

{ 20 }

Jessie's Cafe

Morning came early but just as the day before Justin was already up walking the beach and greeting the staff as they set up for the day. After his walk he made his way back to the main resort where he was greeted by Norman,

"Morning, it's a beautiful day for an excursion.

Justin greeted Norman when Uncle Pete walked up, "it sure is."

Startled, Norman leaned back, "dang, where did you come from, Unc?"

Joseph interrupted,

"Aunt Gerti kicked his scrawny but out for the day, knowing that she couldn't wait to be alone."

"Damn you two are starting already," Travis said walking up with Kerry.

"So, what's on the agenda for today?" Kerry asked.

"We are doing some resort hopping, going to a famous cigar spot, and hitting up the world-renowned Jessie's Café, that's what the pamphlet says," Norman said.

Confused Justin asked, "we got up this damn early to go to a cafe for food or something?"

Just then a loud booming voice sounding like a Caribbean James Earl Jones came from the front office,

"No, my brother Jessie's Cafe is not only the greatest bar on the island, but also one of the best bars in the world."

Justin turned to see if James Earl Jones had moved from Zamunda to the island. They were surprised when a rather small, framed man came walking up to the group introducing himself as Fitzroy Lewis with one of the deepest voices they had ever heard. He continued,

"Jessie's Cafe has some of the most beautiful sunsets in the world and the cliff diving there is second to none."

"Oh, damn cliff diving, I'm down for that." Kerry said.

"You can have it," Joseph said, "I'll be at the bar."

"Order enough for us," Travis added, indicating that Kerry would be jumping alone.

"Forget all of you scary asses."

Fitzroy asked, "if there was anyone else coming?"

Uncle Pete quickly answered, "maybe but they are late so we can go."

"Typical Unc," Norman said.

Norman could remember the times he was left behind because he was late. The guys boarded the shuttle as Fitzroy announced,

"Let the journey begin."

Pulling out of the beautiful resort Fitzroy continued,

"Our first stop is our sister resort to see if any more

people want to join our fantastic voyage."

As the guys chilled on the shuttle Fitzroy began to explain details about the island, he pointed out all the pivotal locations they passed.

"If you look to the right, you will see The Great Rose

Hall, a beautiful mansion overlooking the city."

Great Hall my foot Fitzroy said before explaining it was one of the biggest slave plantations on the island but now it is a museum. The guys looked on nodding their heads as to say yea we have those also. Fitzroy continued,

"On a happier note, down this road is the

Rob's nude bathing beach but don't get excited be-

cause of tropical storm Cholena there hasn't been any

nude bathing there for years."

"Damn that's too bad," Kerry said.

As the drive continued, it was hard not to notice the income disparity which Fitzroy pointed out more than once. At a stop light he had the guys look all the way to the top of a cliff,

"You see that green beautiful mansion; it belongs to some Hollywood ass that paid/bribed the local government to cut the road off so no one can drive up."

"Damn that's crazy," Norman said as he sat back in his seat.

"That's life here on my island."

Pulling up to the sister resort Fitzroy told the men that they had access to everything and that the shuttle would be departing in 45 mins.

Leaving the shuttle, they couldn't help but compare the resorts as they walked around. Uncle Pete was the first to voice his thoughts,

"Damn I'm glad we chose the other resort; this place is a shit hole."

The others quickly agreed as they moved to the bar to wait for Fitzroy.

"I hope no one joins us, I like the roominess we have right now," Travis said.

"Me too," Justin agreed.

The group watched as seagulls landed and walked into the resort only to be chased out by the unfortunate staff constantly. Fitzroy told them to finish up their drinks so the tour could continue. Wanting to leave as quickly as possible without a word the men chugged their drinks and happily made their way to the shuttle. Thankfully for Travis there was only one family waiting. *It's a family of three, they couldn't take up much space* Travis thought. Relieved, Justin and Travis high-fived each other as they got back on the shuttle. Fitzroy got a head count,

"We're off, next stop is some of the best cigars in the world."

Pulling out of the resort Fitzroy continued to tell the travelers about the island and all the benefits the Caribbean people have given to the world. Pulling into a parking lot an aroma swept through the shuttle pleasing everyone. Everyone except Jarell who was not happy that his preteen was subjected to this. The preteen and her mom didn't seem bothered, they in fact liked the fragrance

which made Jarell sulk even more.

Before them was one of the largest cigar bars on the island called Ev's Spot. Fitzroy began to tell the story of Ev's Spot. He told them of a kid who grow up on the island before going to the states. Ev, short for Evans joined the US military to better support his family. He would send money back for his mom and brother as often as he could. During his time away he and his younger brother would often talk about opening a cigar lounge once he came back to the island. Fitzroy looked down and paused before continuing, a few months before his first deployment would have been over, his Humvee was hit by an IED. Thankfully, he made it through the IED blast and at least one more deployment before his time was up and he was preparing to come back to the island. As he was arranging to come home, he was hit by a drunk driver who was trying to beat a damn red light. Unfortunately, he did not survive the crash and that bumboclaat kept going.

"What the Hell?" Kerry asked.

"Yes, my brother but at least they found the batty hole (asshole) but I'm unsure of what happened to them."

With the insurance money, Ev's brother and mother honored his memory by fulfilling his dream of opening the lounge. Fitzroy fell silent for a few moments as he gathered his composure. The shuttle, especially the veterans, took this time to compose themselves as well. Ev's story was one that each of them had either heard before or unfortunately had firsthand knowledge of. Fitzroy attempted to regain the joyfulness of the tour by asking who wanted to go first.

Joseph was the first off, the shuttle, seeming to skip as he went into Ev's Spot quickly followed by the others. Joseph was truly happy bouncing from aisle to aisle touching everything he could,

"How much is this, how much is that, oh look at this?"

Norman said, "damn, man relax," but Joseph was too busy loading his bags.

"I like this, and my baby would like that."
He and the other men knew that most of the items were for him. They decided to let him have his moment. Travis and Justin found themselves looking at the cognac infused cigars which had a robust body to them.

"Damn this shit smells great," Travis said with Justin agreeing.
Kerry came over with a monstrous 18-inch cigar that was infused by not one but three different liquors. They looked on in amazement at the massive cigar, a passing

Uncle Pete said "damn," as he made his way to check out with a box of Rum infused cigarillos for after the vow renewal.

Long after everyone was on the shuttle Joseph was the lone shopper. Fitzroy had to go into Ev's Spot to hurry him along saying your uncle wants to leave you. Knowing his uncle, Joseph quickly paid and left with two bags of cigars.

Now back on the shuttle Fitzroy poked fun at Joseph,

"Did you plan on buying out the whole store?"

Uncle Pete joined, "Nephew, you're going to look like a smuggler at the airport."

Fitzroy resumed talking about the island, telling them the tour used to include a tasting at the island's biggest Rum distillery, but it's closed for maintenance.

"Well damn, I could use a drink," Travis said.

"Well, you're in luck my brother we are about to pull up to Jessie's Café."

As the shuttle emptied, they came face to face with what can only be described as a movie backdrop. Jessie's Cafe sat to the left of the stairs and directly ahead of them was a cliff with a winding staircase down to the water.

"This is beautiful, but I wish I knew a bigger word than that," Justin said.

There was seating cut into the cliff to give you a viewing like no other. A large booming voice could be heard coming from the DJ booth,

"If you want to dive just sign up my brothas and sistas."

"Well, that's my cue," Justin said as he made his way to the bar.

After ordering the first rounds of drinks Justin took a seat in the chair that was in ankle deep water.

"Come on, one of you has to try it with me."

"Shitting me," Justin said as he splashed around in the ankle-deep pool.

"I'm here to relax, not break my damn neck," Joseph said, chiming in.

"Diving sounds crazy as hell," Travis added as he pushed past Kerry to take the last seat in the pool.

"You guys are just too old to be cool."

"I'm ok with that, I'll will sit my old self right here in this pool and have multiple drinks. Have fun young fella." Uncle Pete said.

Travis busted up laughing as he got up to take a few selfies. While Justin and Uncle Pete were joking Kerry, they heard Travis and Joseph screaming,

"Shots, Shots, Shots" from the bar.

"Come on let's go," Joseph said, egging them on.

"Fine, but I better not lose my spot." Justin said.

They gathered around the bar and toasted Uncle Pete and Aunt Gerti's 45years of marriage.

"That was harsh," Norman said as he choked the shot down.

"Come on nephew, you spilled more than you drank," Uncle Pete said.

"Well, we have to do another one," Travis said, waving over the bartender.

"I would but someone might take my seat," Justin said as he grabbed a beer and ran back over to his seat in the pool.

The guys laughed as they took the second shot, this time Norman handled the shot slightly better than before. They joined Justin back in the pool and continued to relax until Jarell joined them with a large coconut dyed pink. They waited for him to pass it to his wife, but he drank it instead which surprised the guys but more importantly it surprised his wife. She stared a whole in the side of his head, but he was doing his best to ignore her. Uncle Pete advised,

"Son you better get her a drink, or you may not leave this island."

Jarell tried to shrug them off and pass the coconut to his wife, but she smacked his hand away on the way to get her own drink. When she returned Travis gave up his seat trying to smooth things over, but she pushed Jarell in the water instead. Now extremely satisfied she sat down to enjoy her drink smiling. The DJ called Emma to the cliff.

"Ok, my Sista, you want 8ft, 10ft, 25ft, or the death defying 55ft, which one do you want?" the DJ asked.

She choice the 10ft platform after her dad ruled out the 25ft and 55ft options. After a quick selfie Emma jumped from the 10ft platform into the crystal blue water, with little hesitation. When she emerged to the top of the water the crowd let out a huge roar. Returning to the pool the guys all high-flied her which made her feel even more accomplished.

"Dude you have to do it now," Travis said pointing to the 25ft platform.

"I ain't no punk, 25ft is nothing."
He had to wait before diving because a local diver was about to jump off the 55ft platform.
The crowd cheered as the diver made his way up the ladder; he looked out over the crowd before waving to them. He leaped off the platform doing a swan dive, but he hit the water harder than he expected. Seeing the pain on his face Kerry eased his way down from the 25ft platform line. He snuck down to the less life threatening 10ft platform.

"You're up!" The DJ said as Kerry looked around to see if anyone in the group was looking.
Seeing that they were temporarily distracted he quickly jumped from the 8ft platform. Assuming he was in the clear he came back to the pool area and demanding they all take turns buying him drinks, letting them believe he had jumped from the 25ft platform. They all agreed since none of them

were crazy enough to jump. Seeing this Emma burst his fun bubble by showing Justin pictures she took of Kerry jumping from the 8ft platform.

"This bitch," Justin said before apologizing to Emma for cursing.

With this revelation he proceeded to snatch the drink from Kerry's hand calling him a fraud. Kerry tried to defend his action but once the photo was circulated all he could do was call Emma nosey. She took the insult in all fun, but Justin and Travis came to her defense making fun of Kerry being too scared to jump. Kerry went to redeem himself but the 25ft and 55ft platforms were closing due to high winds and a possible weather front moving in. They hung out by the pool side for another hour before Fitzroy came back to get them. He asked if anyone jumped, the guys said,

"Yes, Emma jumped from 10ft and lil Kerry jumped from 8ft."

"Oh, that's great my kids used to jump from 8ft."

"Yea but this guy isn't a kid," Uncle Pete said laughing.

"Oh, well never mind."

"Dude, you aren't helping," Kerry said feeling a little salty.

The sun beaten travelers loaded onto the shuttle, all they wanted to do was to have a nice easy ride back to the resort, however Mother Nature had a different idea for them. Pulling out from Jessie's Cafe it began to rain, Fitzroy downplayed the rain which put the shuttle at ease. As they traveled down the road, they started seeing cars along the road leading to a huge sheet metal building. Curious Uncle Pete asked,

"What is that?"

Fitzroy jumped up,

"Oh, did I not mention Jr's Jerk shack? It's hands down some of the best local restaurants you will ever have."

Now even more curious and intrigued Joseph asked,

"Is it possible for us to stop?"

"We can always stop but the rain may catch us."

Kerry dismissed the rain, "a dive champ such as I need to eat."

Emma said, "champ? You must not need a big meal then." which made everyone laugh.

They entered the dirt and gravel floor shack which made Jarell uncomfortable. He refused to eat at Jr's Jerk Shack, but his wife and Emma quickly jumped in line like it was nothing. Fitzroy told the group this was a true island place and not a tourist trap. Justin and Travis were the next up and caught the eye of some of the local women. Their skin was perfectly bronzed and flawless as it glistened in the dim lighting. Some of the locals did not care for the tourists being in their local eatery and looking at their women. Seeing this Joseph, a seasoned traveler thanks to the Air Force, asked the bartender for shots which he passed out to lighten the mode. Norman and Kerry stood in amazement as their food was being chopped and prepared on a large table, the smells were infectious. Out of nowhere Uncle Pete surprised the shack by playing the spoons with the live band. His nephews looked on as he and the band began to freely play music. What was meant to be a quick pit stop became a jam session.

After taking several pics with the patrons of Jr's Jerk Shack, the travelers boarded the shuttle.

> Fitzroy asked, "if they wanted to learn more or just ride and listen to the music?" Everyone respectfully said, "music please."

> "Good, I'm tired and I want to eat," Fitzroy admitted, turning the music up.

While Fitzroy was eating, a news report interrupted the music stating some of the roads were washed out. Unfortunately, the shuttle was so engulfed in Jr's Jerk Shack they forgot about the rain. Now looking around they noticed that the rain had picked up and water was starting to form on the road.

Looking ahead the road seemed to be washed out making them all nervous.

"Man, we have that dinner tonight," Norman said.

"We might not make it. Gerti told me I better be on time," Uncle Pete said.

"Well, looks like you failed," Joseph said laughing but he stopped as water splashed up on the window. Smaller cars were being turned around, but the buses and shuttles were allowed to try to make it through. The group looked on as the shuttle in front of them drifted to the left as it hit the large water trail on the road.

"Here we go," Justin said as it was their turn in the trench.

 Kerry looked out the window as the water began to rise. Travis closed his eyes as he felt the shuttle begin to drift. Thankfully the driver was a pro, he drifted and shifted his way through the trench. Uncle Pete started to clap, and cheer followed by everyone on the shuttle, this hyped the driver up who was now speeding through the narrow streets. Seeing this Justin decided to close his eyes and get some rest figuring they would either make it back to the resort or he would meet his maker.

Justin was awakened at the sister resort and not in heaven when the shuttle rolled over a speed bump. As the family got off, Fitzroy asked if they wanted to stretch their legs before leaving. They quickly declined the offer remembering their dislike of the resort. Getting back on the road the shuttle passed a huge event with neon lights and thumping music. After reading the sign Kerry asked,

"What's Club Raas?"

"Loosely it means Club Ass."

"Oh shit, we should definitely go there," Kerry said with Uncle Pete agreeing.

"Absolutely not," the other married men said in unison, not wanting any problems from their wives.

"I'm getting married tomorrow, we should go."

"Definitely not," Norman said.

"Besides, you're already married. This is just a vow renewal," Joseph said.
Justin added in saying that he was trying to make it to 45yrs like him and Gerti.

Fitzroy put an end to the debate, "sorry my brothers, it doesn't matter, we can't go there anymore."

"What happened?" Kerry asked, disappointed.

"Well, some tourists didn't know how to act when those Caribbean curves hit them. So now tourists are largely banned."

"Damn tourist!" Kerry yelled.

Pulling up to their resort Uncle Pete realized they had just enough time to meet the women for dinner. Fitzroy refused the tips that were being offered stating that the resort had a strict policy on asking for tips or gratuity. Not having time to argue but wanting to do something for the driver and Fitzroy, Uncle Pete and the others left money on the shuttle seats and ran to meet the ladies.

{ 21 }

Excursion

As Morgan sat enjoying her second or third mimosa, Lina came in and plopped down beside her taking her mimosa from her,

"Girl, I can't wait for this spa day."

"I totally understand," Morgan said, ordering her a new mimosa thanks to Lina. "I think it would be cool to go to Jessie's Cafe, but I got some stress in these shoulders that only a strong island man can get out."

"Oh, I feel you."

Shawn and Sarita came next in bikinis and wraps,

"Oh, look at you two sexy devils," Lina said.

"Oh yes I am," Sarita said as she swished her mimosa in her glass.

"My kids are home, and my husband is gone, so mama is about to have some fun," Shawn said.

"I'm not even mad," Morgan said as she raised her mimosa to Shawn.

After enjoying fresh fruit and omelets the ladies laid out by the pool waiting on Aunt Gerti and Mrs. Carolyn. While the four women laid out enjoying the sun Aunt Gerti and Mrs. Carolyn came up in a much different outfit startling them. Morgan sat up and just watched as the matriarchs walked around in khaki shorts and boots.

"Aunt Gerti, what are you wearing?" Shawn asked, surprised at what she was witnessing.

"I'm dressed for a full day of excursions."

Morgan spoke up, "Aunt Gerti, I planned a day of spa treatments for us all, it will be a nice and relaxing day."

Aunt Gerti and Mrs. Carolyn looked at each other and started laughing,

"First off we don't need to be so formal, we are one of the girls today so call us Gerti and Carolyn, second we are taking ATV's off-road, then we are swimming with dolphins, and lastly we're doing the historical Rum tour."

Morgan and the others sat in disbelief and thought for a moment that Gerti was joking. Their hopes were crushed when she told them to go change so they could get going.

"But Aunt I mean Gerti wouldn't you rather enjoy a hot island man getting the knots out of your neck or a seaweed wrap?" Sarita asked.

The two matriarchs again started laughing this time uncontrollably,

"Heck no, I'm here to have some fun. I love my husband to death, but he can be a stick in the mud sometimes."

Carolyn agreed, "I have been married to the same man for 40 years and it has been a chore at times. I have raised two boys who are grown with their own families, it's time for me to have fun. My husband is old and stuck in his ways so I'm here to enjoy myself."

"I can understand what you're saying but some of that sounds a little dangerous," Lina said.

"Being married for decades to the same man without killing him is dangerous."

"You got that right," Carolyn concurred sipping her mimosa.

"You ladies are young, we have raised children, worked for decades, and it is our time to cut loose and have adventures."

The four women all nodded in agreement after being schooled slightly.

"Now get your young butts up and go put on some clothes so we can go kick up some damn mud!" Gerti yelled, taking Morgan's mimosa.

Morgan said, "yes ma'am," as the others gave their mimosas to a thirsty Gerti and Carolyn.

A few purple paradise's later, Morgan, Lina, Shawn, and Sarita came down to see Gerti and Carolyn singing to the live music.

"Are you guys alright?" Lina asked.

"Yes, we're fine just enjoying the wonderful purple paradises," Mrs. Carolyn said.

"I assume you beautiful ladies are waiting for me," a stranger voice spoke.

The group turned to see what Gerti, and Mrs. Carolyn would call a strong strapping lad with muscles rolling down his body.

"Morning ladies, I'm Dominic and I'll be your guide for all of your adventure excursions today, are we ready to go?"

"Oh, I'm ready," Carolyn said as she walked close enough to smell him, from her smile he must have smelt pretty good.

When the group finished loading on the bus Dominic could not hold his intrigue any longer as he expressed his amazement at the idea of the women booking the excursion. Stating that most women opt for the relaxation packages instead. He quickly said "no disrespect intended" as Sarita gave him a who are you talking to stare. Morgan who did not take offense to his statement told of her desire to relax and get pampered today. Gerti and Carolyn both let out boos as the purple paradises settled into their systems. Dominic smiled,

"Well, I can't promise pampering, but you may end up with a mud mask during the off-road safari."
Gerti and Carolyn cracked up at the joke made at Morgan's expense.

As Dominic talked about the island and what to expect a soulful Caribbean song came on and with the multiple purple paradises in her system Carolyn said,

"Sit down sexy and turn the music up."
A Genuinely shocked Dominic did just as he was told and sat his sexy self-down and turned the music up. The younger ladies of the group were embarrassed at the time but as the music started playing, they simply laid their heads back and nodded to the rhythm. Sensing a shift Dominic began to introduce and narrate the songs instead of talking about the island.

This change in focus pleased the ladies. As an older sounding song started Dominic stood up,

"This is my song."

He began, describing the song to Morgan and the others.

"This song is about a forbidden love between lovers from what you would call different sides of the tracks."

He began to sing the first verse in English sounding pretty well, *I long for you, I live for you, and I'd die for you.* When the hook finished Dominic now feeling it lowered his head and raised his voice as the second verse started, *the smile on your face gives me life, the feel of your lips will never leave me.* Gerti and Carolyn hummed along to the song as if they knew it. When Dominic finished his impromptu concert, he sat down to the applause of everyone on the bus. A little confused, Sarita leaned in close to Gerti,

"Do you know this song?"

Gerti looked at her, "girls, we lived this song."

Even more confused and intrigued, Morgan and Shawn joined Lina and Sarita in the aisle in search of further explanation. Carolyn looked at the women,

"Ok, you might be old enough to hear this."

Carolyn began her story,

"Now keep in mind this was before meeting my husband and just as Gerti met Pete. Pete worked on the farm back then just like most of the men in our town, we would go over and visit with him after school."

Morgan smiled, "visit with him."

"Not like that with your fast self," Gerti said as she popped Morgan on the leg. "We visited Pete on the farm whenever we could."

Shawn asked if Gerti and Carolyn went together to visit Uncle Pete all the time.

Gerti told them, "Yes in southern Virginia during that time there was safety in numbers."

"There was so much hate to watch out for, plus Gerti was a little to smittened by Pete, always necking."

Gerti laughed and told Carolyn to finish her story. One day as we visited the farm, a man came walking up with Pete looking like a bronzed god. His name was Samson, and he looked every bit of the heavenly being. He worked with Pete on the farm.

"He was so sweet, so when I visited with Pete, she would visit with Samson."

"Dang, Carolyn," Shawn said.

"This sounds like the beginning of a love story," Lina said grinning.

"It should have been, and it started that way, but it didn't end that way at all."

"Why not?" Sarita asked.

Samson was white and in the south that was not something you did. The sun had bronzed his skin and Carolyn loved it. The problem was that everyone else other than the four of them did not love it. This was back when we had to stay in our place, not like the generations today. Samson wasn't welcome in many places on their side of town, and they definitely were not welcome anywhere on his side of town. Despite that they still tried to make it work, needless to say it was very difficult.

One night all the hostilities came to a head between the southern hate and their love. The two couples were in one of the few bars that they were welcomed at. After some dancing and partying they left the bar together. They dropped Gerti and Pete off first, as Samson was taking Carolyn home, he noticed that they were being followed. Instead of leading them to Carolyn's parents' house he drove around hoping they would leave. When it was clear they would not leave he went back to town, he pulled in Graham's auto and got out. Carolyn begged him not to, but Samson took the fight to them in true form. Lina and Morgan grabbed hands as they all started to tear up.

Samson was outnumbered and they beat him badly; Carolyn tried to help but she was tossed aside. She got up and ran to help her Samson. Her screams startled the men, they had never seen anything like her yelling and swinging.

>"If I was going down, they were going to earn it. We were able to fight them off that night, but my Samson was hurt pretty bad." Carolyn said as she consoled a weeping Shawn.

As the story continued each of the ladies tried to place themselves in Gerti's or Carolyn's places which made them all feel sad. Carolyn finished up her story saying,

>"He was a good man but a better friend, after the war he married a different black sista and I was with my love. We remained good friends until his death a few years back."

Lina and the others began to express their sorrow for her loss until Carolyn stood up and yelled,

>"I want the pink one!"

Confused, the ladies looked around and noticed that they were not only at the first excursion, but that Dominic and the driver were also listening in on Carolyn's story. Dominic stood up giving Mrs. Carolyn a hug,

"Out of my way sugar, I want to get to that 4wheeler," Carolyn said as she made her way to the pink ATV.

Morgan and the others stayed seated for a minute until Gerti spoke,

"Look, that was over 40 years ago, ok. It took years but we dealt with it. Get off the bus."

Now off the shuttle Dominic handed a set of keys to Gerti and one to Carolyn. The two would be off roaders turned to pick their riders,

"I'll take Shawn and Sarita," Carolyn said as she got into the pink 4wheeler.

Shawn and Sarita nervously followed behind her.

"Load up," Gerti said to Lina and Morgan.

Morgan received a quick and emphatic, "no," when she asked if Gerti wanted one of them to drive. Dominic began to explain what was going to happen as he got onto an ATV. The shuttle is going to be waiting at the dolphin enclosure. We will ride there and do a little swimming. You will feel these majestic mammals pull you along with their dorsal fins or even better you can get a push from them through the crystal-clear water. There is a 30ft slide if you're still looking for thrills, oh there is a natural lagoon surrounded by colorful birds also. Feeling the need for speed.

Carolyn said, "ok, ok let's go let's ride," with Gerti agreeing as she revved the engine.

"Ok I get it, well let's ride," Dominic said as he headed down the trail.

The women were amazed by trails breathtaking natural beauty. Dominic described the passing sites over the CB radio. He told them about the slave quarters that had been turned into one of the first churches for freed slaves on the island. He pointed to other landmarks which helped them feel even closer to the island.

Gerti said, "I want to feel the wind in my hair," as she asked Dominic to speed up.

"Oh, it sounds like you want to take a walk on the wild side."

"Oh, yea baby, you're speaking my language," Carolyn said as she sped up.

Speeding through the lush tropical foliage Gerti hit several mud patches giving Morgan the mud bath Dominic had promised. He took them deeper and deeper into the tropics until he stopped suddenly giving them all an added mud bath. He directed their attention to what felt to be a hidden piece of paradise, before them was what had to be a 40ft waterfall. Dominic told them they could jump if they wanted to, but no one took him up on his offer. He got off his ATV,

"Once you're done taking selfies, we can take this easy trail down or we can take this one which is a little harder but way more fun."
Morgan and Lina spoke first,

"Easy please, I have eaten bugs and had more mud on me than I ever wanted."
Shawn and Sarita quickly seconded the request, Gerti looked at them like they were snitching or something.

"Fine if we take the easy one, we will race down it," Carolyn said.

"Ok, it's a straight shot."
Before Morgan or the others could continue their debate, Gerti and Carolyn hit the gas leaving Dominic in the dust. Morgan and Lina both closed their eyes at the same time while Shawn and Sarita docked down as far as they could. Barreling down the trail towards the dolphin enclosure Gerti and Carolyn emerged from the woods at the same time yelling,

"Who won but there was no one outside to see!"

Dominic made it shortly thereafter praising the two daredevil drivers while trying to console their passengers who looked like they had seen better days.

"I'm so glad that is over," Morgan said while trying to catch her breath.

Dominic unlocked the shuttle to let them grab their bags to change,

"I'll be here when you're done."

After trying to rinse off in what can be described as a sprinkler head, they all emerged ready for their next adventure (well the matriarchs at least). Dominic brought out the dolphin instructors

who asked, "who will be the first to treat themselves to the experience of a lifetime?"

Gerti and Carolyn both stepped forward grabbing life jackets in the process. Dominic said

"How did I know you two would be first?"

Once in the water the dolphins swam up to the waiting Gerti and Carolyn. To Morgan they looked like sharks which freaked her out. She was freaked out a second time when she noticed iguanas walking around freely. Gerti told her to calm down as she herself was pushed through the beautiful water by a dolphin. The ladies marveled at the joy that was on Gerti's and Carolyn's faces, so much so they each gave them their tickets to the dolphin ride. They wanted to argue but the encounter was a thrill like no other; they simply said,

"Thank you."

Dominic showed the landlubbers around the habitat pointing out the different types of birds flying around. He failed in his attempts to get Lina or Shawn to hold an exotic snake. However, Morgan agreed to be wrapped in the yellow boa. Dominic explained that it was a protected species that loves to sun itself on rocks before hunting. Sarita held a thunder snake that was dazzling to look at because of its vibrant color pattern.

Fresh from their extended dolphin swims, the mermaids also took part in the reptile experience.

"Come on, it's fun," they said.
Lina and Shawn remained steadfast in the decision. After holding the snakes Gerti asked Dominic about the 30ft slide that he promised.

"It's not far, we just need to take these mini boats to the other side."

"Ohhh, we will drive?" Carolyn asked.

"Sorry, we have to drive them," Dominic answered to the delight of Morgan and the others.
Dominic loaded the boats and began the drive across the lake. During the journey he pointed out the stingrays underneath them.

"This is one of the most magnificent things that I have ever seen," Gerti said.

"Well, I thank you on behalf of my island," Dominic said, looking around at the natural treasures.

They rounded the bend as the sight of the slide came into view,

"Oh damn," Lina said as they looked up at the 30ft monster.

Before them stood a 30ft yellow and green slide, Morgan was at the base of the slide looking up from the mini boat wondering why anyone would get on the slide.

"Any takers?"

The normally adventurous matriarchs both sat back with hell no written on their faces. Dominic was trying to convince someone to give it a try when a weather report came over the radio.

"Sorry ladies, a storm is rolling in, we have to get off the water."

"Oh man I wanted to do it," Sarita said before she quickly backed down as Dominic told her he would wait for her.

"The good news is if we leave now, we still have a chance to do some ziplining."

Confused, Morgan asked, "who the world said anything about ziplining?"

"We did," Gerti said to the dismay of the bevy of ladies.

Dominic made his way back to the shuttle Morgan, Shawn, Sarita, and Lina each took turns praying that the rain would come.

The shuttle pulled into the large zipline park ranging from easy to hard skill levels. Thankfully, it seemed that their collective prayers for rain did not work. Morgan, Lina, Shawn, and Sarita were dragging behind the speed walking Gerti and Carolyn as they tried to beat the storm. Scripture states,

"God may not come when you call but he is always on time."
When Gerti and Mrs. Carolyn finished getting instructions for the course, Morgan's and the others' prayers came true. Heavy rain began to fall as Gerti, and Carolyn stood watching disappointed. Morgan and Lina hugged as they were unable to control their excitement. Shawn and Sarita high-fived a little more discreetly, seeing Gerti giving Lina and Morgan the death-stare. When Dominic came to tell the group the bad news the younger ladies were already on the shuttle. Surprised, he chuckled to himself as he saw the anger on Gerti's face.

"Do you want to try and wait it out?"
This brought hope to the eyes of Carolyn and Gerti while bringing despair to the once happy souls on the shuttle. After several tense moments for Morgan and the others Gerti said,

"No, it is ok we can go."

When Carolyn boarded the shuttle Morgan was the first to go in for a hug to thank her, but Gerti tried to stop her. Seeing this, the others ran up and joined in on the forced group hug. Carolyn and Gerti tried to fight but they were outnumbered.

"Ok you got your hug now get off me you heathens," Gerti said as she sat down.

Carolyn said, "turn the music up and let's roll."

"Yes ma'am."

The rain danced on the window as each woman took power naps after their adventurous day. The silence was broken when Lina asked,

"How do you do 45yrs?"

Gerti and Carolyn looked at each other and said, "painfully." Morgan asked the question again. Seeing the four attentive faces looking back at them this time Gerti took the question a little more seriously,

"You take it one day at a time, some days I hated my husband, some days I loved him, and some I wanted to kill him but underneath I knew we were in it together."

Carolyn said, "I thought I had fallen out of love with my husband, but it was more like our love was entering a different stage."

Gerti said, "We married for life back then not like to-day, it was for keeps."

"Now don't get me wrong, if he's a beater then shoot his ass and leave," Carolyn said.

Lina and the others hung onto every word that came out of Gerti's and Carolyn's mouth.

"You all have good men so cut them some slack and above all else cut yourselves major slack," Gerti said.

Mrs. Carolyn said, "the biggest thing I had to learn as a young wife was that my love was not there to make me happy. I had to find happiness in myself. Once I did, our marriage improved drastically."

As the counseling session was concluded the shuttle arrived back at the resort. Just like with Fitzroy, Dominic tried to turn down the tip, but Gerti and Carolyn were a little more forceful than Pete. Walking into the resort lobby Carolyn saw a purple drink and made a b-line to grab one with Gerti right behind her. Once at the bar she ordered a round for everyone bringing an official end to the adventure. Carolyn had built up such a rapport with the bartenders that all their drinks were turned into doubles.

"Wow, is this what you guys have been drinking?" Morgan asked, trying to catch her breath after the first sip.

Shawn added saying, "I can only do one, anymore and I might not make it to the dinner."

Each woman went their separate ways to change as Carolyn ordered her second round to go.

{ 22 }

Don't Be Late

The women gathered at the front of the restaurant marveling at its breathtaking design. The restaurant looked to be cut into the side of a mountain which was confusing and somewhat out of place at a Caribbean resort. The hostess noticed their confusion and came to assist she explained that this was the resort's Italian-Caribbean fusion restaurant styled after the Ristorante Grotta Palazzese located in Italy. The light bouncing off the rocks added to the ultra-romantic setting overlooking the Adriatic Sea but, in their case, it was overlooking a wonderful, secluded beach. As the women made their way inside, they compared the pictures of the Italian views on the wall to the resort's interpretation on it and despite a little island flavor the rendition was amazing. Once they were seated at the beautifully decorated table each woman took a turn complimenting a different area of the restaurant. Aunt Gerti talked about how nice the chairs where, Lina focused on the flowers blowing in the breeze, Morgan spoke of the uniqueness of the floor design, Sarita took several pictures of the last bit of sun as it cascaded across the water, Shawn twirled in her chair as the light bounced off the man-made rocks, and Mrs. Carolyn admired the strength of the drinks. Morgan looked around for Travis,

"How much do you want to bet that the guys are going to be late?"

"That's an easy bet," Shawn said.

"He better not be late," Gerti said as she asked the waiter to give them a few more minutes before ordering.

"For their sake I hope they aren't," Morgan said as she smiled at Gerti.

"Look this man has been blaming me for being late for 45 dang years, I'm early for once and as I said, his tail better be on time."

As Gerti was making her declaration, the guys ran off the shuttle to change and make it to dinner.

"Damn if we're late, I'll never hear the end of it," Uncle Pete said as he hurried the group along. Thankfully the men in the group all had thoughtful wives, the women had taken the time to lay out the attire for their husbands. They either did it to be nice, or they knew the guys had a better than chance of being late. Whatever the reason it was a life saver as it allowed the men to make it downstairs in good time. The hostess walked the out of breath track stars to the table as they to marveled at the wonderful sites of the restaurant. Gerti looked at her watch which prompted Uncle Pete,

"We made it on time, woman."

"Haven't you always told me if you're early you're on time and if you're on time you're late?"

As if on cue, Uncle Pete being the wise old married man replied,

"When you're in international waters that doesn't count."

Gerti tried to hit him as the table erupted in laughter. During the laughter Kerry was brought over by the hostess.

He sat down, "I can't believe you guys left me."

"Hey, we waited but you took too long," Justin said.

"I had to iron my clothes, how in the hell did you get ready so fast?" Kerry asked taking Travis's drink.

"Well, my lovely wife pulled out my clothes," Justin said with each guy agreeing and thanking their wives.

"Oh, ain't that something."

"Well, get a woman instead of a girl," Lina said, dumping on Kerry even more.

Unable to respond Kerry simply sat there and sipped on his stolen drink.

After the appetizers were ordered Morgan asked Uncle Pete if he enjoyed his excursion.

"I had a wonderful time sweetie; I was able to learn so much about the island and the sites at Jessie's Café were ridiculously beautiful. Oh, and I watched people jump off the cliff."

"Oh wow, did you try it?" Morgan asked, looking at Travis.

"Nope, I got some drinks and sat in the pool."

"Did anyone jump?" Shawn asked, looking at her husband.

"Kerry was the only person who took the leap," Justin said, smirking.

"Why are you smirking?" Lina asked, sensing something was up.

"Well, ask him," Norman said, trying not to laugh.

"Hey, I jumped, I didn't see any of you guys doing it."

"True he did jump from 8ft," Uncle Pete said.

"8ft is good," Aunt Gerti said.

"True my love but toddlers were jumping from the 8ft platform."

"Oh," Gerti said, trying to avoid eye contact with

Kerry.

Trying to turn the attention away from himself Kerry went on

the attack,

"Well at least I didn't spend my life savings getting a

few cigars."

"Oh, yea we did go to a cool little cigar shop named

after a fallen veteran," Uncle Pete said.

As the women looked around to see which of their loves

spent said fortune Joseph began to fiddle in his chair.

"How much did you spend?" Shawn asked, looking

intensely at Joseph.

"Who me?"

Shawn repeated her question as she leaned in closer to him.

Joseph looked angrily at Kerry,

"Thanks," as he tried to avoid answering the question.

"Better you than me."

Shawn, still waiting on an answer, looked as if she was going

to explode. Uncle Pete tried to defuse the situation,

"Don't get us kicked out of this resort the night be-

fore my vow renewal."

Shawn sat back in the chair and said, "yes, Uncle

Pete."

"Thanks baby girl besides it's not like we had to drag him out of there or something," Uncle Pete said which made the guys laugh, well all except Joseph.

The stare down was broken up when the chef sent out an order of his signature special crab cake appetizers after hearing about the couple's 45yr marriage vow renewal. With tempers dialed down slightly, Aunt Gerti asked the waiter to thank the chef as Uncle Pete shook his hand. Everyone tasted the crab cakes; Mrs. Carolyn was the first to ask if it tasted funny.

"Yea it tastes as if it came from a can," Morgan said. Lina and Sarita agreed as they pushed the non-fresh appetizer aside. Kerry thought the crab cakes were great, he took both the discarded appetizers from Shawn and Sarita. Despite some at the table being disappointed in the crab cakes they praised the chef for his infusion ideas when he walked up. He bragged about his credentials before telling them about the specials. He explained there was a choice between flash grilled steaks or garlic shaken chicken. Justin was unsure about the chef's infusion descriptions so he suggested that Lina order the steak and he would order the chicken just in case. The other couples followed suit by ordering both the steak and chicken. Kerry tried to order both meals, but the hostess told him due to other parties that he could only have

one. He tried to charm her but struggled badly trying to pro-
nounce her name.

"Raaeena," he said with attempt number one.

"No, sir."

"Raenu."

"No, sir."

Kerry looked closer at her name tag, "Raquon."

Even with the second look she responded with "No,
sir."
Unable to continue witnessing this massive train wreck, Aunt
Gerti stepped in,

"Love, please put him out of his misery by telling him
your name."
She smiled at Aunt Gerti,

"Yes mam, I am Raeni (Ray-knee), and it means Caribbean queen."
As she walked away, she turned back and told Kerry he could
still only have one order. Kerry sat there stunned at Raeni.

Trying to take the attention away from Kerry's utter failure,
Justin began to explain how they almost got stuck at the other
resort thanks to the raging storm.

"Wow babe, that sounds crazy."
He continued explaining how the road was washed out in
spots and as they drove how the water was so high it reached

the bottom window of the shuttle. The women looked con-cerned, until Uncle Pete explained how the storm had a silver lining. He told them about stopping at a local jerk chicken spot that was freaking amazing.

"Oh yea, babe I was going to bring you some," Travis said looking at Morgan.

"I love jerk chicken," Morgan said before Travis could finish telling her he ate it all. You ass."

"I'll be that. It was freaking good."

"How was your day of relaxing and pampering?" Norman asked.

The table fell silent with the younger women looking at each other. Mrs. Carolyn broke the silence,

"We didn't do any pampering. We went out and tasted life."

"I tasted bugs and mud but I'm not sure I tasted life," Morgan said in retort.

Aunt Gerti answered for the women,

"We went off-roading in ATV's, dolphin swimming, and held some snakes. We were supposed to go ziplining, but we got rained out."

In shock, the husbands looked at his wives and said a version of you did that. Everyone except for Uncle Pete, after all he helped plan it with Gerti.

"Wow, babe that sounds amazing," Justin said.

> Lina reluctantly agreed, "It was crazy at first and com-
> pletely out of the box, but we got some great photos
> and saw an amazing waterfall."

Morgan seconded what Lina was describing and added that relaxing would have been perfect and despite nearly dying thanks to our elderly drivers it was a good day.

> "I got your elderly," Mrs. Carolyn said pointing her

finger at Morgan.

As they laughed, the waiters started bringing the meals to the delight of everyone. As discussed, each couple got separate meals, and Raeni gave Kerry the chicken. She was not playing with him. For a few moments, the table fell silent, all that could be heard was forks scraping off plates and the occasional umm or mumbled damn. Uncle Pete broke the silence,

> "Hot damn this steak is juicy, tender, loaded with
> freaking flavor, and it has just the right amount of
> fat."

He cut a piece of the steak and gave it to Gerti as planned. She too loved the lean cherry-red part of the meat. Unfortunately, they were the only couple to follow the preset rules. Morgan gave Travis some of her steak while asking him about his chicken.

"This damn chicken is one of the most well-prepared things I have ever had. It's juicy but not at all too rich or overpowering."

Morgan, now intrigued, tried to get a piece as he leaned away from her. Surprised, she looked around the table to see if anyone else was having as much trouble as she was. After hearing the description, it should not be a surprise that no one was sharing, Lina tried to stab Justin as he went in for a piece of her chicken. Norman got a piece of Sarita's steak when she was not looking but he quickly put it back when she stared at him. Joseph gave Shawn a piece of steak so small she had to take a picture of it for future reference. Mrs. Carolyn had a bit of her steak and gave the rest to Kerry opting for more sides than a main course. Uncle Pete and Aunt Gerti sat back and laughed at how selfish the couples were being. After dinner Uncle Pete and Aunt Gerti were leaving when he turned,

"I don't know at y'all but I'm trying to get a little nookie," tonight.

Aunt Gerti slapped his arm and told him not to be nasty.

The group walked out of the beautiful restaurant when Uncle Pete looked up,

"It's a beautiful night'."

Aunt Gerti grabbed his hand, "yes, it is."

Kerry walked behind them,

"I don't want the night to end, let's check out that pub."

"Oh yea, I've been wanting to go in there," Mrs. Carolyn said changing directions.

"Ok, we can go for a minute, but we have to get up early tomorrow," Aunt Gerti said.

"Yes dear, I only plan on having six to ten tequila shots."
Kerry held the big wooden door saying welcome to The Royal Oxford Pub.

Lina said "thanks," and slapped him on the back of the head as she walked in.

"Good evening welcome to the Royal Oxford Pub, we have a wonderful Shepherd's pie, fish n chips, Banger'n Mash."
She could tell by the looks on their faces that the term bangers n mash confused the hell out of them,

"Ok, bangers n mash is a British term for sausage and mashed potatoes."

"Ok, I was wondering what kind of place this was," Justin said laughing.

"Shit it sounds like a place I visited in Nam," Uncle Pete said laughing.

"A place you what?" Aunt Gerti asked, holding a fork to Uncle Pete's arm.

"A place I heard about… just heard about, baby."

"Right, heard about," Joseph said laughing,

"Shut up, fool," Uncle Pete said.

"Don't tell my favorite nephew to shut up when you said it," Aunt Gerti said.

Morgan told the waiter that they were just here for drinks trying to take some of the heat off Uncle Pete.

The waiter laughed as she passed out the drink menus instead. Travis looked over the menu,

"Bring me the Tyger-Tyger beer and what is the Tyger-Tyger beer."

"Oh, sir it is a clear, bitter apple flavored beer with a citrus finish."

"That sounds complicated as hell, I will have the Huntsman Ale," Justin said.

"Great choice, the Huntsman Ale is a heavy lager with a bold malty flavor."

"Yea that's what I thought."

"Whatever, bring us a dozen tequila shots please."

Lina said as she took the menu from Justin.

"Oh, you guys are trying to party I see."

"You better believe it," Uncle Pete said.

The waiter laughed as she went to put in their drink order.

"Hey, I didn't get to order," Kerry said.

"You do know those shots are for everyone right," Morgan said looking at Kerry.

"Oh, I thought she was about to turn up to the max."

"I hear you, let's turn up," Uncle Pete said.

"Nope I will not have you drunk at the altar again so you will be turning down," Aunt Gerti said.

Collectively the table looked at him, "damn, Uncle Pete."

"Come on Gerti it wasn't my fault, Carolyn's husband took me to the starlight and had a bottle of shine," Uncle Pete argued looking at Mrs. Carolyn.

"Oh, you two fools smelled just like a liquor barrel," Mrs. Carolyn said.

"I know and I will not have that again," Gerti said.

"Woman, I plan on being drunk all day."

Aunt Gerti cocked her head to the side, "excuse me."

"You heard me," Uncle Pete said before getting up to put some distance between him and his beloved.

"You better run," Aunt Gerti said as Uncle Pete tried to cover up the fact that he ran by helping the waiter bring the shots to the table.

After passing out the sizable tequila shots, Uncle Pete gave a toast,

"All jokes aside, I want to thank you all for being here with Gerti and I. I've loved this woman long before I knew how to love, and she has put up with me for 45yrs and I thank her for that."

Gerti stood up,

"Thank you, my love, but we're still going to talk about you in Nam."

Everyone busted up laughing as they clinked their glasses together.

"Oh, that's smooth," Shawn said.

Sarita stood up, "another round garcon!"

"Girl sit down," Aunt Gerti said.

It was too late; the bartender was already making the second round for the table. As the drinks were being made a group of young attractive women were checking Kerry out. However, for some unforeseen reason he was not returning their energy. Travis got Justin's attention so he could witness the documented womanizer avoid eye contact and invitations from the table.

After the second shot was taken Justin asked Kerry if was feeling ok.

"Yea I'm good what are you talking about."

"What I am talking about, I'm talking about how you're knowingly ignoring those women."

"Oh that, I'm good for the night," Kerry said which completely confused his friends.

Justin and Travis tried to continue their inquiry but were blocked by their wives.

"Look he doesn't feel like hooking up with random people so drop it," Morgan said with Lina backing her the whole way.

After some much appreciated water to wash down the second shot Aunt Gerti took Uncle Pete's hand,

"Let's take a walk my dear."

Uncle Pete kissed hand, "yes dear."
The two said their goodbyes to the group before making their exit.

Shawn grabbed Joseph, "that's sweet, let go see the water honey."

"I'm sleepy, I want to go to bed," Joseph said but Shawn was already pulling him towards the water.

Kerry said, "let's keep turning up, no need to go to sleep."

Norman said, "count us out too, we got one more kid free night and I'm trying to hurt myself."
He grabbed a blushing Sarita's hand and scampered off.

"Oh, let me guess, you guys are leaving also."

"Nope not yet," Lina said as she and Morgan got up to dance.

Travis ordered a round of Tyger-Tyger for the table but almost on cue after tasting it they simultaneously put the draft down,

"No thanks."

Now sipping on a better draft beer Justin looked at Kerry,

"Dude, you really aren't trying to go over there."

Kerry again turned down the chance.

"Ok, I don't know what's up but it's cool with me," Travis said as he sipped on his beer.

After dancing to some classic 90's Hip-Hop Morgan put her head on Travis's shoulder,

"I need to get some sleep; I have that hair and makeup appointment in the morning."

"Girl you better go," Lina said as she got up to hug her goodbye.

"Yea and I'm trying to see what the hype is with these morning beach walks," Travis said.

"Trust me bro, you'll love it."

Kerry was the next to leave, he decided to go to his room alone. Justin and Lina were leaving when the DJ put on *Spend My Life With You* stopping them in their tracks. They had to take the opportunity to dance to their wedding song in a British Pub in the Caribbean.

{ 23 }

Vows

The next morning, Travis woke up early as planned so he could walk the beach and receive some of the peace that Justin had been raving about. As he moved around like a ninja trying not to wake Morgan the alarm clock began to chime, Morgan rolled over,

"I'm up."

"Ok you're up for what?"

"I have to meet Aunt Gerti, so we get our hair and makeup done for the vow renewal," Morgan said sitting on the side of the bed.

"Oh damn, you're starting early, just put it in a ponytail."

"Shut up fool, we're meeting at 06:30 so we'll have time to do everything," she said while getting out of the bed.

"Ok good luck with that," Travis said before kissing her and leaving for the beachfront.

Justin was already walking on the beach when Travis approached and told him Red's plan.

"Damn, that's a lot."

"I know right, I tried to tell her."

"I hear you; Lina wants me to wake her at 07:30 for an 11 o'clock event."

"Dude these women are crazy," Travis said with Justin nodding in agreement.

While walking they passed Shawn and Sarita who were making their way to join in on the hair and makeup festivities. After his morning walk, Justin went to wake his wife for her own glam session. Walking back to his room Travis began to hear someone call his name. He looked around for a minute but saw no one.

"Up here!" Morgan yelled.

"Oh hey, what's up?" Travis answered after seeing Aunt Gerti and Morgan on the balcony.

"Do Not let my husband have too many drinks before this ceremony." Aunt Gerti yelled sternly pointing at him.

Travis stood there confused until he remembered Uncle Pete saying he was going to tie one on before walking down the aisle again. Morgan reiterated Aunt Gerti's words and added,

"You better not be drunk either!"
Travis tried to reassure them that he and Uncle Pete would be on their best behavior but neither of the women believed him.

Now back in his room, Justin gently woke Lina with a kiss to her forehead,

"Morning love."
Lina responded by kissing him on the cheek trying not to share her morning breath with him. She got up to get ready and to make a second attempt to skype the kids who were obviously having a great time with grandma and grandpa. They tried to talk to the kids, but grandpa was about to take Triston fishing and grandma was taking Jasmine shopping, so Justin and Lina got a cliff note version of their vacation before getting hung up on.

"Damn, our kids don't even need us," Justin said as he hung up the phone.
His disbelief was short-lived when he turned and saw Lina picking out clothes naked. He caressed his wife's curves until she put him on hold until after the vow renewal. With his plans put on hold Justin got in the shower to cool off, Lina joined in the shower moments later. Justin thought it was to tempt him, but Lina had other things on her mind as well. After enjoying each other in the shower, Justin sat on the bed

watching Caribbean football while Lina continued to get ready,

"I am almost done!"

This prompted Justin to get up and get dressed. After a few selfies the two made their way to breakfast where they ran into an extremely happy Kerry.

"Dude, what's going on with you?"

"I'm just happy!"

"Is he high?" Lina asked.

"He might be," Justin said as he laughed.

Justin held the door as Mrs. Carolyn was walking in shining like Patti LaBelle,

"Wow, you look amazing."

"Thank you, baby, so do you," Mrs. Carolyn responded as she asked them to join her.

Travis interrupted Justin ordering breakfast asking him to come with him to make sure Uncle Pete was still kinda sober for the ceremony.

"Hey babe grab me a muffin or something and I'll be right back."

"Ok I got you," Lina said as Travis and Justin went off with a skipping Kerry. Lina looked at Mrs. Carolyn, "ok let's eat.

"Yes, let's eat and have mimosas."

When the guys made it to Uncle Pete's room they were met by Norman and Joseph.

"Hey, did Uncle Pete call you guys?" Joseph asked.

"No, Aunt Gerti told me not to let him get drunk." Travis said.

After knocking for a few seconds Uncle Pete came to the door wearing nothing but boxers and socks.

"Unc cover that thing up," Norman said as they entered the room.

"It's my room; besides, I was getting dressed and having some fun with the mini bar."

"Aunt Gerti told me to make sure you don't have too many so how about you slow down a little." Travis said.

"Oh, are you a narc? You know what snitches get."

Kerry laughed, "I haven't seen anything as long as I can have a little taste."

"Of course, everyone is welcome, well maybe not the narc," Uncle Pete said as he poured drinks for them. Not trying to be offensive, Travis took the drink offered to him,

"That's my boy."

"Ok, but just one, I'm not trying to get my ass kicked today."

"Ok deal, I need to finish getting dressed anyway."

"Yes you do and put some lotion on them elbows," Joseph said, cracking himself up.

Dressed and now downstairs Uncle Pete and the groomsmen made their way to meet with the hotel's liaison. As they waited out front Lina and Mrs. Carolyn came up and met them,

"Ok we are here now what?" Uncle Pete asked. A tall resort liaison came and told the group that the women were slightly delayed, and they were going to have to wait at the hammock bar.

"Shit that sounds good to me," Uncle Pete said as he started to make his way to the bar. The group made its way down the beach wondering what a slight delay meant. After meeting at 630 the bridal party took a shuttle to get their hair and nails done but of course there was traffic. When they finally arrived at the salon a mix up limited the number of staff, so they had to wait, which was not put into the time budget. To top it off, the salon messed up the colors of their nails and even cracked one of Shawn's real nails as they tried to fix their previous mistake. After several delays they were finally on the way back to the resort to get dressed in their reserved VIP suite. Meanwhile, back at the hammock bar Uncle Pete and the others moved from one side of the bar to the other trying to avoid the pounding rays from the sun. Travis's mission was successful at first but that was mainly due to the bar still being closed. His job got harder when the heavyset bartender opened the bar. Trying to avoid danger Travis ordered a round of purple paradises for everyone thinking the mixed drink would help keep the alcohol level down. This effort proved futile; unfortunately, Uncle Pete persuaded the bartender to add extra shots to their drinks and to turn the music up.

Now back at the resort the bridal party made their way to the VIP suite, unfortunately when they arrived their liaison had the wrong keys. So, as she ran off to find the right pair, Aunt Gerti and the others had to sit and wait with barely any shade from the intensity of the sun. After skipping breakfast to get her hair and makeup done Aunt Gerti was starting to get real DAMN hangry. By the time the resort liaison made it back some of their makeup needed to be touched up. Now in VIP, Moran texted Travis to explain her awful morning. Travis tried to reassure her that things would be ok and suggested ordering room service for the starving ladies. She took his advice and ordered a fruit and cheese platter that proved to be a lifesaver. The sampler helped Aunt Gerti to relax as she and the bridesmaids began to get dressed. Back at the bar, the groomsmen and Uncle Pete continued to hide from the sun,

Lina however was sitting out enjoying every ray she could find. After three or four purple paradises complete with extra shots the resort liaison came in yelling,

"Ok let's go, we have a celebration to get to!" as she clapped her hands loudly.
Uncle Pete finished his drink,

"Let's get me hitched again."
Lina wanted more time in the sun, but she got up as the party headed to the venue. The venue was a church that was overlooking the water with floor to ceiling windows, it was decorated in gold and off white with all the doors and windows open to maximize the breeze. As Justin followed Lina to their seats, he stumbled a little, Lina looked back at her,

"Damn those purple paradises may have been stronger than I thought."

The music started as Uncle Pete walked down the aisle which was his only request followed by Travis and Morgan who was in a beautiful off the shoulder gold shimmery dress, next up was Joseph and Shawn who was in a form fitting dress with 6-inch spiked heels, and lastly Norman and Sarita came in wearing a wonderful flowing gold dress with white accents. The doors to the church opened prompting everyone to stand as Aunt Gerti made her way down the aisle. Aunt Gerti walked in wearing a gorgeous sleek wedding dress that gripped her waist perfectly as it fell to the floor just below her hips. She walked down the aisle to their original song of *At Last* by Etta James. Uncle Pete could be seen pinching himself to make sure he was not dreaming.

The music stopped as the preacher said take your seats, he started:

> "We are gathered here to celebrate love, not just love but a 45-year love affair. Most of us in this room are not 50 years old yet, their love is simply amazing. You two have seen so many things together, been there, fought, hated, loved and circled back around again."

As the preacher continued the guest could not help but notice that the groom and groomsmen were swaying from side to side. The extra shots were catching up with them as the breeze pushed the smell of purple paradise throughout the church with every exhale. The preacher asked Uncle Pete to face his bride and repeat after him, as he began to recite his vows Aunt Gerti cut him off and asked if he was drunk. Uncle Pete tried to look as sober as possible when he answered her with an of course not, the question and the answer made everyone laugh except for Aunt Gerti. The preacher sped up the remaining parts of the ceremony up. That was until it was time to sign as a witness, Norman gave a half assed attempt to sign the document as those purple paradises were talking to him. The Preacher had him sign twice before the wedding was over.

As the wedding party exited the church the bride and groom were snagged for pictures. Now outside the bridesmaids began to question their husbands about why they were so drunk. Travis tried to defend them,

"We only had one or two."

Morgan quickly shot that down, "you never just have one or two."
Norman was the second to try and defend their actions, but Sarita shut him up before he could utter a sound. Joseph seeing the two failures he did not even try to mount a defense, Shawn looked at him,

"Yea just keep quiet."
Justin cracked the tension when he asked if the video camera caught Aunt Gerti's question, it lightened the mood as they all chuckled. After the bride and groom were done taking photos it was now time for the remainder of the renewal party to have their photos taken. Lina complemented Aunt Gerti how beautiful her dress was.
Uncle Pete asked Justin,

"Can you believe what Gerti did?"
Justin, however, tried his best to avoid involving himself in that trouble.

"Oh, please you had way too many drinks," Aunt Gerti said.

Uncle Pete looked around for help, but he stopped before asking Lina assuming she would tell the truth. As the group took photo after photo the liaison said,

"It's 1:30 now, your reception will be held at 3pm in the state room."

 "Word," Kerry said as he kissed the bride before skipping back down the beach.

"Ok, he might be drunk," Uncle Pete said.

Each couple made their way down the beach to their rooms separately but they each had similar stories after arriving at their. Justin was rubbing Lina's hair on the way back but fell asleep as she undressed, Travis sat on the bed talking to Morgan about having a little fun before the reception but he passed out sitting up, Sarita had to help a sleeping Norman off the toilet, Joseph barely made it to the room before passing out in the chair, and lastly Uncle Pete was unable to consummate his remarriage as he too passed out.

When Lina was unable to wake Justin, she decided to take a walk on the beach. As she made her way down the beach she was joined by Morgan and Shawn. They passed Sarita as she was laying out on a chair, she decided to join in the walk as well. They met Aunt Gerti and Ms. Carolyn at the hammock bar,

"Dang we're all here," Morgan said.

"Yup, I'm sure your men are sleeping just as mine is," Aunt Gerti said.

They all agreed and took turns telling how each one of the husbands fell asleep. They decided to have a few purple paradises as they enjoyed the afternoon breeze. After some much needed time relaxing in hammocks and having rum punches and purple paradises, Aunt Gerti said,

"Ok ladies, let's get these men up so we aren't late." They finished their drinks and headed back to wake their sleeping beauties. Lina had an easy time waking Justin who sprung up as she opened the door to the room. It took a splash of cold water to wake up Norman who was sleeping too hard for normal actions. Joseph was nearly rolled onto the floor before he finally got up, Travis begged Morgan to leave him alone, but she continued to nag him until he got up. Aunt Gerti had the toughest time waking Uncle Pete, he asked if he could skip the reception to a resounding hell no from Aunt Gerti. She got dressed as he was laying there like he was dead or at least wishing he were, she told him if he was late then do not come at all as she walked out the door. Uncle Pete laid there a little longer before getting up and forcing himself to get ready. Each couple made it there, but you could see the struggle on each of their faces. They entered the reception hall and saw a friendly face; Linford was the DJ for the event. He pumped up the music as soon as Aunt Gerti and a sober-ish Uncle Pete came in, they danced to *These arms of mine* by Otis Redding.

Linford had the reception jumping as the guys forgot all about being too drunk to do anything earlier. As the party raged on the hostess Raeni (Ray-knee) came in to assist at the event and because Linford was the DJ. Kerry assumed she came for him.

"Oh, damn I see you," Linford said, which made everyone take a second look at Raeni who was in her normal clothes.

"Is this why you were skipping around all day?" Lina asked Kerry.

"No."

"Way to redeem yourself," Travis said.

"You know me," Kerry said, not wanting to get into the real reason he was skipping.

"Did you just look to see where she was?" Justin asked.

"Shut up."

"Oh, scared already," Travis said laughing.

"What's wrong with him being respectful?" Morgan asked Travis, who was unaware she heard him.

He tried to change the subject. Morgan looked at him as she walked off.

"Oh, but I'm the scare one."

"Shut up fool, she might still be looking," Travis said. Linford played a good mix of old and new jams, in no time everyone was dancing and sweating like they did when they were teenagers. The party continued until the event manager came in a second time telling them to shut it down, just as she had to do during the Rum party. Linford told the renewal party that he was DJing that night at a festival if they wanted to continue the party. The couples declined his offer worried they would miss their return flights in the mornings.

{ 24 }

Leaving Paradise

The next morning, Justin continued with his daily routine of strolling down the beachfront. During his walk, Justin greeted a couple who walked by him without speaking in return. He was not offended by their actions; he assumed that they had just gotten to the resort and that the calm of the island had not settled in them yet. He dabbed up Kerry who was taking a few selfies before boarding the shuttle for the airport. They met Travis at the shuttle as he was bringing down Aunt Gerti's bags.

Kerry said, "I forgot you were staying longer; I should have extended my stay."

"It's cool, I figured Lina needed more time in paradise," Justin said.

"True and after hearing about their excursion I'm sure they'll be good with our surprise," Travis said.

The group took a few more photos before Fitzroy came off the shuttle,

"I'm sad to see you leave but I will be happy to drop you lovely people off. All I want to know is if you had fun in my home?"

"We had an amazing time, I'm just sad it took us so long to make it here," Aunt Gerti said.

With the group now on the shuttle, Fitzroy began to tell them about the friendship festival planned for the upcoming week-end. He told them that the festival was established to unite the island's newcomers with the locals. He explained how the entire island turns out for the party with restaurants supplying the food and local DJ's taking turns entertaining the crowds.

"Man, I wish we would have known that." Joseph said.

"Don't worry my friend, I will take pictures for you." Fitzroy passed the party off to Bob who was waiting to get them through immigration as quickly as he had done once be-fore. Once at the gates the couples sat around looking at the pictures from the week, before boarding their return flights. Kerry boarded his flight eager to get home. After a connec-tion or two he made it back to the city. After waiting on his bags, he walked out to a waiting BMW,

"Hey beautiful I missed you."

Back at the resort, Lina met Justin on the beach as Morgan and Travis sat on the deck enjoying the sunshine. Standing in silence, Lina and Justin held hands as they listened to the water crashing on the rocks.

"I want to live on an island."
Her statement sparked an old conversation that the two had from time to time throughout the years.

"Yes, I agree, we should start looking as soon as we get back."

"Thanks babe, I know you don't really like the beach."

"Normally that would be true but this island feeling along with the clear water makes it a harder decision." After a few more moments staring at the water Justin and Lina grabbed a round of purple paradises and joined Morgan and Travis on the deck. The couples sipped on their drinks as a refreshing breeze swept by.

"Man, this is great," Travis said.

"Agreed."

"What are your plans for today?" Morgan asked.

"Oh yea, you guys made the ATVing sound great, so we signed us all up." Justin said.

"Excuse me?" Lina asked, looking at Justin.

"It will be great," Travis said, egging Justin on.
Looking for answers, Lina put down her drank,

"You better be freaking joking."

"Yea, we're joking," Travis said to the relief of the women.

"So, what is on the agenda for today then?" Lina asked.

"We're doing a glass boat tour."

"Really, I don't want to do that," Morgan said.

"What do you guys want to do?" Justin asked.

"I'm trying to relax," Morgan said.

"Well, you are in luck, Justin and I are doing the glass boat tour and you two are having a spa day."

"Are you serious, babe?"

"Yea, I'm serious."

"When do we go?" Lina asked.

"It's an open appointment; all you have to do is show up and get started." Justin said.

"But before you guys run off, I want to grab some food," Travis said.

"Rain check hun," Morgan said as the two women ran off to change.

Lina blew a kiss as she and Morgan ran past Justin and Travis who were still on the deck. The ladies entered the beautiful spa and overheard,

Discover a completely unique mind body experience that transforms you - inside and out.

"Damn, I want some of that." Lina said as the hostess came out to greet them.

"Welcome Ladies, we have been expecting you," the host said, introducing himself as Trevor.

"Thank you, we are excited to be here."

"Have a seat and we'll bring a menu of our services," Trevor said before directing them to the waiting room.

The ladies sat in a waiting room adorned with large floral patterns, inspired by the beautiful traditions and majestic natural backdrops of the Caribbean scenery. Trevor brought out service menus and two waters infused with cucumbers.

"Thank you," Morgan said, taking the menu.

Lina tasted the water and said, "wow, this is amazing."

"Thank you, I adore the water as well," Trevor said as he took a seat.

He went on to explain that their husbands left a blank balance of whatever the ladies wanted,

"As I told your significant others, a blank balance was unnecessary, but they insisted that you two get whatever your heart's desire."

"Oh wow, how I love that fool," Lina said.

Morgan agreed before asking about the Caribbean Flame.

"It is an organic renewal wrap that utilizes dynamic minerals to warm, firm, tone, and leaves you with silky irresistible skin."

 "Oh, I want that," Morgan said, putting her menu down.

"I'm torn between the Seaweed Body Treatment and the Victorian Lemon drop."

"Those are two wonderful choices; the Lemon Drop is a plush polishing from Finland with reverse-aging properties. It soothes dry patches while washing away impurities. The Seaweed Treatment forms to your body and hydrates the skin while reducing the appearance of cellulite. Either choice will be Phenomenal."

"OH, yes, I will take the Lemon Drop but keep the Seaweed wrap close just in case."

With their selections now chosen each lady was led into a warm dimly lit room to prepare for their pampering. Lina's Lemon Drop started by her being wrapped in thermal blankets to ensure her body released stress and toxins. After 30 minutes she showered before receiving a therapeutic massage including reflexology. Lina was already relaxed from the thermal blankets, but the feeling of the massage pushed her into a deep sleep. Morgan's organic renewal wrap began with a light body brush exfoliation, followed by an application of micronized minerals. Unlike Lina, Morgan fell asleep instantly. She had to be woken up for her treatment to continue but soon after repositioning she fell asleep again. Lina was waiting in the recovery room as a still groggy Morgan was led into the room,

"Wow, you look almost too relaxed."

"I feel too relaxed," Morgan said, taking a seat. As they talked about keeping the plush robes and slippers, they were taken to get their nails done. Lina chose bright pink for her feet and hands; Morgan chose an alternating combination of silver and sky blue. Morgan warned the manicurist before she started that she was extremely ticklish. The manicurist assured her that she would take her time. Lina was in her own world as she ran her hands up and down the robe with her eyes closed while receiving her pedicure. Morgan on the other hand was trying to hold her laughter in as the manicurist started on her pedicure, *So far so good.* She giggled and grabbed a hold of her face trying not to be too loud. Morgan was the only one giggling, the manicurist was worried about getting kicked. Lina looked over and laughed. Thankfully, she did not kick anyone. The pampering day came to an end, as they were given their plush robes for bringing some comic relief to the spa.

While Lina and Morgan settled into their spa treatment Justin and Travis embarked on their excursion. They waited near the dock for their ride, the "Unfriendly Rumor." Travis was unimpressed as the lackluster boat began to dock,

"Are you sure this is the right boat?"

"Yea, they said just wait here for the "Unfriendly Rumor," Justin responded.

As the boat docked Travis was hit in the leg by a volleyball. He turned to see a group of kids playing on the beach.

"Sorry sir, can you throw the ball back?"

Justin looked at Travis and secretly wanted to play but was unsure how committed he was to the excursion. He threw the ball back to the waiting kids and turned back towards the "Unfriendly Rumor". Justin looked at the kids playing,

"Dude, I want to play."

"I'm down," Travis said walking away from the docks.

"We got next."

The kids agreed to play Justin and Travis but only if it was kids vs grownups. The adults agreed and began to stretch.

Travis looked at Justin and said, "we got this Goose." referring to *Top Gun.*

"Goose, Goose, if anything you're Goose," Justin responded, rejecting the nickname.

"Goose my ass, if anything I'm Iceman."

"Ok, then I am Maverick."

"Fine that will work, you be Maverick, and I'll be Iceman."

"Really it shouldn't matter, they are just kids after all." The kids finished their game and called Justin and Travis over. As the two players stepped within the square block of sand, Justin looked around at his and Travis's competition. They both noticed they were extremely outnumbered by a ratio of 4:1.

"Bru, was it this many kids here before we accepted their challenge?"

"I think they multiplied but it's cool we have to hit the open spots," Travis said, thinking of a strategy for the game.

Justin looked on as the kids began to rotate and assign positions based on height. *Clearly, they have done this before* Travis thought to himself.

"First one to 15 wins, call out of bounds," Justin said, explaining the rules.

Travis served the ball and quickly the team of two found themselves in trouble. A short round island kid hit the ball to set up a spike. Justin moved in to block the attempt, but his efforts were in vain as a kid quickly shifted gears tapping the ball into an open spot in the sand. Travis and Justin realized they were not only outnumbered but probably out skilled as well. However, they had the height advantage, so they were able to score some points. They ran from one side of the sand to the other, onlookers stopped and watched the over-matched duo. The problem was that no one joined in to even out the odds at all. The bystanders watched and even took a photo or two before continuing with their beach activities. The battle raged on for eternity in Justin's mind but despite their age, the duo was still alive in the match. Travis looked at Justin as they huddled up,

"Bro, we need 3 points."

"We can do it," Justin said as he struggled to get off his knee after the huddle was over.

Travis served and scored easily, *1 down, 2 to go*. He served again and after a lengthy rally, Justin was able to spike and get a point.

"One more, come on bro," Justin said.

"I got you," Travis said, hoping he could pull it off. He served a deep ball that was returned quickly, Justin hit a line drive that was again returned. Justin dove, hitting a bullet to Travis who was able to spike it down.

"Out!" one of the kids yelled.

"Nope, it was on the line," Justin said.

The disagreement continued until one of the kids' dads said it was on the line. Justin and Travis ran off with the victory before the kids could ask for a rematch.

Leaving the Spa Lina and Morgan were extremely relaxed, they decided to walk the beach while the guys finished their excursion. As the two walked and talked, they walked past what they thought were older men sleeping in beach chairs. It was not until Morgan heard one of them say Red, did they realize that the two old men, were their two old men. Lina walked up to a depleted Justin,

"What's going on babe?"

Justin tried to speak but his words were jumbled.

"Babe, are you ok?" Lina asked, now concerned.

"Yea, I'm good just worn the hell out."

"I thought you guys were on your boating thing?" Morgan asked.

"We were but we ran into some kids playing volleyball and decided to join in," Travis said.

"That sounds awesome Babe."

"Sounds good is the key word, those little fuckers ran us to death."

"I mean we won but it feels like we lost," Justin said, rubbing his back.

"Looks like you got beat up," Morgan said sitting down.

"Forget all that, we won, and they lost!"

"How many games did you play?" Lina asked, feeling the rock type knots in Justin's back.

"Just one."

"Babe, I don't think you could have survived a second game," Morgan said, massaging his knee.

"That may be true, how was your spa day?" Justin asked Lina, shifting the conversation.

"It was freaking amazing, thank you for sending us!"

"Yes, it was great, and we got great robes!" Morgan screamed.

"You stole robes?" Travis asked, trying to high-five Morgan.

"No fool, they gave them to us!" Morgan said, trying to hit Travis' hand.

He moved his hand; after learning she was given the robe instead of taking it. Travis liked to collect gym towels or robes from nice hotels.

"What are we doing tonight?" Lina asked.

"I need a nap and some icy-hot," Justin answered.

"Ok, let's go and get some advil grandpa," Morgan said, knowing Travis would need some.

"I will hit you up if we leave the room," Lina said as the group separated to get icy-hot and advil.

Neither of the couples left their rooms after acquiring the medication needed and alcohol. On their last morning in paradise Lina joined Justin on his now routine walk. As they walked hand and hand Travis and Morgan walked up from the opposite direction.

"I see we all had the same idea," Justin said as he laughed.

"Man, these walks are amazing."

"I would love them more if they happened around noon," Lina said.

"Well, it's about that time," Travis said as the couples made their way to the airport shuttle.

Justin looked back one last time as the two couples boarded the shuttle bound for the airport. Fitzroy welcomed them as he began to tell them of the fun they were going to miss out on before taking them back to the beautiful suite inside the airport to wait for Bob. He again guided the couple past immigration and security with little resistance just as he did before. This time on the flight back both Justin and Lina slept much of the way home. They took a crowded train ride to baggage claim. After grabbing their bags Justin sped out of the airport towards gam-gam's house. At the red light, Lina looked at Justin,

"Let's have one more kid free night and grab them in the morning. After all, they seemed to be thrilled being with their grandparents."

"Word, let's do that."

Travis and Morgan were the last to leave the island and unlike their flight, their return trip was perfectly calm. They held hands as they walked to their car.

"Just think, that will be us in 40 years," Travis said.

"True but I want a pampering trip not a dang ride on the wild side," Morgan said remembering the excursion from hell.

About the Author

D. L. Meadows is a proud military veteran, family man, and a lifelong storyteller who writes imaginative stories rooted in family, teamwork, and adventure. Based in North Carolina, he shares life with his dynamic family who keeps him on his toes and constantly inspired.

Contact Information

Author Website: dl-meadows.com

dlmeadows5070@gmail.com

instagram.com/d.l_meadows

pinterest.com/dlmeadows5070